Praise for DDC Morgan…

"With each new book, the Calloway Series is developing into a tour de force of British noir – a must-read…"

"A terrific addition to the English Mean Streets school…"

"A brilliant piece of post-war noir…"

"A gem of a find and highly recommended."

"As I read, I had that feeling that I haven't had since I read chandler for the first time."

"I literally couldn't put this down and read the whole thing in under 24 hours."

"A fantastic read, stylishly written."

"Exciting, gripping and enjoyable - what more could you want!"

This edition first published 2023

ISBN: 978-1-914475-53-5

10 9 8 7 6 5 4 3 2 1

www.Fahrenheit-Press.com

F 4 E

Cover Design & Manuscript Typesetting by www.SkullStarStudio.com

Rope & Canvas

By

DDC Morgan

A Reg Calloway Mystery

Fahrenheit Press

Also available from Fahrenheit Press

- *Blood & Cinders*
- *Pills & Soap*

To my wife, for never-ending inspiration and all the best ideas.

ONE

When the drunk took liberties with the barmaid, Calloway broke his nose.

He should have lost his job. But the barmaid was a friend of Trudi Trauber and Trudi had a lot of influence at the arena. The drunk was lucky. If Trudi had got to him first, a broken nose would have been the least of his worries.

Calloway tossed the drunk a beer towel to wipe the blood from his face. Then he yanked him by the collar of his threadbare jacket and dragged him down to the foyer and out through the big double doors. The drunk stumbled down the steps cursing, the blood-soaked towel muffling his empty threats. As Calloway turned to re-enter the building, he heard a familiar voice.

'I expect he deserved it.'

'They generally do,' Calloway replied.

A small, bow-legged man stood in the light of the red neon sign in a well-cut suit that clung to his wiry frame like it was nailed to him. He had the dry parchment skin of the lifelong chain smoker which aged him beyond his forty-odd years. He looked like a jockey with cash in his pocket, which wasn't a million miles from the truth. He grinned at Calloway through his crooked yellow teeth.

'So you're in the wrestling game now?' the small man said.

'I'm in the nose-breaking game, Bert.'

'You should be in the ring.'

'It's lady wrestling.'

The small man chuckled. 'Might be a laugh.'

Bert Webber nodded towards the poster in the glass display case beside the main doors. Fierce painted faces glared back, their muscled bodies squeezed into swimsuits above tightly-laced wresting boots. Trudi Trauber was top of the bill.

'They're a rum lookin' bunch, mind you,' said Webber.

'They'd chew you up and spit you out, Bert.'

Webber pondered this. 'I don't think my Elsie would approve.'

Calloway pulled a Navy Cut from a battered gun-metal case and offered one to Webber.

'It's been a while, Bert.'

'Over a year, I reckon.'

'You don't strike me as the lady wrestling type, so I assume this isn't a chance encounter. How did you find me?'

'Called round your old gaff. There's Irish living there now. They had a forwarding address. So I called there and they told me you was working here.'

'You've clearly been to a lot of trouble.'

This made Calloway uneasy. Webber was part of a life he'd done his best to leave behind.

'Yeah, I had to go round the houses. Didn't think it was a good idea to ask Pat.'

Patricia Moxon. Speedway promoter. Former boss, former lover and the cause of a whole lot of trouble for Calloway. Bert was one of her riders. Calloway had been her head of security.

'Does she know I'm here?' said Calloway.

Webber dragged on the cigarette. He shook his head. 'Look, can we go inside?' he said. 'I don't really want to be seen outside this place. If the *Sunday Pictorial* caught me on me tod hanging around lady wrestlers, Pattie would do her nut.'

Webber was a proper star now. Pulling in six thousand a year, Calloway had read.

He nodded and looked at his watch. 'My shift finishes in twenty minutes. Wait for me in the bar. Tell the barmaid you're a friend of mine. She'll serve you after hours.' Calloway noticed blood spots on his cuff. 'She owes me a favour,' he said and returned to the arena.

The last bout had finished and the punters were leaving. Calloway was there to ensure an orderly exit. They were an odd bunch. Old biddies with a blood lust, couples on a night out, single men of certain tastes. Those were the ones you had to watch. The ones with their hands in their pockets all night and shameful looks on their faces when you caught their eye. There was the odd drunk, like you get anywhere hard-working folk gather to let off steam. If they got punchy, Calloway would turn up with an arm lock or a sly jab to the guts.

He met Bert in the bar. It was closed now and Trudi's friend was clearing the tables and emptying the ashtrays. A fug of bitter beer, body odour and cigarette smoke hung in the air. Bert sat at a table in the far corner smoking a cigar. In his well-cut suit and handmade shoes he looked like a mobster from an American B movie. That's what happens when the boy from Bermondsey gets six grand a year, thought Calloway. He was pleased for Webber. He was one of the good ones. A fearless little rider and everybody's friend. He also knew everyone's business, which had been an asset to Calloway in his former job.

'You're looking well, Bert.'

Webber swilled what looked like scotch around in his glass and took a sip. 'Can't complain. I've had a couple of good seasons.'

'Still in the prefab?'

Webber rolled his eyes. 'Elsie won't leave it. She hated it when the corporation first moved us in. Now she says it's home. I keep telling her, we can live anywhere now. Bromley, Beckenham, somewhere decent. She won't have it.'

A cleaner was clanking around the floor with a can of bleach and a bucket, smearing the dirt around with his sodden mop. A roll-up fag dangled from his lower lip. The smoke from the fag aggravated the tick in his eye.

'Lift yer feet,' he grunted in Webber's direction. The small man took one look at the grey swill heading in the direction of his handmade shoes and put his feet up on the chair opposite him. When the clang of the bucket had died down, Calloway cut to the chase.

'This isn't a social call, is it Bert?'

Webber looked sheepish and shook his head. 'I came to ask a favour.'

Calloway was done doing favours. They'd never done him much good. He nodded towards the arena. 'Need a few wrestling tips? I reckon I can get you those.'

Webber glanced back at the posters pinned to the varnished wood panelling behind them and winced.

'I'll pass, if you don't mind.'

He drained the whisky glass and lit another cigar, puffing at it instead of getting to the point. It irritated Calloway.

'Say your piece, Bert. We've both got homes to go to.'

'Yeah, I've seen yours. Not much of a place, is it, if you don't mind me saying.'

'I do mind,' said Calloway.

Webber realised he'd crossed a line, but he was right. Calloway was all but on his uppers. The big man lived in a single room in a rat-infested building that should have been condemned. When he'd taken the job at the arena two years ago, he'd argued for the title head of security. In reality he was a bouncer and a cheap one at that. His shoes were down at heel and his dinner suit smelled of damp. The once proud military man had lost much of the fastidiousness that had been second nature. What spare cash he had, he gave to Doreen. Her need was greater.

'It's me brother-in-law, Stan,' said Webber.

Calloway had a vague recollection of the man. He'd eaten with Webber at the cafe where Stan's wife Vera worked. Vera was a blowsy brunette with big curves and a dirty laugh. The stuff of shameful thoughts.

'What about him?'

Webber spat out a shard of tobacco and stubbed out the cigar out like it suddenly tasted bad. 'He's dead.'

Calloway's meter flickered red. He tried not to let it show. 'Sorry to hear that, Bert.'

Webber drained the last of the whisky and looked like he needed another. The bar was empty and Trudi's barmaid friend had clocked off for the night. Calloway crossed the room and helped himself to two doubles from the optics. When he returned, Webber took a large slug before continuing.

'Stan's a short-haul lorry driver. Well, he was. He was working away from home. Running ballast from the quarries to the building sites at that new town they're building up at Stratton-Fenwick.'

Calloway had read about the new towns. They were building them around the country to relocate families bombed out of their homes during the war. Entire towns built from scratch. All modern and orderly. Homes with indoor bathrooms, heating and hot water. A far cry from the close-knit, oppressive pit villages of his own upbringing.

'He told Vera he'd be away for a few months. He'd never been away that long before, apart from the war. Vera didn't like it, of course. Kept on at him to come home weekends. Stan told her the fares home would cost too much. And he said he needed the overtime. He was saving to buy her a television. Vera's been on at him for ages to buy one, even more so when she heard I'd bought one for Else.'

The little man looked sheepish, as if owning a television made him a traitor to his class. 'Anyway, after a couple of months this bloke turns up at her door. Stan's boss, he said he was, although Vera says Stan had never mentioned him. He had a copper with him. They sat her down and told her they had some bad news. Stan had been killed in an accident.'

'What kind of accident?'

'Crashed his lorry, they said, on the fourteenth of last month.'

Calloway shrugged. 'These things happen, Bert.'

Webber shook his head like his big friend was missing the point. 'They sent his things back to her, his wedding ring, his watch, his clothes. All wrapped up in a brown paper parcel. She went through everything, wanted it clean, wanted him to look his best when they laid him out. I told her, don't bury him in his wedding ring. I know them undertakers. They'll have that down the pawn shop before he's gone cold and have pissed the proceeds up the wall by the time they put him in the ground. She wouldn't have it. "He's keeping it on," she said. "Wherever he's going next I want them to know he's married." Never really trusted him, see. Not since the war. Old Stan had a good war, if you know what I mean. Vera knew it. She knew he'd been putting it about in Egypt for starters. He was stationed in Alexandria. Got a liking for the local bints. His love letters home were all sweetness and light, but she knew. Knew him of old. After he was demobbed she kept him on a short leash.'

Calloway glanced at his watch. He should have been clearing the place and locking the gates by now. The punters had all left but through the open doors of the bar he could see lights on in the wrestlers' dressing room at the end of the corridor.

Webber noticed him looking and gave him a nudge. 'She found this in the lining of his best suit. It had slipped through a hole in the pocket.'

Webber passed a printed card to Calloway. It was crumpled and garishly coloured. It said *Club Continentale* in lettering cheap establishments think looks sophisticated. Below it were cheesecake images of pinup girls dancing with feathers.

'So Stan found a clip joint on his night off. Hardly surprising, given his past form.'

Webber shook his head. He looked around him to see who might be listening, even though the bar was empty. He behaved as if he and Calloway were conspirators. He nodded at the card, like he was saving the best for last.

'Turn it over.'

There was an address on the other side, on Potsdamer Strasse, Berlin.

'That ain't no new town, Mr Calloway.'

Calloway passed the card back. He wanted rid of it.

'So?' he said.

'Why would he have that in his pocket?'

'Could be any number of reasons. Could have been there for ages. Had he ever been to Berlin? Was he ever stationed there?'

Webber shook his head. 'Just North Africa. Before that, Blandford Camp. He was Royal Signals. He was demobbed by forty-six. He was never posted to Germany.'

'So maybe a pal passed him the card. Recommended the Club Continentale. Maybe he was planning a holiday by himself. Slip the leash for a bit.'

Calloway knew this was unlikely.

Webber scoffed. 'Do you think our Vera would have let him go to Berlin? On holiday by himself? She did all she could to stop him going to Brighton for the races on bank holidays. It was only 'cause it was his job that she let him go. It was good money and she knew it.'

Calloway drained the last of the scotch. It still had the previous customer's lipstick on the rim of the glass. The arena was that kind of establishment.

'There's any number of ways that card could have ended up in Stan's suit. The man's dead, Bert. What does it matter? Can't you leave Vera to mourn him in her own way, suspicions and all?'

Webber sulked like a child that thinks it's been chastised unfairly. 'Vera's not having it.'

The small rider dug into his pocket again. He pulled out half-a-dozen postcards and pushed them across the table. 'He sent her these.'

Calloway leafed through them. They were picture postcards of the sights of Stratton-Fenwick. There weren't many sights yet, clearly. Three of the six postcards were the same: a collection of boxy, flat-fronted buildings and a couple of rows of saplings which they called the town square. The rest showed the town sign next to some kind of sculpture Calloway couldn't make out. The messages from Stan were bland. 'I'm alright', 'how are you?', 'how's the weather?', 'missing you'. They were written by someone who felt obliged to write but had nothing to say.

Calloway's irritation showed. 'What's your point, Bert?'

'Six postcards in the six weeks before his accident.'

Calloway shrugged.

Webber rolled his eyes in frustration. 'Stan wouldn't write that often. He's not like that. He wasn't the romantic type, not in that way. He'd have been happy to be away, not missing her enough to write to her once a week.'

'You know what they say about absence, Bert.'

'Yeah but in Stan's case it usually meant a fondness for playing away.'

They both looked through the bar windows towards the arena as the lights went off one by one. Calloway looked at his watch again. He was tired and his knuckles hurt from the punch he'd given the drunk.

'Go home, Bert,' he said, as kindly as he could muster. 'It's late and you're a good hour from your place. Give your sister-in-law time to grieve. There could be any number of reasons Stan had that nightclub leaflet. It doesn't mean anything.'

Webber wasn't having it. He reached into his pocket and pulled out a small slip of printed paper and slid it across the table.

'Then what's this about?'

It was a ticket for the Berlin U-Bahn.

'Why did Stan have a Berlin underground ticket in his pocket, dated when he was supposed to be in Stratton bleedin' Fenwick?'

Calloway picked up the ticket and turned it over in his big hands. Webber sat back in his seat and shook his head repeatedly.

'Vera's beside herself and I don't blame her. All she's had from Stan's boss is flannel. They seem to think that because she'll get a pension now, she don't have to worry.'

'Is it usual for short-haul lorry drivers to get a pension?' said Calloway.

'Search me, squire.'

'Has she mentioned Berlin to Stan's boss?'

'Of course she has.'

'What did he say?'

'Told her he didn't know what she was talking about. Made out she was hysterical. Offered to take her to one of those Harley Street doctors for her nerves.'

'Harley Street?'

Webber raised his eyebrows and gave a knowing by nod. 'Yeah, that's what I thought. That's pushing the boat out, innit? They could send her up the Maudsley on the National Health for nothing. Something ain't right.'

'Who's she been dealing with at the haulage company?'

'A fella named Denton. Oily git, by all accounts. He was the one that turned up with the copper to give her the bad news. He said she'd be well looked after, if she didn't make a fuss.'

The whole business smelled rotten. Calloway knew that smell. It followed him around.

'What did you come to me for?'

The little man smiled. He knew he was getting somewhere. 'Sniff about, that's all. See if you can get some proper answers. You've got a knack for it.'

It was a knack Calloway could do without. But ten years in the military police and six in the Intelligence Corps gave a man certain talents. Talents which can get you into a lot of bother in civvy street. That's how he and Webber had become friends. A bad business at the speedway stadium they'd both played a part in fixing.

'Vera needs peace of mind, Reg,' said Webber. 'All this not-knowing is tearing her apart. Just see what you can find out. I'll pay the going rate. I've got money and it looks like you need it.'

Calloway bristled. 'I'm not for hire, Bert, unless you want me to throw someone out of somewhere. That's what I do these days.'

Webber looked Calloway up and down. 'Yeah, and it don't pay much, I can tell. When I first met you, you was straight out of battledress and straight into Moss Bros, like they used to say in the adverts. Sharp as a pin.'

'I was straight into Allkits, Bert. My commission was temporary, remember?'

'Suit, yerself. But, no offence, Mr Calloway, you look like a sack of shit.'

Calloway had knocked men out for less, but Webber was right. The past year hadn't been kind to him. A succession of scrapes and lost jobs. His standards had dropped.

'Look, there's no shame in being down on your luck,' said Webber. 'And there's no shame in accepting good money for a job, neither. That's what I'm offering. I'm good for it.'

He looked Webber up and down. Handmade shoes, chalk-stripe suit, a showy signet ring with the initials *AW*. Webber was good for the money and flash with it too. Qualities not normally endearing to a man like Calloway, who should have sent the little rider packing the moment he showed up at the arena doors. But Webber ranked among the very few that Calloway considered a friend, to the extent that he'd ever had real friends. And the money was tempting. Doreen could do with some help. The pound or two Calloway gave her every other pay day didn't go far.

'I'll talk to Vera,' he said, regretting each word the second it formed in his mouth.

Webber beamed. 'That's the ticket.'

He reached into his inside jacket pocket and pulled out a wad of pound notes. He peeled some off and passed them to Calloway.

'That'll get you started.'

Calloway nodded and pocketed the money, but unlike Webber, he wasn't smiling.

TWO

There were boys playing cricket in the street, in spite of the weather. They had a dustbin for stumps and a charred plank scavenged from a bomb site for a bat. Fielders in hand-me-down shorts shivered in the chill of the damp afternoon while a lanky lad in oversized corduroys walloped a tennis ball towards Webber's car. The wet ball scudded across the windscreen leaving a greasy smear.

'Little sod did that on purpose,' said Webber through a wheezy cackle. A cigarette dangled from his lip as he wound down the window.

'Oi, Dennis Compton,' he shouted. 'Watch where you're hitting that ball.'

The boy flicked a V-sign. His entourage giggled.

'Serves me right for driving a flash car I s'pose,' said Webber. 'Especially round here.'

Webber had picked Calloway up in his new motor. A pale grey Buick with red leather seats. Calloway had watched pride fight with inverted snobbery on the speedway star's face when he wound down the window and asked Calloway to jump in. Webber still wasn't quite used to that six grand a year.

They'd driven south along the Old Kent Road towards Deptford. They'd taken a left down Canal Road, past the speedway stadium where Webber and Calloway had met. Where Calloway had met Pat Moxon. He felt his stomach knot as they drove alongside the old tin fencing around the stands. He remembered the day over a year ago that he'd walked out on all of them. It was a memory that pained him. He was grateful when Webber turned into the grubby backstreets of Deptford.

‘I can’t promise she’ll be up and about,’ said Webber. ‘Been sleeping odd hours since the news about Stan. The place’ll be a tip too. She’s all but given up on housework, my Else says. Not that she was a big one for it in the first place. She was happier with a milk stout inside her and a fumble on the couch with Stan. They was always like that, even when they was courting.’

‘I’m surprised she wanted a television,’ said Calloway.

Webber sniggered. Then he looked thoughtful. ‘She’s a good girl, Vera is. Solid, you know. Won’t take no truck from anyone.’ He shook his head. ‘This business with Stan has changed her. She’s losing her grip, if you know what I mean. She flips from being angry half the time to being all maudlin. And she’s necking gin like the country’s running out. Starting early too.’

Webber turned into a narrow, cobbled street. Only half the houses remained. Mean little two-up, two-downs. Old dockers cottages by the look of them. They stood in a row along one side of the street. The other side was still a mess of rubble. Deptford had taken a pounding in the Blitz. Two little girls with mucky chops pushed a rusty doll’s pram over the cobbles. An impudent-looking fox terrier sat upright in the pram, like he was lord of this manor. Webber pulled the car up by the kerbside. He looked over at the two girls with the dog. One gave him a disingenuous smile. The other stuck her tongue out. The dog gave him a mischievous look.

‘Reckon I’ll lock the car,’ said Webber, pulling out his keys.

Vera came to the door in her housecoat. She’d lost weight since those few times Calloway had seen her in the caff. The kind of weight loss that trouble brings. The housecoat hung on her like it fitted, rather than straining at the seams like it used to. She looked tired and drawn. She’d made an effort with her hair, but it was half-hearted. Her bold, saucy cheeriness of old had packed up and moved out.

‘Bert,’ she said, her voice flat. ‘And Mr Calloway. I’ll get the kettle on.’

She turned and walked into the small dark hallway, leaving Calloway and Webber to follow. Calloway smelled gin on Vera’s breath amid the rancid fug of unwashed dishes. The two men stood in the kitchen in the awkward silence as Vera filled the kettle from the tap above the stone sink. The sink had three days' washing-up in it, Calloway reckoned.

'How've you been?' said Webber, like he couldn't decide whether to sound cheery or concerned.

'How d'you think?' Vera replied, without emotion. She rinsed cups from the sink and put them on a tray.

'Mr Calloway's going to help us, Vera,' said Webber.

Vera looked Calloway up and down but said nothing. She carried the tray into the front room. The curtains were closed and the room was dark, lit only by the half light of the hallway through the door. She turned on a standard lamp in the corner. It cast a sepia glow over the cheerless surroundings. Webber and Calloway sat on the small two-seater sofa, each balancing their cups and saucers on their laps. Vera slumped in an armchair and lit a cigarette. She put the spent match in the saucer of an undrunk cup of tea on the side table. Webber stirred his tea unnecessarily, for something to do.

Calloway broke the silence. 'I'm sorry to hear of your loss, Vera. I really am. Bert here has asked me to help make sense of some things that are troubling you. I'll do my best.'

Vera sniffed. 'Good luck,' she said, 'because they don't make an ounce of sense to me, luv.'

Bert nudged Calloway. 'Ask her about the man who came to visit, the one with the copper.'

Calloway tried not to show his irritation. This was going to be hard enough without Bert chiming in.

'This man Denton said he was from Stan's employer. Had you met him before?'

Vera shook her head. 'Stan worked all over. I never really knew who he worked with. They weren't the sort of jobs where you get to take your missus to the annual dinner dance. I'd never heard of this Denton until he turned up on the doorstep to tell me my Stan had been killed in an accident.' She pursued her lips and drew smoke through the gap in her clenched teeth. 'Said he came off the road on a bend. Going too fast, swerved to avoid a car coming the other way. The weight of the ballast in the tipper had him over. Cracked his head on the side of the cab, Denton said. I asked if I could see Stan's body, you know, say goodbye, but they told me I couldn't. Can you believe that?'

'It would have been quick, Vera,' said Webber. 'He wouldn't have felt nothing.'

Vera shot him a look. 'Oh, yeah?' she said. 'And how the hell would you know?'

Webber stuttered. 'I was only trying to...'

'Well don't,' she said. 'I'm a big girl, Bert. I don't need you to kiss it all better.' She looked at Calloway. 'My Stan's dead and someone's not telling me the truth. I'll grieve for the poor sod later, God rest his soul, but right now I want to know why this Denton said Stan was killed in an accident in Stratton-Fenwick, when I know he was in Berlin, of all the places.'

'We don't know that Vera. Not for sure,' said Calloway, half-wishing he hadn't.

'Then how come he had a Berlin train ticket and a flyer for a local girly bar in the pocket of his best suit? Explain that, if you're supposed to be so smart.'

Bert shuffled, looking uncomfortable. He said, 'Mr Calloway used to be...'

Calloway stopped him. 'There's a dozen reasons Stan could have had those things.'

'What reasons?' she said, pinching the butt of the cigarette and grinding it into the saucer on the side table. 'Find me a reason that makes sense and I'll buy you a toffee apple. Nothing makes sense, apart from the fact that I'm a fucking widow and I'm being fed a load of bullshit.'

Bert backed into the sofa. Calloway heard him whisper, 'She's proper angry now.'

Vera stood up and crossed the room. She lit another cigarette and held it in her mouth while she reached for the bottle of gin on the sideboard. She poured herself a good-sized slug.

'What else did this man Denton say?' said Calloway.

'He said I'd get a payoff. That the company's insurance would pay out, even though the accident was Stan's fault. Reckless driving, he said.'

Bert rolled his eyes. 'They all drive reckless, those short-haul boys. It's not like Stan was any worse than the rest.'

'Has there been an inquest?' said Calloway.

Vera shrugged. 'If there has, nobody told me.'

'That strikes me as unusual.'

'Does it?' she said. 'How would I know? I've never lost a husband before.'

She was agitated. Tense. On the edge of snapping.

Calloway adjusted his tone. He summoned up what passed for a bedside manner. 'I know this is difficult, Vera, but if I'm going to help, I need to ask questions.'

Vera knocked back the gin and poured another.

Webber said, 'Go easy, Vera girl.'

'Don't lecture me, Bert Webber. You haven't been through this. You've still got your Elsie. Nice and cosy in your little prefab. I've lost my Stan. It's just me now. And I'll bloody well drink when I want.'

She took another gulp of the gin. Bert and Calloway lit up cigarettes. They both needed one.

'He was no angel,' said Vera. 'He could be a right old devil when he wanted. I mean I could never really trust him. He was a good-looking man and he got the attention. He liked it an 'all. But I kept him close. Kept him fed, made him laugh, made sure he didn't go short of the other.'

Bert shuffled in his seat. 'Steady on, girl,' he said.

Vera waved it away. 'He was a rogue, my Stan. An opportunist. Always a bit sly.' She laughed. 'I mean, he'd done a stretch, hadn't he?'

'Stan had been to prison?' said Calloway.

'Glasshouse,' said Bert. 'An army prison in Egypt. Got caught selling the signals corps' radio valves on the black market to local shopkeepers. They banged him up for a bit. Must have behaved himself 'cos he got out early, as I recall.'

'He was no angel, my Stan.' said Vera. She drew on the cigarette. 'But he was mine.' Her voice wavered and her eyes welled up.

Webber stood up and put his arm around her. She pushed him

away.

'You've no need, Bert. I'm alright.'

Her stoicism looked skin-deep to Calloway. It was to be expected. But there was anger too. Plenty of it.

'What else did Denton talk about when he visited you?'

'Funeral arrangements,' she said. 'He said the company would arrange it all and that I didn't need to worry about the cost. They'd pay for a nice send off.'

Webber whistled. 'They must've liked him, Vera. Not many firms offer perks like that.'

They certainly didn't, thought Calloway.

'He had a load of questions too. About Stan,' she said.

'What sort of questions?'

Vera sat back in the armchair. She was calmer now. Must be the gin, thought Calloway.

'He asked if I'd seen Stan since he first left for Stratton-Fenwick. Had he come home to visit at weekends? That kind of thing.'

'Anything else?'

'He asked if he'd written me letters or called. I told Denton I'd had regular postcards, which surprised me to be honest, although I didn't tell him that. Stan wasn't the writing kind. I can't recall him ever writing me a love letter, even when we were courting. He expressed his affections in other ways, if you know what I mean.' She rolled her eyes and shook her head. 'I got six postcards in as many weeks. Part of me suspected it was guilt. That he'd been up to something while he was away.'

The room was getting stuffy. The earlier drizzle must have cleared up and the afternoon sun was shining on the front of the house. Calloway wished Vera would open the curtains, but he knew she wouldn't, and it would be impolite to ask. It was tradition. You closed your curtains when there had been a death in the family. Like flying the flag at half-mast.

'Bert tells me this man Denton offered you help from a private clinic when he visited?'

'That was the second time he called,' she said.

Webber and Calloway exchanged looks.

'You didn't tell me he'd been again, Vera,' said Webber.

'Last week,' she said. ''Cause I'd been calling him up. Demanding to know what was going on. He kept fobbing me off, but I wasn't having that. Told him if he didn't give me answers, I'd take it somewhere else.' She looked across at Bert. 'You know, David,' she said.

Webber read Calloway's quizzical expression. 'One of her nephews,' he said. 'He's a reporter on the *Mercury*. The local paper.'

'That got their attention,' Vera said, with satisfaction. 'Two of 'em turned up on the doorstep.'

'Two of them?' said Calloway. 'Did Denton bring the policeman again?'

Vera shook her head. 'He brought a doctor. Talked to me about how I was feeling, how grief plays tricks with the mind. Gave me some pills for my nerves.' She scoffed. 'Nerves, I said. What nerves? I've just lost my husband. I'm not likely to be in the best of spirits, am I? I haven't got nerve trouble, I said. I'm tough as old boots.' Calloway didn't doubt it. 'But this doctor, he kept on about it. Like he was trying to convince me I was losing my marbles, you know, because of the grief.'

'Private doctor?' said Calloway.

Vera shrugged. 'Smartly dressed. Blazer, cavalry twills, nice striped tie. Good looking sort.'

'Did he give his name?'

'If he did, I can't remember. I was all at sixes and sevens.'

'Have you still got Denton's telephone number?' said Calloway. 'And the name and address of the haulage company?'

She stood up and crossed the small room to the sideboard. She was a good woman, Calloway thought. Confident, engaging and smart as buffed-up buttons on a tunic. Even in the half-caring dishevelment of grief, she retained an innate dignity. Stan had been lucky to have her. Whether she had been lucky to have Stan was another matter. She opened one of the sideboard drawers and rifled around.

'Here,' she said, passing him a business card with Denton's name and number on it. There was no address or company name.

She also handed him a payslip on headed paper.

'Thank you,' said Calloway, slipping both into the pocket of his suit jacket. 'Just one more thing,' he said. 'What does Denton look like?'

She thought for a moment. 'I don't know. Skinny fella, I s'pose. Dark hair with a widow's peak. Bit big in the chin.'

She turned her back to them and poured herself another large measure of gin.

They left Vera's house and stepped out onto the street, their eyes adjusting to the late autumn sun. The two little girls were sitting on the running board of Webber's Buick. The fox terrier stood sentinel by their side.

'We minded your car, mister,' one of the girls said.

'Give us a shilling,' said the other.

Webber pulled a coin from his pocket and tossed it towards them. As he unlocked the driver's side door, the dog cocked its leg against the Buick's wheel.

THREE

It was full house at the arena. A rough-looking lot too. All the local chancers, with their women in tow. Adult artful dodgers in too-wide suits, their hats pulled down over their eyes, their faces set firm. None of them smiling, except to greet others like them with a mean little grin and a nod. They sat close to the ring, at tables with tablecloths and candles in wine bottles. Mr Finnegan's nod to nightclub sophistication, and an excuse to charge half as much again for ringside seats. The men stared through the ropes, their eyes fixed on the action. It excused them from chit-chat, or any other concession to perceptible enjoyment. These were the local hard men, in their own eyes at least. They gave no quarter where emotion was concerned. They weren't much of a date for their women, these local faces, thought Calloway. Their dates sat there in their vulgar faux-couture, sipping their gin-and-Its, looking bored. It was a different story in the cheap seats, the long, hard benches you had to excuse-me along to get to the bar or the peanut stall. This crowd were packed in and revved up. They hollered encouragement and abuse in equal measure, singling out their heroes and villains from the night's bill. Couples, groups of lads and girls in pairs. The lads stared transfixed at the fighters in the ring, their hungry eyes devouring the female flesh, as it grappled and bounced. They would nudge each other, winking, eroticising the contortions of the fighters in their oversexed young minds. The girls sought a different pleasure from the display, projecting the rivalries of their everyday lives onto the women on the canvas, like living voodoo dolls. For the couples it was a way of just being together, sharing in the fun, such as it was, holding hands and nuzzling up, lost in the throng.

And the smell of the crowd. God, thought Calloway. It was

enough to turn your stomach. Five hundred unwashed bodies, basting in their own sweat, stale inside their overcoats. A monstrous odour, and more than a match for the cloying scent of the Brylcreem in their hair, or the lavender behind their ears, or the smoke of the Woodbines that hung from their lips.

A man in a loud check suit emerged from the office that overlooked the arena and adjusted his garish, fat-boy tie.

'Mr Finnegan,' said Calloway with a deferential nod.

Frankie Finnegan was the promoter. He ran the arena.

'Good crowd tonight, eh, Mr Calloway?' he said. He shot his cuffs and rubbed his hands. 'Bodes well for the title fight.'

The two men looked down onto the ring from the gallery.

'Trudi's on form,' said Calloway, for want of something to say. He watched Finnegan's star attraction bouncing a fighter half her size off the ropes, to the boos of the crowd.

'They love a good villain,' said Finnegan. 'That's what they pay to see, and Trudi's the best.'

The big fighter slammed her opponent onto the deck, like a butcher slapping meat on the block. The crowd hurled abuse. Trudi deflected it with a shaking fist. She bared her teeth and snarled.

'She certainly puts on a show,' said Calloway. How they called this a sport, he couldn't fathom. Finnegan pulled a gold cigarette case from the inside pocket of his dog-tooth suit. He offered Calloway a cigarette and lit it with a shiny new gold lighter.

'Hand-rolled,' he said. He was a flash bastard, Finnegan, thought Calloway. But he had to admit, he'd never smoked a fag so good.

George the cleaner scurried up to the two men, panting, an expression of disgust on his old, sagging face.

'There's one in the gents again,' he said.

'I'll deal with it,' said Calloway. He ducked through the fire door and walked along the corridor at the back of the first-floor gallery. The smell of cheap pine disinfectant hit him as he approached the lavatories. There were three stalls inside, opposite a row of rank-smelling urinals. Two stalls were empty, one was occupied. Calloway kicked the closed door open.

'You should put that down, pal,' he said. 'Before it goes off in your hand.'

A middle-aged man in a gabardine mac let go of his manhood and scrabbled to pull up his trousers. The man stepped out of the stall, his face flushing red. He edged past Calloway's big frame, avoiding eye contact.

'Don't forget to wash your hands,' said Calloway. 'And don't come back.' He left the man in the mac to it. His work was done.

At the end of the night, Calloway made his rounds of the arena, turning out lights and testing the doors. The light in the wrestlers' dressing room was still on. Calloway knocked and entered.

The room smelled of sweat and cheap talcum powder. Trudi Trauber was alone in the room packing her kit into a shabby canvas hold-all. She wore high-waist American jeans with a check shirt rolled up at the sleeves and men's penny loafers on her size-nine feet. Her dark hair was up, with a roll at the front and a ponytail behind. At just shy of six foot with big square shoulders, she looked like a bobby-soxer crossed with a fire door. Someone you wouldn't want slamming into you.

'Reggie, *liebchen. Wie gehts?*'

It took someone of Trudi's height and build to speak German so openly. Wounds still ran deep in these post-war years.

Calloway shrugged. He'd just taken on a new burden and it showed in the lines chiselled into his face. He answered in German. He was out of practice and barely fluent, not like during the war when he interrogated German POWs as a sergeant in a field security section. But he could still hold a conversation.

'I've just agreed to something I may live to regret,' he said.

'The story of my life,' said Trudi. She kissed the fingertips on her man-sized hand and touched his cheek. 'Thanks for defending my friend's honour. I'm glad chivalry is alive and well.'

'I'm not sure the man whose nose I broke will agree when he wakes up tomorrow. Or Mr Finnegan, for that matter. I'm waiting for him to haul me up on the incident.'

'Frankie won't do anything. I've had a word,' said Trudi.

Trudi was the star attraction. She was worth a lot of ticket sales to Finnegan, which meant she could call the shots.

'I'm grateful,' said Calloway. He changed the subject. 'You started wrestling in Berlin before the war, didn't you?'

Trudi laughed. 'Mud wrestling. Not so much a sport as a sideshow.' She looked around the dressing room. 'Back then we wrestled in nightclubs, not arenas.'

'Ever hear of a Club Continentale?'

Calloway passed Trudi the flyer Bert had given him. She looked at the gaudy image on the front. She shook her head. 'I don't recall it,' she said, then turned the card over. She gave Calloway a wry smile.

'Potsdamer Strasse. I can guess what kind of club that is.' She handed back the card. 'Are you planning a little holiday, Reggie?'

Calloway flushed red. He shook his head. 'Enquiring for a friend,' he said, and then regretted it.

Trudi raised an eyebrow. 'If I didn't know you better...'

'I trust that you do,' said Calloway, cutting her short. 'Give you a lift home?'

He could barely afford to keep a car on the road these days, and it wasn't much of a car at that, a 1938 Morris 8 with more dings and dents than a panel beater's workbench. It was a small car for a man Calloway's size, smaller still once the six-foot wrestler had climbed in. The pair of them wore it as much as rode in it.

'So what have you agreed to that is causing you so much angst?'

A good German word, *angst*, thought Calloway. The feeling of fear that comes from the immense responsibility of the power of choice. He'd chosen to help Bert against his better judgement, against his instincts even. And now he was committed. He had Vera's expectations to think of too.

'I have a habit of getting involved,' was all he said.

It was a twenty-minute drive to Trudi's place that time of night. The roads were deserted, save for the odd cab and a street cleaning bowser spraying disinfecting water to dilute the filth in the gutters.

'How does a Berliner end up wrestling in East London?' said

Calloway. He had often wondered this since taking the job. This was the first chance he'd had to ask.

'When the national socialists came to power, they closed down the clubs. The Resi, the El Dorado, the Heaven and Hell. They all went. Too decadent for the new German ideology. The Nazis turned the El Dorado into a headquarters for the Brownshirts. Can you believe that? After that, I found it hard to work. I wasn't cut out for a regular job.' She laughed to herself. 'Or a regular life, for that matter. Not regular enough to fit in with the expectations of the thousand-year Reich. I'd never been one for *kinder, küche, kirche*. And I had no intention of producing offspring for the master race.' She paused, thinking for a moment. 'You know they gave a medal to any woman that could produce more than four children for the fatherland.' She shook her head. 'My talents lay elsewhere.'

'Like throwing young girls around the ring to entertain the populous?'

'They're not so young, believe me. And don't dismiss all-in wrestling as entertainment. It's strictly Lord-Admiral Mountevans rules.'

Calloway wasn't convinced. Trudi's ironic tone said she wasn't either, although she was quite happy to play along. Admiral-Lord Mountevans and his radio-star pal, Commander Campbell, may have created sportsmanlike rules, weight divisions and formal championships, but Calloway couldn't help sharing the more sceptical views of the press. From what he'd seen at the arena, the sport still relied on fakery and gimmicks, as much as sportsmanship.

Trudi pulled a cigarette case from her hold-all. She lit two cigarettes, passed one to Calloway and wound down the window a couple of notches.

'So did you leave Germany for Britain?' he said.

'No. I went to Paris first.' She laughed. 'I didn't have much choice. Ideology wasn't the only reason I had to leave Germany. There were more pressing considerations.'

'Such as?'

She took a long drag on the cigarette and blew smoke out of

the half-open window. 'Let's just say I found myself on a side of the law that wasn't conducive to a long and fruitful life.'

He was curious, but it was idle curiosity.

'In Paris I met a French promoter,' she said, changing the subject. 'He was taking wrestlers to Portugal, to fight at the Campo Pequeno in Lisbon. He added female wrestling to the bill.' She looked reflective for a moment. 'The Campo Pequeno was some arena, I tell you. A grand old bull ring. The atmosphere at the fights was electric. The best I've known.'

'So you sat out the war in Portugal?'

She nodded. 'A neutral country seemed the best place to be. I moved to London in forty-seven, when the formal championships started up. That's when Finnegan picked me up.'

She stared out of the car window, as they passed row after row of bombed-out buildings, their remains still to be demolished.

'I miss Berlin,' said Trudi. 'Or whatever's left of it.' She turned to Calloway. 'Have you been there?'

Calloway had been there in forty-six, when he was still in the army. He had been recalled from his posting in Palestine to support the war crimes trials that were just starting up. He had experience with war criminals. Too much experience. He'd been part of a unit that had liberated one of the first concentration camps the British forces found. He'd interrogated members of the *kommandantur*. He'd read their files, files recording the camp's procedures and processes, cold and meticulous in their detail. His role in Berlin was escorting prisoners to Nuremberg for trail. One of them spoke out of turn, justifying himself, sneering and remorseless. Calloway had punched out his front teeth and broke three of his ribs. He avoided a charge but was advised by his CO to leave the army, quickly and quietly. Since then he'd been scraping a living as a jobbing security boss, in jobs that had a habit of turning sour. He didn't share Trudi's affection for Berlin.

'I've been there,' he said. 'There's not much left of it.'

He dropped her outside a block of flats. One of those low rectangular blocks with curved metal windows and a portico over the entrance. Not a palace, but not half-bad either. Trudi was pulling in a few bob as Finnegan's star attraction.

'See you Thursday,' he said. 'Big night.'

Thursday was the Southern Area title fight. Mr Finnegan would be upping the ticket prices. Trudi climbed out of the car and raised herself up to her full six feet.

'I'm big every night, *liebchen*,' she said, with a deep, throaty laugh.

It was past midnight when he arrived at his street.

'You've got a visitor,' his landlady said. She stood beside the stairs in a dressing gown that had seen better days. Her arms were folded.

'No visitors after ten,' she said. 'That's the rule.'

Calloway looked at his watch, although he knew the time.

'I'm not expecting anyone,' he said. 'Not my fault if someone turns up when I'm not about.'

'Rules are rules,' she said.

He looked around the hallway, with its peeling wallpaper and brown stains on the ceiling. The smell of cat piss hung in the air.

'A house in this state doesn't deserve rules,' he said, shaking the loose banister in his big hand. He felt her eyes boring into him as he climbed the stairs.

Doreen stood outside his door, half-hidden in shadow, little Maggie cradled in her arms. The toddler was asleep. Doreen looked relieved to see Calloway. She also looked scared.

'I'm so, so sorry Reg, but I had nowhere else to go.' Her voice quivered, on the verge of tears.

'It's alright,' he said, as softly as his gruff voice would allow. 'What's happened?'

She hesitated, backing further into the shadow of the door well. She was turning her head to one side, shielding the right side of her face from his view. Calloway stepped towards her. She flinched. He cupped his hand under her chin and turned her head towards the insipid light from the bare bulb in the hallway. The side of her face was swollen. A bruise was coming up under her eye.

'Jimmy,' she said. 'He's been round again.'

FOUR

Calloway had set off early for the drive north, dropping Doreen and young Maggie home on the way. He'd let them stay the night. His landlady could go to hell. Doreen and Maggie shared the bed in his small room, while he'd slept as best he could in his armchair. It wasn't the best night's sleep he'd had. Doreen had woken him with a cup of tea around six-thirty. Her black eye was up good and proper. He knew he would have to pay Jimmy a visit, set him straight, but that would have to wait. He was on Webber's time now and had to fit in his enquiries between shifts at the arena.

Drinkwell's Haulage had a depot eight miles outside Stratton-Fenwick. The address was on the payslip Vera had given him. The depot was a collection of wartime huts behind a high fence, most likely part of a decommissioned RAF station. He drove through the open gates and pulled up outside the building that looked like an office. There was a sign by the door that said 'no soiled boots' and a scraper set into the concrete step caked in congealed clay mud.

The office was warm inside, despite the chill of the morning. A three-bar electric fire radiated dry and dusty heat. A young female voice from behind the counter said, 'If you're looking for work, we've no vacancies.'

'I'm not looking for work,' said Calloway. 'I'm looking for Mr Denton.'

She stood up from behind her desk and peered at him over her cat's eyeglasses. She wore a candy-stripe shirt tucked into high-waisted trousers that buttoned down one side. Her kitten heels would have been no match for the boot scraper. She looked out of place in the run-down Quonset hut, with its grubby box files and posters advertising spark plugs. He guessed this wasn't the kind of place she'd always dreamed of working.

'Is he one of the drivers?' she said, running her finger down a clipboard.

'One of the managers,' said Calloway.

'I've not heard of a Mr Denton,' she said. 'But then I'm new here. Only started a fortnight ago.'

'Could he be at another office?'

'We've only got the one,' she said.

He passed her Denton's business card. She took it and frowned, then shook her head.

'Doesn't say Drinkwell's on it,' she said. 'Have you tried calling the number?'

He had. Three times. He couldn't get past the switchboard operator.

'Perhaps I could speak to someone that's been here longer.'

'Mr Drinkwell's here, but he's over at the workshop.'

'Then I'll wait, if you don't mind.'

'Suit yourself,' she said and returned to her desk.

Calloway called after her. 'You could do me a favour, while we're waiting. I'm actually here about one of your drivers. Stanley Deakin. I heard he had an accident. I wanted to get some details.'

She thought for moment.

'Are you sure he's one of ours?' she said. 'He's not on the current roster.'

'He was working here for a few months, running ballast up to the building sites at the new town. Perhaps I could see his file.'

She hesitated. 'I'm not sure I can do that. Personnel files are private.' She held the clipboard close to her chest. 'And I don't even know who you are.'

'Rude of me. Sorry. My name's Calloway. Army field security,' he lied. 'We think a deserter might have signed on with you in the name Stanley Deakin. Heard rumours he'd been killed in an accident. Clearly we need to look into it.'

She looked uncomfortable. 'I think you need to speak to Mr Drinkwell.'

Calloway looked at his watch. He gave her a plaintive smile. 'Looks like he's going to be a while and I've only got till noon before I need to be back at the barracks. I won't half get it if I'm late. Are you sure you can't help me out?'

She looked out of the window towards a hut he assumed to be the workshop. 'I'm not sure,' she said, her voice wavering.

'I've already been late twice this month. Three times and they'll dock my pay. Not to mention the balling out I'll get from my Sergeant-Major. Terrifying he is. A giant of a man with a violent temper.'

He tried to look forlorn, in spite of his bulk. She frowned, weighing up the options. Then she smiled. 'Alright,' she said. 'But quickly. I don't want to get in any trouble either. Not this soon into the job.'

She pulled down a box file marked H to J from a shelf behind her and laid it on the counter. She opened the lid and walked her fingers through the manilla folders.

'Here he is,' she said. 'S Deakin.'

Calloway took the folder and opened it. He read down the entries. Stan's start date tallied with Vera's account. He'd received a pay packet every week, with deductions for damage and speeding fines. His last payday was the day of his death. There was a pencilled entry beneath this final pay date. It said, 'Terminated following accident.' There were no other notes on the file.

'Who said you could look at that?'

A stout man in his fifties stood in the doorway, in a worn tweed suit and bowler hat. He didn't look pleased.

'I'm sorry, Mr Drinkwell,' the secretary said. 'This gentleman's from the army. He's asking about one of the drivers.'

Drinkwell peered over at the file, reading the name on the front. 'And what would the army want with Stanley Deakin?'

'Possible deserter,' said Calloway, already worried that the lie was wearing thin.

Drinkwell eyed him suspiciously. 'Do you have identification?'

Calloway reached in his pocket and handed over his old army identity card. He'd smeared the date with spit so you could no longer see that it had expired more than four years ago. He was far from convinced it would hold up to scrutiny. Drinkwell looked at the card, frowning. He handed it back to Calloway.

'Our personnel records are confidential,' he said. 'Even to the army.'

He glared at the secretary, who looked on the verge of tears.

'Miss Fisher, please escort Sergeant Calloway off the premises,' he said. 'And ask Wally to lock the gates. He shouldn't be leaving them open.'

Miss Fisher walked beside Calloway across the hard standing towards his car.

'I'm for it now,' she said.

'I reckon his bark's worse than his bite,' said Calloway, not convinced that it was. 'Anyway, you've done nothing wrong, not really. He'll probably forget about it by tomorrow.'

She looked at him and smiled, only half-reassured.

'I hope you're right,' she said.

'I hate to ask you one more thing,' he said, 'after you've been so helpful, but where can I get a decent lunch round here? An army marches on its stomach, as they say.'

'I'm not sure,' she said. 'I bring packed lunches.'

'Then where do the drivers eat?' he said. 'I bet they love a good fry-up.'

She thought for a moment. 'There's a transport caff a couple of miles up the A1. I've heard them talk about going there.'

Calloway thanked her and opened the door of his car. He glanced back at the office before climbing in. He saw Drinkwell through the window, looking back at him and speaking into the telephone.

The caff was in a pull-in, set back from the main road. A low slab of a building, little more than a box, but with black timbers fixed to the facade in a misguided attempt to give it a cosy, mock-Tudor feel. The red gingham curtains that grinned through the steamed-up windows did little to add to the effect. Nor did the tin signs advertising Coca-Cola, Lyons Cakes and Capstan cigarettes. But he was in the right place. There were five Dodge tippers lined up in the car park. They each had Drinkwell's livery.

The fug of frying grease hit Calloway as he entered. Somewhere beneath it, the smell of bacon and chops. He ordered tea and an egg banjo. He'd not eaten yet today. He'd given the last of his bread to Doreen and Maggie for toast. The five Drinkwell's drivers sat at a chipped Formica table by the window. They were unmistakeable, in their brown leather jerkins, gum boots and berets. Calloway sat at an adjoining table. He looked across to them as he ate. One of them caught his eye, a parchment-faced old timer with a red nose and thick black hair in his ears.

'Hungry work, eh?' said Calloway, above the din of their chatter. 'You Drinkwell's boys?'

The old man nodded. 'For our sins,' he said, jamming a fork full of pale pink bacon between his yellow teeth.

'Know my mate, Stan Deakin?' said Calloway.

Four heads turned to face him. None of them were smiling. The fifth driver sat at the head of the table with his back to Calloway.

'Who wants to know?' said one of the four, a small, weaselly man, with keen black eyes and a sharp, oversized nose.

'Just a mate. The name's Calloway.'

The driver with his back to Calloway stood up and turned to face him. He took out a pack of Woodbines and offered one. Calloway accepted.

'They call me Spanner,' the man said. He was Calloway's height and just as broad, with wiry red hair and a face like a mastiff. 'I know Stan.'

Calloway held out the cigarette for a light from the Zippo the man called Spanner was holding in his tattooed hand. Spanner shook his head. 'Not here,' he said. 'Outside.'

They stepped through the caff towards the door, the other four drivers watching them. Calloway saw one grimace. Another grinned. It wasn't reassuring.

Once they were outside, Spanner held out the lighter. Calloway leaned in to accept the light.

The first blow knocked him sideways. The second one floored him. Spanner was on top of him, big hands gripping his lapels and slamming him against the hard gravel of the car park.

'Where's my hundred and fifty?' he spat. 'Where's my fucking money?'

The four other drivers were outside now. Calloway heard cries of encouragement. Amid the cries, a heavily-accented voice said, 'For Christ's sake, Spanner, you'll bloody kill him.' The owner of the voice leaned forward and pulled Calloway's attacker off him. Calloway scrambled to his feet, spitting blood and gravel dust from his mouth. The driver with the accent took Calloway's arm and led him towards one of the trucks. Spanner and his three pals shouted abuse. Spanner picked up a fist full of gravel and hurled it at the two men. Calloway felt chippings sting the back of his bloodied head. He heard Spanner and his pals advancing towards them.

'You'd better get in,' the man with the accent said, holding the passenger door of the Dodge truck open. 'Quickly, if you know what's good for you.'

FIVE

The truck driver floored the accelerator and drove out of the car park, spraying gravel in his wake. Calloway looked back and saw Spanner shaking his fist, while his little gang of acolytes shouted obscenities.

'Thanks,' said Calloway, 'whoever you are.'

'Marek,' the driver said. 'Mad Marek, they call me.' He laughed. 'I'm a crazy, mad bastard.'

He spoke broken English with a Central European accent.

'Your pal Spanner looked like the crazy one.'

'Different kind of crazy. I'm crazy behind the wheel. He's crazing in the head.'

'I got that impression,' said Calloway. He felt the back of his head with his hand and winced.

'I'll pull over,' said Marek. He bumped the Dodge up onto the roadside verge and slammed on the brakes. The wheels slid along the damp grass before the truck jerked to a halt. Marek reached under his seat and pulled out a canvas haversack. It had a faded red cross on the front inside a circle of blanco. He fished inside and pulled out a bottle of iodine and some sticking plaster.

'Lean forward,' he said. He cleaned the wound on the back of Calloway's head and stuck the plaster on it. 'Just a nick,' he said, 'but head wounds bleed more. I got the dirt out. Now you won't get sepsis, eh?'

'Thanks, Marek. I'm Reg, by the way,' said Calloway. The two men shook hands. 'So what was all that about?'

'Stan did a bunk owing Spanner money,' said Marek.

'One hundred and fifty pounds?'

Marek nodded. 'That's a month's wages for a short-haul

driver. A lot of money Stan owes.'

'What do you mean, Stan did a bunk?'

Marek pulled a pocket watch from his jerkin and checked the time. 'I must drive. Must get my runs in. You ride with me, I tell you about Stan and Spanner.'

Marek revved the engine hard and let out the handbrake. The heavy truck shot forward, throwing Calloway back in his seat. Marek pushed the pedal to the floor and the truck gathered speed. The speedometer hit sixty. They gained on an old Austin Seven. Marek pounded the horn.

'Slowcoach bastard,' he shouted.

He yanked the wheel and swung the truck over the white lines into the right-hand lane of narrow the two-lane road.

'Christ,' said Calloway. A single decker bus was heading straight for them. Marek pounded the horn again. He revved the engine and changed down. When he was within feet of the oncoming bus, he heaved the truck back into the left-hand lane. The two vehicles clipped mirrors as they passed. Calloway caught the ashen face of the bus driver through the window. Marek laughed.

'Like I tell you. Crazy mad bastard.' Calloway had to agree. 'I beat every driver for the most runs in a shift. Today I need to make time on account of stopping to fix your damn head.'

'For which I'm very grateful,' said Calloway, 'along with saving me a kicking from your mate Spanner.'

'He's not my mate,' said Marek. 'He's mad in the head. Stan saw him as soft touch. Tried to win his money. Stan underestimated Spanner. He's a canny bastard, Spanner is. He looks like a big orang-utan. Orang-utans are smart monkeys.' Apes, thought Calloway, but he wasn't inclined to correct his crazy mad bastard saviour.

'How did he try to win Spanner's money?'

'Cards,' said Marek. 'In the back of the workshop, after their shift. Kept losing, kept trying to win it back. Night after night. Spanner is a good card player. Ran rings around Stan. Took him for a hundred and fifty quid, before Stan threw in the towel.' Marek sat upright, suddenly alert. 'Bastard truck's blocking the road.' One of Drinkwell's trucks was overtaking another ahead of them, taking up both lanes. 'Hold on tight, my friend,' he said.

Calloway saw what was coming, although he hardly believed Marek was serious. He gripped the sides of the passenger seat and braced himself. Marek pushed the accelerator to the floor until he was almost rear-ending the left-hand truck. He tugged the steering wheel to the left. The truck mounted the narrow verge. Marek let out a battle cry. He drove through the gap, trees scraping his left flank, an inch to spare on his right. Calloway heard the squeal of metal on metal as the two trucks scraped wheel arches. Sparks flew upwards. Marek went rigid as he pushed the accelerator through the floor. He swung his truck back onto the road, cutting up the truck behind him from the inside.

'Ha,' Marek shouted in triumph. Calloway's heart thumped harder than during his first parachute jump.

'Do you know why I am the fastest driver? Because I have no fear. I lost my fear during the war.'

He pushed the speedometer to seventy-five, as if to prove the point.

'Did you serve?' said Calloway.

'I was a partisan, in Slovakia. I am Slovak. I lived in the mountains for a year attacking the Germans.' He went quiet for a moment. 'When I returned to my village, all my family were dead. The Nazis killed them all in reprisals.'

Calloway had lost a loved one to the Nazis. *The* loved one. Lost to their brutality, their bestial self-entitlement. He shook the thought from his head. 'How did you end up in Britain?' he said, in an attempt to shift the conversation to something less painful.

'After the war, some of us partisans fell out of favour with the new Czech government. It was a good time to leave and I had no reason to stay. I worked my way through Europe taking what little work I could. It wasn't easy. Then someone told me about a displaced workers' scheme, where you could work in this country. Proper wages. I lived in a workers' camp outside town called King's Lynn, with Poles, Latvians and Ukrainians. Do you know Kings Lynn? They talk funny there. We spoke better

English than they did. I took a driving job. Got my license, all proper. But I fell out with some of my fellow workers. It was best I left the camp. I ended up here, at Drinkwell's. Mr Drinkwell is a miserable sod. But the pay is okay.' He smiled to himself. 'I like it.'

Marek swung the lorry into some kind of works. There was a conveyor belt dumping aggregates into a big, rusting hopper. The whole area was caked in a thick layer of dust.

'Good,' he said. 'I beat the others.'

He reversed the truck, expertly positioning the tipper right under the spout of the hopper.

'Are all the drivers this competitive?'

'Of course. We make four shillings an hour and seven shillings a load. More loads, more money. Simple mathematics. Everyone competes, but I am the best. Other drivers make ten runs a day, I make fourteen. I do crazy mad speeds, eh?'

'Do you ever get caught? For speeding?'

Marek shrugged. 'Sometimes. We all pay our own fines. That's the rule.'

He gestured through the widescreen to a worker standing near the hopper. 'You wait here,' he said to Calloway, climbing down from the cab.

Marek exchanged a few words with the worker. Then he grabbed a shovel and headed towards the rear of the truck. Calloway heard an almighty crunch as a big load of gravel landed in the tipper. A cloud of dust billowed around the truck. Calloway looked behind and saw Marek standing on top of the gravel, evening out the load with the shovel. Then he jumped down and climbed back in the cab.

'Quick, yes? I am the quickest. Now hold on.'

Calloway gripped the seat again and braced his legs against the sloped floor of the footwell. The Dodge's engine growled like a cornered beast. Marek reversed away from the hopper. He took the corner out of the depot and onto the road at such a speed that a thick spray of gravel crashed onto the kerb. Calloway wondered how much of it would be left by the time Marek reached his destination.

'We make good time,' said Marek, satisfied.

Calloway lit a cigarette and offered one to Marek.

'When did Stan do a bunk?' he said.

Marek thought. 'Maybe two months ago.'

'That long ago? Are you sure?'

According to Drinkwell's file, the haulier had been paying Stan until three weeks ago, up to the time of the accident. He'd also sent postcards from Stratton-Fenwick more recently than that.

'I'm sure,' said Marek.

The Slovak driver hadn't mentioned any accident, let alone Stan being dead. He was talking about him in the present tense. So was Spanner, who was still wanting his money.

'Did Stan have an accident?' said Calloway. 'A road accident?'

'Stan? Speeding yes, accident no. He was a good driver.' He laughed. 'Lousy card player, but very good driver.'

'Did he give you any clue as to where he was going when he disappeared?'

'He said he knew how to get the money he owed Spanner. He told me there was more to him than driving trucks, whatever that meant. Frankly, I thought it was bullshit. Just an excuse to welch on his debt. But who knows?'

'Did Stan ever say anything about going to Berlin?' said Calloway.

Marek screwed his face up, as if Calloway question was nonsensical. 'Berlin? No. Why would he go to Berlin?'

'That's one thing I'm trying to find out,' said Calloway.

Marek dropped Calloway at the transport caff on the way to the new town site. He gave a cheery wave and shot out of the pull-in, narrowly missing a school bus heading in the opposite direction. Crazy mad bastard thought Calloway and smiled. He crossed the car park to the Morris. It was slumped on the gravel, lower than it should have been.

Spanner and his gang had let all four tyres down.

SIX

He arrived back at his digs as the sun was setting. He'd had to wait at the transport caff for a driver that would lend him a pump for his tyres. A salesman who travelled in cleaning products obliged him, insisting he buy Calloway tea and an Eccles cake afterwards. He subjected Calloway to an hour of mindless chat on the relative merits of powder and cream for cleaning sinks.

When Calloway stepped into the hallway of the rooming house, he found his belongings sitting at the foot of the stairs. Two battered suitcases and an orange crate, hastily packed, and not by him. The landlady stood beside them, her arms crossed and her face like granite.

'No overnight guests,' she said. 'It's a house rule. The penalty is forfeiture of lodgings.' She snorted through her nose, like it hurt to do so. 'A woman too,' she said.

She pushed the orange crate towards him with her carpet slipper.

'This is a respectable establishment,' she said.

'The only thing respectable about it is the money I pay you to live in this hovel,' he said. 'I'll be happy to see the back of it.'

She shot him a look like she'd just been slapped. He piled the two suitcases on top of the orange crate and carried them to his car.

His bravura had ebbed by the time he reached the kerb.

'Congratulations, Reg,' he muttered under his breath. 'You've just joined the ranks of homeless ex-servicemen.'

He had keys to the arena. There was no wrestling that evening. He let himself in and carried his belongings up the darkened rear stairs to the second floor, where he had a small office, in reality an unused store cupboard with a desk and chair. He dumped the cases and crate in the corner and went back down the stairs to the small gymnasium behind the auditorium, where Finnegan's wrestlers trained. The ingrained smell of sweat and embrocation stung his nostrils. He took a floor mat back to his office. It would serve as a bed until he sorted himself out. There was an old army blanket and a Primus stove in the crate he'd brought with him. This wasn't the first time in the past year or so he'd roughed it between lodgings. He switched on the wireless and tuned it to the third programme, for the classical music. He listened to Mendelssohn while he heated a tin of oxtail soup. Home sweet home, he thought.

There were footsteps in the corridor. Soft and tentative. Like someone was creeping. Odd, he thought. It was past eight now. He put his canteen of soup down and reached for the door handle, then yanked the door open, quick as a flash.

George the cleaner gasped. His dentures came loose. His mottled hand shot up by reflex, to push them back in his mouth.

'Sorry to make you jump, George,' said Calloway. 'I thought I had the place to myself.'

'I'm putting in a spot of overtime, Mr Calloway,' the cleaner said, clenching a rolled-up fag in the corner of his mouth. 'Mr Finnegan wants the place spick and span for the regional championship fight.'

Spick and span was a tall order, thought Calloway, especially for an old boy armed only with a mop and bucket. The arena's grime was ingrained. George peered onto Calloway's office and saw the floor mat and blanket.

'Staying over tonight?' he said, with a degree of suspicion. The tick in his eye went double time.

'Let's just say I'm between lodgings,' said Calloway. 'My landlady and I didn't see eye to eye.'

George nodded, like he was familiar with the scenario. 'Kicked you out, eh?'

'Strictly speaking I walked out, but the end result is the same.'

'Hard to find places these days,' said George, drawing on the wet end of the roll-up. 'People bombed out, still not rehoused.

Servicemen back from the war, still with nowhere to go.'

'Tell me about it,' said Calloway. Since the war he'd gone from one dingy boarding house to another. One job to another too, usually leaving under a cloud.

'How long you planning to kip here?' said George.

Calloway shrugged. 'As long as it takes.'

It wasn't going to be easy finding a place. Calloway knew that much. He'd been a fool to walk out of his digs. He could have smoothed things over with the landlady. But impulsiveness was ingrained in him like the dirt in the nooks and crannies of the arena. Sometimes his impulse got ugly. It was best he backed off, even if it did leave him homeless. It wasn't as though he couldn't afford new digs. He had Webber's money in his pocket. But he had other plans for that.

'You like this music,' said George, inclining his head towards the wireless.

Calloway nodded. 'Reminds me of happier times.' All too brief times. A few precious weeks. Learning to love music. Learning to love. And then learning loss.

'I prefer a dance band, me'self. Bennie Goodman. I used to cut a rug to Bennie back before the war.' He tapped the side of his leg. 'Before Jerry knackered this for me.'

George took another drag on his cigarette, thinking. 'I might be able to get you a room. Up Kensington way. Hotel.'

Calloway raised an eyebrow. 'A Kensington hotel? Sounds way beyond my slender means.'

George tapped the side of his nose with a grubby finger. He gave a conspiratorial wink. 'Not beyond the means of old soldiers like us.' He picked up his mop and bucket. 'Give me a couple of days,' he said, then clanked his way back down the darkened corridor, dragging his leg.

Calloway hadn't noticed George's limp before. There were enough damaged men around since the war for things like that to be unremarkable. Everyone was damaged in some way. Calloway's damage was the kind you couldn't see. At least not until it raised its ugly head.

He drove south of the river the following morning. He'd slept badly and his eyes were bleary. Even the coffee he'd drunk from Syd's stall in Shoreditch couldn't compensate for a cold night on the old gym mat. The weather didn't lift his spirits either. The meagre wipers on the Morris struggled to maintain a clear view of the road through the thick drizzle.

Bert lived in a prefab between Peckham and New Cross. The six grand a year he trousered as one of Bermondsey Bullets' star riders couldn't prize him and his wife Elsie from the little flat-roofed building, one of thousands thrown up by the Ministry of Works to house families bombed out by the Blitz. Bert's Buick glistened in the rain outside his temporary home. It looked as incongruous as pearls on a washerwoman. Bert had at least made some concessions to stardom.

Elsie opened the door to Calloway like he was some kind of royalty. Odd considering he was still wearing his demob suit and his car looked like scrap compared to her husband's.

'Oh do come in Mr Calloway,' she said with an unconvincing plumminess in her voice. 'Would you care for some tea?'

He heard Bert shout, 'Ooh, listen to her swank,' from inside.

Elsie held the door for Calloway, undeterred. A small table beneath the living room window was laid for tea. They'd brought out the best china by the looks of it. A small television, little bigger than a large wireless, took pride of place on a stand in the corner. Elsie saw Calloway looking at it.

'Our television,' she said, to confirm the fact.

'Leave it out, Else,' said Bert. 'Mr Calloway didn't come here to listen to you boast about your worldly goods.'

Elsie frowned at him. 'Says the man that got up early this morning to polish his trophies.'

Bert's speedway cups sparkled on the mantle of the tiny, tiled fireplace.

Elsie poured the tea and Calloway made a show of enjoying it. It was a good cup of tea. She dropped the frown and smiled at him. He could see the likeness to Vera, but the differences were obvious. Elsie had chosen well. He knew Bert doted on his missus, in spite of the ribbing he gave her, and it seemed like the feeling was mutual. The little house and the little couple in it radiated contentment, and the pair retained the spark that must have drawn them together in the first place. Vera, by contrast, had picked a bad boy.

'Well,' said Bert. 'Find anything out?'

Calloway hesitated before reporting on his enquiries at Stratton-Fenwick. He wasn't sure how much Bert had shared with his wife about the situation with her late brother-in-law. Bert sensed this and said, 'You can talk in front of my Else, Mr Calloway. It was her idea that I come to you in the first place. She's as worried about her sister as the rest of us.'

'I've never known her like this,' said Elsie. 'She's swinging from tears to tantrums at the drop of a hat. Sometimes she rambles and doesn't make any sense. What with that and the drinking, well...'

Bert lit up and Calloway joined him. Elsie lit one of her own filter tips with a box of Swan Vestas. Calloway said, 'I asked for the man called Denton at Stan's workplace. They hadn't heard of him. I managed to get a look at Stan's personnel file, which showed that the firm had been paying him up to the date of his accident. Then I got short shrift from his boss, Drinkwell, and had to leave.'

'So he couldn't have been in Berlin when he died,' said Bert, in a way which suggested relief that the matter might have quickly been resolved.

'On the face of it, you're right. But then I met some of Stan's workmates. Other drivers for Drinkwell's. They were adamant Stan did a runner about two months ago, owing a one-hundred-and-fifty-pound gambling debt.'

Bert whistled. Elsie looked surprised, but not exactly shocked.

'Cards, was it?' said Bert.

Calloway nodded.

'Figures,' said Bert. 'He weren't ever much of a card player. But that never stopped him. Wouldn't be the first time he'd tried to take a bloke's shirt and ended up losing his own.'

'He was a silly sod,' said Elsie, shaking her head. 'Nice looker, mind, and a lovely dancer.'

Bert gave her a disapproving look. 'Steady on, girl.'

‘Oh don’t give me that, Bert Webber. It’s not as if you never snuck the wrong sort of look at my sister.’

Bert reddened.

Calloway continued, to spare the little man more embarrassment. ‘I spoke to one of the drivers, a chap called Marek, a Slovakian, a decent sort. He said Stan claimed to know a way to make the money back and settle his debt. Stan had told Marek there was more to him than driving short-haul trucks. Any idea what he could have meant?’

Bert shrugged.

‘Had he always been a driver, since being demobbed?’ Calloway asked.

‘Yeah,’ said Bert. ‘Different firms, but always driving.’

‘And before that?’

Bert glanced over at his trophies. ‘He was a rider. Rode up Hackney, in the thirties, with the Hawks. That’s how me and Else met him. He was alright, but nothing special.’

‘How easily could he get back into speedway racing? Could he make decent money in a hurry?’

Bert didn’t hesitate before answering. ‘Nah, mate. No one would have him. He got himself a bit of a reputation, see. Disruptive influence on the other riders, if you know what I mean. Things like that follow you around in speedway.’

Calloway thanked them for the tea and left. He told Bert and Elsie he’d keep working on making sense of things, but short of trying the man called Denton’s number again, he was unsure what to do next. He checked his wristwatch. The pubs would be open. It was as good a time as any to pay a visit to Doreen’s friend Jimmy.

SEVEN

He pulled the car up outside a pub called the Lord Nelson, at the corner of Doreen's street. He'd been there just the once. The night he'd met her.

He'd been especially down that night. A real black mood. The kind he fell into more and more since he'd returned from the war. Sometimes he slept them off. Sometimes he drank them away. That night had been a drinking night. He'd wandered into the pub after walking aimlessly for an hour. He was already half-cut when a young woman who looked no more than twenty introduced herself as Doreen and asked if he wanted company. He did, and he told her so. It was unlike him. He'd normally decline, even in the army. That night was different. He responded willingly to her contrived flirtations. He drank pint after pint while she nursed a gin and lime, cheering him along with compliments and impressed looks on her pale, pretty face. While they talked, he caught the eye of a well-built young lad in a flashy suit sitting at the bar. The lad kept looking at them. Sometimes the young woman Doreen caught the lad's eye too. Through his increasing inebriation, Calloway sensed something conspiratorial between them. When the landlord called time, Calloway went with Doreen to her lodgings, a few doors up from the pub. He swayed as he walked, with her clinging to his arm, steering him in as straight a line as he could manage. Inside the dim hallway of the tall, terraced house, she made him wait while she went upstairs. He heard another female voice, old and croaky, then footsteps and the shutting of doors. She whispered down the stairs for him to come up. He stumbled through the door to her room and slumped on her bed. He leaned forward and grabbed her arm, pulling her towards him. She pulled away.

'Not so fast, you,' she said. 'Good things come to those who wait.'

The line sounded fake. Part of a repertoire she'd grown tired of delivering. She stepped back and stood in front of a shabby chintz curtain that divided the room. He watched her slip off her heels and take off her skirt and sweater, revealing a slight, undernourished body. She turned for a second and peered behind the curtain. A hint of caution crept into Calloway's beery consciousness, subsiding as she stepped forward and sat beside him on the bed. She started to unbutton his shirt.

There was a sound from behind the curtain, movement, someone else in the room. Calloway thought of the well-built lad in the pub and the conspiratorial looks he exchanged with Doreen. Was it a setup? Was he being rolled? He jumped up and lunged across the room, tugging the curtain aside. Behind it was a cot. In it was a girl of eighteen months, two at most. She called for her mother.

Calloway felt sick. Bile rose in his gullet. Doreen grabbed the child and held it to her. Only then he realised how threatening he must have looked. He'd squared to his full height, to see off the lad from the pub, expecting a cosh or a knife. Expecting to be robbed. Now he was terrifying a woman he'd never met, as she stood half-naked and vulnerable, fearing for herself and her baby girl. He put his hands up to signal he had no bad intent. He stepped back and fell on the bed like a heavy sack, apologising, telling her not to be afraid, disgusted with himself. Doreen was whispering to her little girl, trying to calm her. Then Calloway started to weep. Doreen looked down at him with pity.

'I should never have come here,' he said. 'I don't do this.'

She looked confused. Moments ago he'd been pulling her onto the bed, a boozy lust coursing through his veins. Now he was a mess. A weak, pathetic mess. He poured out more apologies and opened the door to leave.

The lad stood on the landing, blocking his path.

'You're not running out on us now, are you, big man?' he said, with a confidence that defied his youth. 'Don't seem like you've sealed the deal.'

The lad looked past Calloway into Doreen's room. He leered

at her as she stood framed in the doorway, still in her underwear.

'That's a nice little piece,' the lad said. 'Worth the price.' He held out his hand. 'Ten bob and you can finish the job.'

Calloway snapped. He clamped his big hands around the lad's arms, lifted him a foot in the air and threw him down the stairs. The boy bounced off the banisters like a ball in a bagatelle, banging his head on the bare wood stair treads and crashing onto the hard tiles of the hall floor. He let out a yelp and clutched his arm. Calloway went back into Doreen's room. He reached in his pocket and pulled out his wallet. He took out all the cash he had and laid it on her bedside table. It was payday at the arena and he had a week's worth of wages on him.

'For you and your daughter,' he said. 'It doesn't excuse anything, but I want you to have it.'

He closed the door behind him and walked down the stairs. He felt stone cold sober now. The lad lay on the floor, nursing one arm and squealing though clenched teeth.

Calloway leaned down to him. 'I'll be round this way a lot now. And I'll be watching you. You're going to leave that young woman alone. If I hear or see otherwise...'

He stepped on the lad's injured arm with his full weight and walked into the street to the sound of screaming.

Since that night, he'd called on Doreen and little Maggie once or twice a week. She was cautious at first. In time they became friends, of a sort. He had no intentions, and she came to realise it. He insisted on helping her out. He'd leave her money, what little he could afford. She'd protested at first but took it by necessity. She couldn't make ends meet with her part-time job, and working full time was not an option. Mrs Grant, the old lady across the landing, would only watch Maggie three days a week, as she had her own work, Doreen had explained.

It was a strange arrangement, him calling and helping her out, watching her go about her life with her daughter, listening to her chit-chat while she poured him weak tea. It was just something he felt compelled to do. A compulsion rooted in his past. In the war. In his profound sense of loss. It went a little way to filling the great emptiness he felt every day.

The pub was half-full, in spite of it being Saturday. The smell of last night's beer hung in the air. Sad faces sat at scuffed tables nursing half-pints and killing time. Folks with nothing in their lives save for the work they did to pay for dingy lodgings, fags and enough tinned food to subsist.

'How's the arm, Jimmy?' said Calloway.

Jimmy Jenks stood at the bar with two young girls who were seventeen at most. He was holding court. The girls were giggling. This was the first time Calloway had got a good look at him. He was barely twenty, with hair piled up high on his head and swept back at the sides so that it touched his collar. It was smeared with enough grease to open a chip shop. His jacket looked American. The style matched his hair.

'Getting better, no thanks to you.'

Calloway snapped his fingers and ordered a pint.

'A multiple fracture, so I heard,' said Calloway. 'Quite debilitating. Taking a long time to heal.'

Jenks made a fist with his left hand and punched the air.

'Lucky I'm a southpaw.'

One of the girls laughed. Jenks told her to shut up. Calloway shook his head and took a mouthful of his pint.

'You want to watch this one,' he said to the girls. 'He'll charm you one day and have you taking punters down alleyways the next.'

Jenks mouthed an obscenity.

Calloway cut him off. 'Oh and don't upset him. It'll take a lot of make-up to cover the bruises.'

Jenks coughed up a gobbet of phlegm and spat at Calloway's feet. Then he told the girls to get lost. He slipped his good hand in his pocket. Calloway grabbed his wrist.

'Don't be silly, lad,' he said. 'I just want to talk.'

Jenks withdrew his hand from his pocket. He pulled himself up to his full height and looked Calloway in the eye.

'So talk,' he said.

Calloway took a swig from his pint and set it down. 'Next time you give a woman a black eye, you'll get two from me. And a kicking for good measure. Next time you so much as open your mouth to Doreen, I'm going to fill it with my fist. Do you understand?'

Jenks sniggered. 'What I understand,' he said, 'is that you're trying to install yourself as Doreen's ponce and you want me out of the picture.'

'Don't drag me down to your level, son. I'm not the sort that thinks living off the immoral earnings of a girl is an acceptable career choice.'

'It's not all one way. A girl gets a man in her life. Someone looking out for her. Not to mention a bit of company.'

'There's better company in a cellar full of rats. The only thing a girl gets from vermin like you is bruises, and no more money in her purse than before she was coerced onto the game in the first place.'

Jenks forced a sigh, for effect. 'Spare me the moral crusade, will you.' He squared up. 'You don't get to tell me what I can and can't do. I've got more sway round here than you have. If I want to talk to Doreen, I'll talk to her. If I want to take a few quid in return for keeping an eye on her, I'll take it. If I want a bit of the other, well that's up to me. And if you know what's good for you, you'll keep your nose out of my affairs.'

'That's big talk from a snot-nosed little Caesar in a jacket he's not grown into yet. What exactly do you plan to do if I don't?'

'Someone might get hurt,' said Jenks.

'You? Hurt me?' said Calloway. 'I've had bigger than you with chips.'

Jenks summoned his nastiest grin. 'I didn't mean you.'

That flicked the switch.

Calloway grabbed Jenks' good arm. He lifted the heavy wood flap in the bar top and brought it down hard on Jenks' hand. Jenks cried. The punters in the pub stared. One punter winced. Another gave Jenks a *serves-you-right* look. Jenks looked down at his crushed fingers and tried to form a fist, before squealing in pain.

'Try hitting a girl with that,' said Calloway.

EIGHT

They heard it before they rounded the corner. The chiming and clanging of carnival music and the diesel roar of engines powering the rides. Then the sickly smell of toffee apples mixed with the electric tang of ozone from the sparks above the dodgems. Then barkers husky from years of shouting. Hook a duck, blue picks a prize. Rifle range, five pellets for sixpence. Calloway hated fairgrounds. He recoiled from their insistent energy. It was distracting, disorientating. It reminded him of battle. Flashes, screams and the fierce growling of engines. A mechanical hell.

Webber didn't share Calloway's distaste. The nearer they drew to the fairground, the more his excitement showed. Calloway saw a glimpse of how Webber must have been as a boy. Too much energy, overexcited, talking thirteen to the dozen, eyes alight with anticipation.

Webber had phoned Calloway at the stadium the previous evening. He'd remembered something. A time just after he'd first met Stan, when Stan, then a speedway rider, was moonlighting. Earning extra cash to pay off a debt.

Webber led Calloway through the crowd. Kids ran around at knee height, fingers sticky with candy floss. Courting couples dallied, boyfriends daring their girls to go on the most daunting rides. Ex-soldiers showed off on the rifle range, aiming at overly tightened tin-man targets that refused to lie down. The fortune teller in her fake gypsy garb caught Calloway's eye. 'Read your future, luvvie?' she said in a flirtatious tone, her slender finger beckoning. Future? thought Calloway. It's difficult enough coping with the past. A gaggle of men in caps and coats were huddled around the front of the boxing booth. A fighter emerged onto a small stage in his robe, dancing around, shadow boxing. The name *Slammer Suskind* sewn on his back in gold silk letters, above the epithet *The Hackney Heavyweight.* Well, well, Johnny Boy, thought Calloway. A fighter now, are we? Last time Calloway had seen Suskind, he'd been lugging crates at the tea building by day and roughing up fascists in the East End by night. Calloway stopped and watched, as the boxing booth barker set up Johnny for the challenge.

'Who'll take on the Slammer?' he shouted in hoarse cockney. 'Which of you fine gentlemen is man enough?' He put on a show of surveying the crowd, his eye cocked. 'Go three rounds, you win five pounds.'

'What's up, Reg?' said Webber. 'You thinking of having a go?'

Calloway shook his head. 'He's an old pal of mine from the war. Ex-paratrooper.'

Webber looked on, his face showing admiration. 'Good strong lad, by the look of him. You wouldn't catch me having a go.'

'Some fool will,' said Calloway.

Some fool stepped forward. He couldn't have been more than five foot eight, but he was broad enough. Young too. He'd have youth on his side. Johnny was only a couple of years off forty, Calloway knew. The crowd gave the boy a cheer as he stepped up. He was pretty, but hard looking with it, with a shock of white-blonde hair and a sparrow tattoo peeking through the open neck of his shirt. The mark of the sailor.

'Let's get a couple of tickets,' said Webber, like the excitable child he resembled, in spite of his own forty years. 'The other business can wait. It ain't going nowhere.'

They joined the crowd around the small ring in the low-roofed tent. The air was thick with the smell of sweat and cigarettes. Suskind was in the ring now, sparring an invisible partner. The young challenger was getting gloved-up in the opposite corner.

Calloway looked at the crowd. They were rugged working men, their faces hewn by toil or adversity. One face stood out though. Different to the rest. Smooth and good looking, in spite of a prominent jaw line. He wore a blue blazer beneath his raincoat. His dark hair was combed back from a widow's peak. Just like the man Vera described. His eyes were fixed on the fighters readying themselves in the ring. Calloway stared at him. In Calloway's experience, when you stare at people long enough, they'll catch your eye eventually. It felt as if this man was making every effort to avoid that happening.

The bell rang. The crowd cheered, shouting encouragement to the pretender. Johnny took a few punches to the head and body, but he took them in his stride. He was letting the lad show what he'd got. He was playing the crowd, softening them up, opening up the prospect of a win for the tattooed sailor boy. Letting him show his good right hand. Johnny kept this up for the first two rounds. The tension mounted inside the tent. It was hot. The sailor dripped sweat in spite of his youth. Johnny hadn't popped so much as a bead. Neither had the man with the widow's peak, Calloway noticed. He was too cool by half.

The bell started round three. The fervour of the crowd grew. A blood lust. They cheered the young blonde David as he took on Johnny's Goliath. Johnny went for an inside slip towards the challenger's right hand and planted an uppercut to his body. The sailor really felt it. Johnny had turned the tables, right on cue. They spun around the ring, before Johnny knocked the young sailor down with three hard punches to his head. The sailor fell to his knees. The referee started the count.

'One, two...'

'Your mate's pretty tasty ain't he?' said Webber. 'Young lad didn't stand a chance.'

'Three times regimental boxing champion,' said Calloway. 'He's used to decking six-foot paratroopers.'

'...eight, nine...'

The challenger gave up any pretence of a comeback. He flopped onto the canvas, resigned to his loss.

'...ten!'

The referee grabbed Johnny by the glove and raised the big fighter's fist in the air.

Johnny caught Calloway's eye. A flicker of pleasant surprise crossed his face. He gave his old pal the wink. Calloway gestured with a nod towards the back of the tent that they should meet.

'Stone the crows, Reggie, old son,' said Suskind, stepping out of the ring. He gave his former comrade a bear hug with his gloves still on.

'You've still got it, Johnny,' said Calloway. 'How come you're back in the ring?'

Suskind grinned. 'Got fed up with lugging tea chests all day long. Decking people is a whole lot easier and it pays better.' He glanced over at the ring. The ref and the barker were lifting the flaccid sailor boy through the ropes. They handed him to his mates, abdicating all responsibility.

'Felt sorry for that one,' said Suskind, unlacing his gloves with his teeth. 'He had a bit of technique. But he was cocky. Fancied himself and let it go to his head.'

Calloway noticed the man with the widow's peak was hanging around. It made him uneasy. He introduced Suskind to Webber. The small speedway rider seemed in awe of the big boxer.

'Any friend of Cab's, as they say,' said Suskind. He rubbed his shoulder and winced. 'Not as young as I used to be,' he said. 'I need to get this a rub before the next bout. You've got my number, haven't you?' Calloway nodded. 'Give me a bell, eh? We'll have a drink.' He turned to Webber. 'You too, mate.'

Calloway said he would, adding, 'I hate to ask, Johnny, but can you do us a favour?'

'Anything, Cab,' Suskind said without hesitation.

'There's a fella over there we don't want to meet, if you get my drift. Can you distract him so Bert and I can slip out?'

Bert looked confused. He'd clearly not noticed the smooth-looking man in the crowd.

Johnny didn't ask for details. He said, 'Anything, Reg, you know that. You risked your neck for me not so long ago. It's the least I can do.'

Johnny had recruited Calloway into his band of anti-fascists. They'd cracked some heads at Mosleyite rallies in the East End.

'Good man,' said Calloway, clapping the ex-paratrooper on the back.

Suskind approached the man with the widow's peak and gave

him some spiel, telling him he looked like a fighter and challenging him to step up for the next bout. Calloway and Webber slipped through a vent in the canvas at the back of the tent.

When they were outside, Webber said, 'Good bloke, your mate. But what was all that about us slipping out?'

Calloway looked over his shoulder. They were clear for now.

'There was a man in the crowd that fitted Vera's description of Denton. Normally that wouldn't be unusual. There must be hundreds who do. But not in a boxing booth full of working men that we happen to be in too.'

'Blimey,' said Webber. 'You sure? It's all a bit Dick Barton, innit?'

'Not sure,' said Calloway. 'But when things don't add up, like your brother-in-law Stan's death, it's best to trust your instincts.'

They wove their way through the crowds between the rides and sideshows. It was busy now. Easier to lose themselves. Calloway kept alert, casting an eye around the faces. Bert pointed to a sideshow at the edge of the fairground.

'There it is,' he said.

It was a brightly-lit, double-height structure, edged with rows of lightbulbs, illuminating a gaudy, painted sign which read, *The Devil's Drome – defying gravity and death!* It had tall open stairways on either side. Between them was a small stage where a motorcyclist was riding a motorcycle on rollers while a barker gave the spiel.

'Roll up, roll up, to the greatest show on wheels. Be amazed as the fearless Cyclone Sid rides the entirely vertical, totally diabolical, Devil's own drome! Witness the sensation of the century for only a shilling.'

Webber was eyeing the bike on the rollers. 'That's an Indian Scout,' he said. 'Or was. They've stripped off the lot. Mudguards, speedo, lights. They've just left a stub pipe for the exhaust. They've shortened the frame and bent the forks back, an'all.'

Calloway knew nothing about motorcycles but he could see the bike on the stage was little more than a skeleton, on which its rider was balanced, his hands in the air. Webber bought a pair of tickets and they climbed the stairway, ducked through the doorway in the tented cover and took their place among the punters on the viewing gallery that lined the rim of the high, circular wall below. They were packed in tight. Perhaps this really was the sensation of the century, thought Calloway. The rider, Cyclone Sid, appeared, wheeling the stripped-down motorcycle through a hidden trapdoor at the base of the drome. He was stocky and muscular, with slicked back blonde hair, an impish grin and a gap between his teeth. The crowd cheered as he entered. The barker followed him, picking up a microphone and continuing his patter, this time through the small Tannoy speakers in the dome of the tent. Cyclone Sid kickstarted the bike, signalling to a third man, his mechanic, who crouched behind the machine and gave it a good push off. The scream of the engine echoed off the planked wooden sides of the drome. The crowd leaned forward as far as the safety wire would allow. Webber did too, and Calloway followed his lead.

'Watch yer hat,' said Webber, pushing his trilby down on his head. 'You don't want to lose that down there. You could have him off.'

The rider made circuits of the gently sloping base of the wall, revving hard and building speed. With a jerk of the long, cow-horn handlebars, he mounted the vertical sides and immediately sped up to the rim, his tyres missing the noses of the crowd by inches. They recoiled, gasping. He fixed them all with his impish grin as he passed them at speed. Their heads circled with every circuit, and each time they relaxed and peered back down into the hole, he shot up to greet them, to more gasps and screams. The barker worked his spiel, building the anticipation and announcing each new trick the rider performed. No hands. Side saddle. Backwards in the saddle. Backwards with no hands. And Cyclone Sid's pièce de résistance, side-saddle, lying flat on the seat with arms flung outwards and legs in the air. The crowd cheered and applauded. Their exhilaration was palpable, their excitement infectious. Calloway felt himself drawn willingly into the collective delight of the moment. He had to admit, the show was thrilling, even to a tightly-wound brute like him. Webber nudged him with his elbow.

'Great, innit?' he said, beaming like a small boy again.

After the show, they hung around until the punters had dispersed.

'Let's grab 'im before they start over again,' said Webber, tugging Calloway by the sleeve and leading him to the stage. The barker looked down at them. He recognised Webber.

'Bert?' he said. He scraped his hand through the big tuft of greasy black hair on his square head.

Webber nodded and gave him a smile.

'Bert Webber, as I live and breathe,' the barker said. 'Gawd, it's been a while.' He climbed down to meet them. 'You still riding?'

'With the Bullets, down Bermondsey,' Webber replied.

'The Bullets, eh?' he gave Webber a knowing look. 'Pretty Patty Moxon's mob, you lucky boy.'

Webber shuffled, looking slightly awkward. 'She's alright, as it happens,' he said.

The barker gave him a sleazy look.

'A good guv'nor, I mean,' said Webber.

The barker gave a grudging nod. 'She was a great show rider in her day, I'll grant you that. Had some balls on her.' He looked at Calloway. 'We've not met, squire,' he said, offering his hand. 'I'm Alfie Shuman. Shuman the showman.' He cackled, shaking Calloway's hand. 'So what brings you here, Bertie Boy? You found that brother-in-law of yours?'

Webber frowned. 'What d'you mean found him?'

Shuman took a Woodbine from behind his ear and lit up. 'Your Stan did a runner, so I hear.'

'From Drinkwell's?' said Calloway. 'The hauliers?'

Shuman pulled a face. 'Never heard of no hauliers. He did a runner from our tour of Germany. Left me right in the lurch. I've got a girl rider over there and fuck all else right now.'

'What tour of Germany?' said Webber.

'Stan didn't tell you?' Shuman frowned at Webber then shrugged, meaning he didn't care whether Webber knew or not. 'I run two dromes,' he said. 'One here, and one for touring. Stan came to see me a few months back saying he needed to get his hands on some money real quickly. I guessed what was up. He'd been gambling, as is his wont, and he'd been losing, as is his habit.'

Webber turned to Calloway. He said, 'Stan used to moonlight for Shuman when he was riding with the Hawks. This was back before the war.'

Shuman nodded.

'Anyway, he showed up a couple of months back looking for work and it just so happened I was starting a tour of the bases in Germany, so him popping up was a bit on the convenient side,' he said. 'I bit his hand off. Signed him up to ride as a double act with this German bint I've got on the books. Hannelore and Herman, we called them, with Stan being Herman, if you know what I mean.'

'What do you mean bases?' said Calloway.

Shuman took a drag on the fag, exhaled and belched. 'US bases,' he said. 'Army, air force, you know. Entertaining the yanks. My business partner's a yank, as it happens, and he fixed it all up. Nice little earner too. Them yanks'll pay through the nose. It's like they don't know what the money's worth.'

'And Stan disappeared?' said Calloway.

Shuman nodded. 'It was all going great guns. The yanks loved the show and we got more bookings and extensions. It was promising to be a nice long run. The show arrived in Berlin where we had a string of dates in the American sector. Next thing I know,' he said, nodding at Webber, 'I'm getting a telegram saying that his toe-rag brother-in-law had done a runner. Didn't show up for a show and hasn't been seen since. When you turned up just now I thought maybe you had some news for me.'

Webber looked down at his feet. He looked up and was about to speak. Calloway cut him off.

'We came here thinking you might know where Stan had got to,' he said. He didn't want Webber mentioning that Stan was dead. 'He's not showed up at home or anywhere, and his wife is beside herself.'

'Perhaps he's run off with a *fräulein*,' said Shuman. 'He always had an eye for the skirt, eh?'

Webber forced a grin.

'When did he fail to show up?' said Calloway.

Shuman dragged the last of the nicotine out of the butt of the Woodbine and flicked it onto the ground. He thought for a moment. 'A month back. The fourteenth or fifteenth, I reckon.'

The date Stan was supposed to have died in the accident, thought Calloway.

Shuman squinted at Webber, furrowing his brow.

''Ere, Bertie Boy,' he said. 'Speedway season'll be finishing any day now, won't it? Don't fancy a nice little trip to Germany, do you? Wouldn't take much to get a rider like you trained up on the wall. The money is handsome, like I said. You could line your pockets and treat your Else to something nice. Not to mention a bit of oompah, oompah, with a local Helga and a couple of her flaxen-haired friends. I've heard they're pretty broadminded over there, Bertie.'

Webber flushed red. He shook his head. 'Nah, mate. Sorry. You won't catch me risking me neck in that contraption,' he said, nodding towards the drome. 'The cinder track is one thing, that's second nature to me, but that bleedin' drome is a mug's game.'

Shuman lent back, faking offence.

'Yes Bertie,' he said. 'It's a mug's game that's putting my two boys through a very good private school, if you don't mind.' He pulled another cigarette from a pack in his pocket. 'Anyway, son,' he said, 'let me know if you change your mind. And if you know of any other mug who fancies a trip to Berlin and a pocket full of Deutschmarks, you know where to find me.'

NINE

'I want you to go to Germany,' said Webber, as they were walking back to his car.

'You're not serious, are you?' said Calloway.

'It's the only way we're going to find out what happened to Stan. I can pay your passage and expenses. You need to get over there and start asking around.'

'You make its sound easy, Bert. Even if I went to Berlin, I can't just go walking into US military bases asking difficult questions.'

Webber considered this for a moment.

'No, I suppose you're right,' he said. 'It's a shame you're not a rider. You could take that job Shuman's offering.' Webber caught the look on Calloway's face and laughed.

'That's never going to happen,' said Calloway. 'I've not ridden a motorcycle in my life and I don't intend to start.' Calloway thought for a moment. 'If anyone's going to join that German tour, it should be you, Bert. Shuman seemed pretty confident you'd shape up as a wall rider.'

As he said this, Calloway was doubting the sense of it. Berlin seemed very far away. The idea of going into a strange city to investigate the mysterious death of an indebted gambler, fairground stuntman and all-round ne'er-do-well seemed ridiculous.

'Shuman's being a bit ambitious,' said Webber. 'It ain't that easy to learn them tricks, no matter how much of a natural you are on a bike. I would if I could, but I don't have what it takes.'

Webber ground through the Buick's gears. His frustration showed in his driving.

'I hate to say it, Bert,' said Calloway, 'but we may have hit a dead end.'

Calloway knew he should have left it there and then. And perhaps he would've done, were it not for the appearance at the fairground of a man matching the description of Denton. Calloway reckoned he knew when something wasn't right, and that wasn't right. The official line on Stan's death made no sense at all. It didn't tally with the facts, as Bert and Calloway had uncovered them. It was a loose end. Calloway hated loose ends. They were the bane of his life. They led him down paths that he knew he should avoid.

Webber dropped him outside the arena and drove home. The little man couldn't have looked more down in the mouth. Calloway climbed the dark stairway to his office and turned in, grabbing what sleep he could on the uncomfortable floor mat. He was awoken the next morning by a tap on the door. George the cleaner stepped in the small room and said, 'I found you a place.'

Calloway was barely conscious. He sat up, rubbing sleep from his eyes. 'What place?'

'A new gaff. Somewhere to live. Somewhere better than this,' he said, gesturing around the pokey office room.

Calloway said thanks and agreed to meet George once he'd freshened up. He washed and shaved in the gents' lavatories, combed his hair in the cracked and mottled mirror and made himself a plate of beans from a can for breakfast. He met George on the pavement outside the arena doors, with his two suitcases and orange crate full of belongings. The two men set off in Calloway's car. They headed west.

Kensington was alive and bustling at this time in the morning. The pavements were already busy with gentrified folk, or shabbier types that aspired to be, heading to work, shopping or walking ridiculous dogs. George gave directions. They turned the corner into a wide side street of tall and ornate buildings. Calloway saw a gaggle of people at the far end of the street.

'What's going on there?' he said.

George said, 'Oh, Christ, they've come for us. It was only a matter of time.'

'What was?' said Calloway, pulling the car over just ahead of the crowd. He saw two dozen policeman, a news crew with a camera and an angry-looking bunch of men and women of a class not normally found in this part of town. They were shouting slogans at the policeman while some threw what looked like food parcels up to the first-floor windows of the corner building, where men were reaching out to catch them.

'The Scott Hotel,' said Calloway, reading the sign above the entrance.

George nodded. He said, 'We've been squatting in it for a year now. The Vigilantes took it over and moved a dozen families in.'

'Who are the Vigilantes?' said Calloway.

'They organise squatting for homeless ex-servicemen and their families. There's enough empty buildings in this city to house the lot of them, but you can't get your hands on them through official channels. Too much red tape and stupid regulations. The Vigilantes started squatting in them after the war.'

'What do you mean "squatting"?' It was an unfamiliar term to Calloway.

'Breaking in, claiming it and moving in those that need a roof over their heads.'

'Why the police?'

'The building's owner wants it back. We knew this was on the cards but wasn't expecting it so soon.'

'So who are the people on the ground, the ones chanting?'

George looked over at the crowd. 'Supporters, other squatters. And the Communists of course, although if you ask me, it's none of their business. This ain't political. It's about respectable people needing a home, like Mrs Churchill said. Good old, Clemmie. She supports us, you know. The reds have jumped on the bandwagon and they're a pain in the neck.'

Calloway watched as the squatters fielded the upward barrage of packets and tins thrown from the crowd below.

'Why the food parcels?' said Calloway.

'It's a siege. Like the Berlin airlift. The squatters can't leave, or they'd lose their spot. The folk on the ground are their lifeline.'

'And that's where I'm supposed to live? Seriously?' said Calloway.

George nudged him. 'Go on with you,' he said. 'You're an old soldier. You've faced bigger challenges. And once you're inside, it's a bit of alright. Proper high class, as squats go. Better than the old military bases they're squatting outside London. All we've got to do is sneak round the back to the service entrance. My pal Jimmy is manning the barricade. He'll let us in.'

Jimmy was a burly man in his mid-thirties. He wore a reefer jacket and flat cap, with a pair of steel-toed boots on his oversized feet. He nodded to George, and eyed Calloway with suspicion.

'This is Reg,' said George. 'He's moving in. Ex-airborne. He'll be useful.'

Calloway didn't like the sound of that. But as he walked through the corridors of the former hotel, he had to admit that as digs went, this place was a cut above. It had retained much of its grandeur, with deep red carpeting, panelled walls and high stucco ceilings. Even the chandeliers were intact. Children were chasing each other up and down the corridors, while their mothers chatted cheerfully from their respective bedroom doors. Men were piling the supplies thrown up to them onto a trestle table, where a studious-looking young man in horn-rimmed spectacles noted down each item in an exercise book.

George said, 'The lifts are out, so you'll have to put up with climbing a few stairs. Your gaff is on the top floor.'

The 'gaff' that Calloway had been allocated was a double bedroom with two floor-to-ceiling windows overlooking the street. It had jazz-age wallpaper and thick velvet curtains, which looked dusty but warm. There was a door in the far wall. Calloway peered in. The room has its own bathroom, with vivid green and black tiles, and angular chromium taps.

'This is what you call a squat?' Calloway said.

'Good, innit?' said George. 'Normally we'd put a family in a room this size, but the roof leaks. You'll have to keep changing the bucket when it rains.'

Calloway spotted the galvanised pail in the corner of the room, beneath a brown stain on the ceiling. He shrugged.

'I can live with that,' he said. He threw his cases on the bed and George lifted the orange crate onto the walnut dressing table.

'Everyone gets chores,' he said. 'It's how we run the building. Yours will involve lifting and carrying, I reckon, seeing as you're a big lad.'

Calloway said this would be fine. A small price to pay in return for free lodgings, even if they were under siege. The chanting below was still going. Calloway glanced down. The police were trying to move the protestors on. Two constables grabbed one of the ringleaders by the arms and led him to a Black Maria. The protestors booed and hissed.

'What are the neighbours like?' said Calloway.

'Most of the building is full of London families. From north London and the East End. People who were bombed out and had nowhere to go when their old men came back from the war. Your corridor's different. They're Poles mostly. Blokes who fought with the free Polish army and air force and didn't fancy living in Poland under the Soviets.' George lowered his voice. 'A word of advice. The Poles don't like the Communists, for obvious reasons, so if any reds show up here, it's best to keep your head down and let 'em get on with it.'

Calloway had met plenty of free Polish serviceman during the war. He'd fought alongside the Polish 1st Independent Parachute Brigade in Europe. He didn't rate the Communists' chances much.

George left Calloway to it.

'Me and the missus are in room 106 on the first floor, if you fancy dropping in,' he said.

Calloway said he might. He returned to the window and stared down at the protest below. Even from this height he could see the faces of the crowd. They were a mix of ages and types. Working-class men and women in their work clothes or their Sunday best, skinny student types, organisers with earnest faces busying around in their raincoats.

And a smooth-looking man in a blazer, with dark hair and a widow's peak. He was looking Calloway straight in the eye.

TEN

'Call for you, Mr Calloway.'

Young Charlie Fowler, Finnegan's gofer, popped his head into the bar, where Calloway was steering a drunk back to his seat. The drunk had been overly familiar with one of the female bar staff, who had complained. He wasn't worth kicking out yet, just sitting down with a warning.

Calloway left the bar and climbed the back stairs to his office. The phone's receiver was lying on his desk.

'Calloway,' he said.

'Reg, it's Bert.' Webber sounded excited. 'I've found a wall rider.'

'Go on,' said Calloway, trying to conceal the apprehension in his voice.

'I can't talk now. Meet me tomorrow night.'

He gave Calloway a place and time.

The following evening Calloway drove out to Custom House, near the Royal Albert Dock. He parked his car in a side street of mean little dockers cottages. His was the only car in the street, apart from a grey Nash which had pulled up a hundred yards behind him. Two men got out and nodded, then turned and walked towards the noise in the distance. They wore belted macs and woollen scarves, like typical sports fans. Calloway followed in the same direction, the noise getting louder. He turned the corner at the end of the street. He could hear the roar of engines, even from this distance. It was a familiar sound, from his days as head of security at Bermondsey Stadium. But this wasn't Bermondsey. This was West Ham. Bigger, grander, almost palatial by comparison. With its Art Deco gates and neon lighting, it resembled a Hollywood studio more than an East London dirt track. He caught the unmistakeable smell of methanol and Castrol R in the damp night air. The smell of speedway. It sparked memories, some he'd sooner forget.

He bought a ticket and a programme and took his place in the crowd. There must have been forty thousand in tonight, if he was any judge. The toffs had Ascot and motor racing at Brooklands. The working man and woman had the dogs and speedway. Dogs for gambling. Speedway for thrills. Dirty, fast and dangerous. Maniacs on machines.

It was the Bullets away to the Hammers tonight. Bermondsey versus West Ham. The last fixture of the season. Webber was riding, alongside others Calloway knew. 'Six Gun' O'Donnell, Billy 'Boy' Riley and Chip 'Clanger' Bellman. Calloway looked in the programme. It was heat nine already. Webber and Riley riding for the Bullets, against West Ham's two Aussies, Lawson and Watson. Calloway checked the scoreboard on the opposite side of the big oval track. It was still close. Everything to ride for tonight. And the Bullets and the Hammers were neck and neck in the league table. Tonight would decide the champions.

Calloway let the atmosphere wash over him. He tried to lose himself in the scream of the engines and the chanting of the crowd. But all the time, his thoughts drifted back to the man with the widow's peak hairline that was following him. He was sure of it.

He snapped to as they announced heat fifteen over the Tannoy. Webber was up again, with the tall American, O'Donnell. The scores were close. This was the deciding heat. Calloway watched the riders line up at the tape, digging in with the heels of their lead-soled boots. A hush descended. The atmosphere was electric. The tape flew up and the four bikes shot forward, revving hard into the first bend. O'Donnell claimed the lead, the Hammers were second and third with Webber a hair's breadth behind them. They broadsided round the bed and into the back straight. Webber let rip, passing both of the Hammers and tucking his bike in behind O'Donnell, as the pair of them entered the second bend. The conditions suited the Bullets. They were used to riding the tightest circuit in the league at home. More circular than oval. A big track like West Ham gave them time to breathe, time to think, time to steal a lead and hold it. This they did. The Bullets fans went wild. Webber and O'Donnell grabbed each other by the shoulders and slapped each other's backs.

Calloway killed time. It would be a while before Webber changed out of his race leathers and could meet him in the bar. His stomach churned. Was it hunger or the jitters? He bought a hot dog, realising he'd not eaten since lunch. The churning didn't stop. He sat at the back of the stands and smoked a half pack of Navy Cut.

He looked at his watch. Time for a drink. He crossed the stands, going against the tide of punters leaving the stadium. He climbed the stairs to the bar, a generous affair more suited to a modern hotel, at least in comparison to the bar at Bermondsey, as he remembered it. And it was full too. Rammed to the gills. Calloway elbowed his way in and ordered a scotch and soda.

Webber was seated at a table by the big windows that overlooked the track. Webber wasn't alone. Someone sat drinking with him, with their back to Calloway. Calloway downed the scotch and ordered another. He picked it up and crossed the bar towards Webber.

'Reggie,' said Webber, his face lighting up. 'Come and celebrate.' He gestured to a seat he'd clearly been saving. He'd had a few already, judging by the glazing of his eyes. If he'd been sober, he might have sensed Calloway's apprehension. Calloway hesitated before sitting. Webber's drinking companion turned to face him.

'Look what the cat dragged in,' she said.

Pat Moxon. Pretty Pattie. Queen of the dirt track. The Bullets' promoter and Calloway's old boss.

And the lover he walked out on without saying a word.

'Hello Pat,' he said.

Webber's smile dropped, as if suddenly realising the significance of the meeting.

'Sit down, Reg,' said Pat. Her tone was gracious. And ice cold.

'Have some champagne,' she said. 'Like Bert says, we're celebrating.'

'Thanks,' said Calloway. 'But I've got a drink already.'

Pat smiled at him. She had a lovely smile when she chose to use it, but right now he struggled to see any warmth in it.

'I'll pour you one anyway,' she said. 'As a chaser. I'm sure your mouth's dry.'

Dry and sour, thought Calloway. He swigged the scotch to take away the taste.

She huffed with mock impatience. 'Well, aren't you going to join us?' She patted the chair beside her. 'I mean, I've saved you a seat.'

Calloway sat. Bert caught his eye. Now he realised. He looked apologetic. Too late for that, Bertie Boy. Calloway downed the scotch and picked up the champagne.

'To the Bullets,' he said.

Pat raised her glass. 'I'd prefer to drink to absent friends, Reg,' she said. She gave an insincere laugh. 'Absent without leave, as I'm sure you used to say in the army.'

She chinked his glass and looked him full in the face. Her eyes were beautiful, and as hard as diamonds. The air turned brittle. Webber cut in to break the tension.

'Pat's gonna ride the wall,' he said, taking a gulp of his champagne. 'She's agreed to do the tour.'

'In Germany?' said Calloway. He found this hard to grasp, in spite of his suspicions. It was hard enough meeting the woman he'd walked out on. Now Webber was suggesting they go to Berlin. Together.

'I told Pat all about it. About Stan and how Vera's doing her nut.'

Pat nodded. 'I know Bert well. I know he's not going to let this go. I can't risk his mind not being on the job.'

Webber shuffled in his seat, looking slightly offended.

Pat responded. 'I know you got a result tonight,' she said. 'Especially in the last heat. But if your mind had been on the job, you'd have taken that first bend and held the lead for all three laps. Instead you played catch-up and scraped second place by the skin of your teeth. I'm not having that carrying into next season. You need to get this business with your brother-in-law sorted out once and for all.'

She was serious. Calloway had hoped Webber had been overplaying Pat's willingness to join the wall of death tour. But she was deadly serious.

'Can you really ride the wall?' he said.

She scoffed. 'Oh ye of little faith, Reggie. How do you think I got set up as a speedway promoter in the first place?' She rubbed her thumb and forefinger together. 'It takes dough, you know. I earned it on the wall. When they banned us girls from speedway in the thirties I became a show rider.' Calloway remembered her telling him this. 'After a couple of years as a warmup act, doing stunts at speedway fixtures, I got offered a crack at the Kursaal drome in Southend. Girl riders were a novelty back then. I made a packet.'

'And you're prepared to join a wall of death tour in Germany, just to get me in there to investigate Stan's death?'

She poured herself another glass of champagne and sipped it. Her lipstick left a ruby red bow on the glass.

'No,' she said. 'Not just to get you in there.' She lit a cocktail cigarette and drew on the gold filter. You didn't see many of those in West Ham. She exhaled with a wistful sigh. 'If you want to know, Reggie,' she said, 'I'm bored. The season's finished and for now I've had enough of wet-nursing the likes of Bert and his cowboy teammates.' She looked at Bert. 'No offence,' she said. Webber gave a small bow, as if to say *none taken*, although Calloway suspected he was hurt by the comment. Pat waved the cigarette in the air. 'I'm bored with the stadium, and the press, and the accountants, and the interfering busybodies at the association. I fancy a thrill. A real thrill.' She cocked her head to one side and looked at Calloway. Her diamond eyes twinkled. 'Not a cheap thrill, Reggie,' she said. 'I've had enough of those.'

She snapped her fingers and a steward brought another bottle. Calloway drank more champagne. The booze calmed him. At least it calmed his churning stomach. Deep down he'd guessed this would happen, the moment Webber told him on the phone he'd found a wall rider. Patricia Moxon. Pretty Pattie. The moniker didn't do her justice. She was bold, confident and handsome. Well-dressed, well-coiffured, well-manicured. She worked hard at being a class act. For a moment Calloway felt something more than the drink.

Pat raised a glass. Calloway and Webber did the same by reflex.

'To Berlin,' she said. They chinked glasses. 'So what's the plan, Reggie?'

'Seems like you're the one with the plan, Pat,' said Calloway. 'I'm just the fella doing the dirty work.'

She leaned into him and pinched his cheek.

'Perhaps that's all you're good for, lover,' she said.

ELEVEN

It was almost midnight when Calloway returned to the hotel. The crowd was gone, and the only police presence was two weary-looking beat coppers at the far end of the street. He parked the car and walked down a side alley to the rear of the building. The service entrance was dark. Burley Jim would have knocked off for the night, now that the police had thinned out. They'd be back with a court order, George had said. But the Vigilantes would hold out. This was their home now and they had plenty of supporters. Clemmie Churchill for one.

He let himself in. The Vigilantes had changed the locks and given everyone a key. The hotel was quiet as he climbed the stairs, save for a baby crying in a distant corridor. The Poles were awake on his corridor. He could hear their chatter and the muted sounds of a gramophone through the heavy door to one of their rooms. He missed his gramophone. He still had a handful of records in the orange crate. Mahler, Mendelssohn, Brahms. He'd learned to love the romantic composers. He had a wonderful teacher, for an all too brief moment in his life. He'd bought gramophone records to remember. He would ask the Poles if he could play them.

He kicked off his shoes and laid out his blanket, rolling up a towel to use as a pillow. The streetlights outside cast a bright glow across the bed. He crossed the room to close the curtains and looked down from the window.

There was a grey Nash parked opposite the hotel.

When he arrived at the arena the following morning, there was a message for him on his desk. Webber had called again. He said they should meet at Vera's house. Calloway sighed. It wasn't that he didn't like the little rider or want to help him. Webber and Johnny Suskind were the closest thing he had to friends. But this business with Vera and her late husband was getting too strange by half. His meter was nudging red all the time now. The Grey Nash turning up in Kensington only made it worse. But Webber's money was good. He had a use for it and there would be more to spare, now that he had free digs at the squat. He looked at his watch. He reckoned he could get to Deptford and back in time to catch Finnegan before the wrestling that night. He didn't relish breaking the news that he'd be taking some leave.

Webber had heard Calloway's car pull up outside Vera's house and was waiting for him on the doorstep. He was smoking and looking anxious.

'She's really bad today,' he said, shaking his head. 'My Else is in there with her now.'

'Bad how?' said Calloway.

'Off her rocker. Speaking in tongues.'

They went inside. The curtains were open, the obligatory darkness of mourning over. Vera was anything but over it though, as Calloway looked at her. Her eyes were glazed, but not like a drunk's. She was staring at the wall, at the wallpaper, concentrating hard, enthralled. She pointed with a limp hand, tracing the outline of the pattern, and giggled to herself.

'Hello, Vera,' said Calloway. 'Bert says you're a bit out of sorts today.'

Bert's wife Elsie looked up at him from the sofa, where she sat holding Vera's hand.

'She's been getting worse all week,' she said. 'Sometimes she's fine. Other times she's away with the fairies.'

'She's been taking them pills for her nerves, but they don't even touch it,' said Webber.

Calloway picked up the pill bottle from the sideboard. It was half-empty. He read the label. Common barbiturates, from his limited knowledge.

Vera snapped to.

'It's that nice Mr Calloway,' she said, crossing the room and taking his hand. She turned to Elsie. 'Handsome devil, ain't he.'

She let go of his hand, returned to her armchair and drank some tea from the cup on the side table.

'Are you going to find my Stan?' she said, in a sing-song voice.

Bert looked at Calloway, uncertain, then turned to his sister-in-law. 'Stan passed away, Vera. Remember? An accident, they said.'

Vera thought for a moment then huffed. 'You don't need to remind me, Bert Webber.' Her tone was suddenly rational. 'I know my Stan's dead. What do you think I am, gaga?'

Webber shrugged.

Calloway had to admit, Vera's mood had deteriorated since his last meeting with her. She would switch from whimsical, to angry to completely lucid within only a few minutes. The nearest Calloway had seen to it was battle stress. That could alter men's minds in strange and disturbing ways. He'd seen it happen.

'Reg is going to Germany, Vera,' said Webber. 'To Berlin. He's going to find out what happened to Stan. It'll settle your mind, girl.' He looked at Calloway with plaintive eyes. 'It will, won't it, Reg?'

It was a tall order. Calloway doubted a few facts about Stan's death would fix Vera's current condition. She needed proper help.

'I'll do what I can,' he said.

He drove north back towards the stadium. He took a left turn at The Nelson into Doreen's street and parked.

She stood by the sink making him tea. Her tightly-cinched dressing gown clung to her skinny frame. She'd lost weight. She had the body of a boy. She played with her hair self-consciously knowing she looked a mess. He wanted to hug her but he couldn't bring himself to, not when he knew she'd had a caller. The small amount of money he was able to give her wasn't enough to make ends meet. She was still relying on other means.

'I'm sorry, Reg. I wasn't expecting you,' she said.

'I should have called first.'

There was a phone in the shared hallway but he didn't know the number.

‘How’s Margaret?’ he said.

‘Alright. She’s across the hall with Mrs Grant. Mrs Grant is very understanding. She looks after Maggie while I’m...’

Doreen looked shameful. Calloway smiled.

‘She’s a good girl,’ he said.

They perched on the unmade bed. The lone armchair she used to own had gone. Pawned, he assumed. They sat in silence for a while before Calloway spoke.

‘I have to go away,’ he said.

‘Away?’ There was a tremor in her voice. ‘Where to?’

‘Not far,’ he lied.

‘But for how long, Reg?’

She took his hand in hers and held it tight, like he was a lifeline. He understood. She would be scared Jenks would be around when he heard Calloway was gone.

‘I’ve taken care of Jenks,’ he said.

He let go of her hand and kissed her lightly on the cheek. Her skin felt cold on his lips. She stood and paced the room, her thin arms clasped tightly around her.

‘If he comes back here, Reg, I swear I’ll kill him.’

Calloway stood to leave. ‘He won’t.’

He pulled out his wallet and put a few notes from Webber’s advance on the bedside table. It made him feel uncomfortable, like the first time he’d been there.

‘I expect Maggie needs new clothes. She’ll be growing.’

She lit a cigarette and drew hard on it with tensed lips.

‘Thanks,’ she said, not looking him in the eye.

Finnegan took Calloway’s request for leave better than he had expected.

‘You could do with a break, Reg,’ Finnegan said. ‘I can’t remember you ever having taken one since you’ve been here.’

It was true. What would Calloway have done with a holiday? He preferred to keep busy. Holidays meant time to think. And thinking brought thoughts he’d sooner forget. There were plenty like him in his generation. The generation that fought. A life of thoughts not thought, and words not spoken, gathered up, nailed down and buried in the war grave of the mind.

‘Growler Grimes is looking for work. He’s one of my old wrestlers, before I started in female wrestling. He can fill in while you’re away.’ He looked apologetic. ‘I’ll have to pay him you’re wedge, though.’

Calloway nodded his agreement. He’d be using Webber’s money anyway.

‘You’re going away?’ said Trudi, when he told her Grimes would be around for the next couple of weeks.

‘Berlin,’ he said. ‘Your old stomping ground.’

‘Marvellous,’ she said. ‘Assuming there’s anything left of it.’

‘I’ll be working,’ he said. ‘After a fashion.’

He told her about Vera, and Stan’s death, the man called Denton and the dates that didn’t tally. It was indiscreet, but in that moment he couldn’t help relieve himself of the burden of discretion. Maybe he was growing weak. Not the stoic, tight-lipped type he’d been since first joining the army as little more than a boy.

Trudi frowned. ‘Be careful, Reggie,’ she said. ‘Berlin is a rotten city if you meet the wrong people. Believe me, I know.’

‘I’ll get by,’ he said.

She shook her head.

‘Don’t be too sure. You’ll need to keep your guard up. Do you have friends there?’

‘I don’t know a soul,’ he said.

She smiled. She unbuttoned her shirt halfway. She had a thin gold chain around her neck. A signet ring hung from it. Calloway hadn’t noticed it before. She didn’t wear it when she fought. She reached behind her head and unclasped the chain.

‘Take this with you,’ she said, handing him the ring on the chain. ‘For luck.’

She reached in her hold-all and took out a wrestling flyer. She wrote a name and address on the back.

‘You may need a friend,’ she said.

TWELVE

D-Day minus one, somewhere over Normandy. Eight young, tense men huddle in a glider, its wood and canvas creaking. The engines of the Dakota tow plane throb ahead of them. There's a smell of piss. Warren kicked over the Elsan. His nervous bladder again. Turbulence sends streams of cold piss in rivulets along the glider's grooved wooden floor, reflecting the red safety light, glowing like rivers of blood.

The glider pilot signals to the men hunched up in the long tubular fuselage behind him.

'Gentlemen, we're about to lose our tow.'

There's a jolt as the tow plane releases the cable, then a bump as the flimsy Horsa glider hits the air beneath and starts its downward glide. It's quiet now. The tow plane's engine noise fades and the airstream whispers around them. The men check their weapons and adjust their webbing.

There's a massive, bone-shaking thud as they hit the ground, throwing them every which way, bouncing their brains around their skulls like snooker balls off the cushion. They scramble over each other, out of the glider and onto the damp earth below.

They approach the radio hut, affixing silencers. Lofty Small dons knuckle dusters. They blow through the door like a hurricane. There's five in the room, a Waffen SS signals unit. Four men, one woman. Lofty floors the officer with a jaw breaker from his brass knuckles. Choc Brown kicks the chair from under the NCO and stamps on his face. Warren, Reece and Cauldwell loom over the other three, pistols held two-handed like Shanghai police. Brown disarms the men. Calloway, their sergeant, opens a canvas duffel bag and starts stuffing in the signals unit's files.

The woman jumps from the chair, her arm raised. She squeezes the trigger on a small Walther pistol at point-blank range and blows Cauldwell's arm from his shoulder. Cauldwell screams. The arm dangles limply in the sleeve of his Denison smock. Blood seeps through the camouflage fabric forming a pool of crimson the colour of his beret.

Calloway raises the Browning automatic in his hand. It spits through the silencer. The 9mm round takes off half the woman's head.

A hand gripped his arm, shaking him.

'Reg, Reggie.'

He awoke, screaming.

'For God's sake Reggie, pipe down. You're scaring the passengers.'

Faces were watching them from the aisle.

'It's the engine noise,' he said. 'It's a DC-3. We called them Dakotas during the war. They towed the gliders to Normandy, the night before D-Day.'

He didn't need to explain any further. People were well used to the hangover of war. They tried to ignore it, deny it, put it behind them, but it wasn't going away. Pat snapped her fingers and summoned the stewardess.

'He needs a large gin,' she said.

The stewardess smiled with forced grace. 'We're not actually serving drinks yet, madam.'

Pat shot her a look.

'It's medicinal,' said Pat. 'And it's Miss.'

Calloway downed the gin in a single gulp. It grounded him. The other passengers had lost interest in the commotion now. Half the seats were block booked for government officials and members of the occupation forces. They remainder of the sixteen passengers looked like business travellers. They had boarded at the new London airport. Calloway remembered when it had been a military airfield sending long-distance flights to the Far East towards the end of the war. Now it had a smart modern terminal, with a bar and cafeteria. They were flying BOAC to

Frankfurt, where they would change to a flight to Berlin. Shuman was all for sending them by boat and train, to save on the fares. Webber had bought Calloway an air ticket. Pat had insisted on paying for herself.

On landing in Frankfurt they transferred to a smaller aircraft operated by the new British European Airways. It was a pre-war twin-engine biplane, an anachronism among the smart new Stratocruisers and Constellations lined up on the tarmac of the airport.

'Christ,' said Pat. 'Is that ours? It looks like something out of a flying circus.'

'We called them Dominies during the war,' said Calloway. 'I think the civil airlines call them Dragons.'

'Well if it starts breathing fire, I'm bailing out,' she said. She pointed to her luggage on the tarmac. 'Take those will you, luvvie.'

He obeyed by reflex, then felt irritated by his own compliance. She was making him pay and he knew it. She strode across the tarmac drawing admiring looks from the ground crew. A steward held her hand and helped her up the small steps into the door at the rear of the plane.

They took two adjacent seats from the half-dozen inside the cramped fuselage. Pat pulled a silver hip flask from her handbag and took a nip before offering it to Calloway.

'Thirsty work carrying my bags, eh?'

He declined.

'Suit yourself,' she said, taking another drink and putting the flask back in her bag.

The little biplane taxied along the runway and glided up into the chill autumn air. Its twin engines made little more than a whisper in comparison with the DC-3. Calloway sat back in the bucket seat and lit a cigarette.

What the hell was he doing?

It was dusk as they made their approach to Berlin. The city lay spread out beneath them, with its endless blocks of gutted buildings and new construction sites. The streets were lighting up, revealing a latticework of routes punctuated with the red and blue neon of cafes and gaudy advertisements. Halfway across the city, the neon stopped abruptly. The Soviet sector, Calloway assumed.

He slid back the window next to his seat and breathed in the cool air. He could see the grand crescent shape of the airport terminal ahead. They were landing at Tempelhof, a swaggering monument to Germany's air superiority. Calloway remembered it from his last visit. If the Roman Empire had airports, they would look like that, he thought.

Tempelhof buzzed with activity. Affluent-looking civilians, sales representatives with sample cases and servicemen in the uniforms of the western allies, all swarming over the mosaic floors, between the travertine columns under the high-vaulted ceiling. The building inspired awe, without a doubt. All part of Nazi architect Albert Speer's megalomaniacal vision for Germania, the new capital of the thousand-year Reich. A liaison officer had given Calloway the history the last time he was here. Calloway had just come through six years of war and couldn't have cared less.

He took a last draw of his cigarette, flicked it to the floor and ground it into the mosaic tiling with the sole of his shoe.

A long line of Volkswagen taxis was lined up outside the terminal like obedient insects. The driver, a worn-down man in his fifties, struggled to get their luggage into the boot at the front of the car. Calloway and Pat eased themselves into the meagre back seat. He felt her warmth against his thigh as they squeezed together.

'This is cosy,' she said. 'Don't get any ideas.'

He ignored her and lit another cigarette, offering one to her.

She waved it away.

'I prefer my own,' she said, taking a brightly-coloured cocktail cigarette from her case.

She made small talk with the driver in English, which he responded to with a series of polite grunts. Calloway looked out of the window and watched the city pass by. This was the American sector. Its bright cafes and illuminated shop windows detracted the eye from the blackened carcasses of the windowless, bombed-out blocks behind them. They passed the derelict stump of the Kaiser Wilhelm church, which stood stubbornly, as if righteously indignant to the damage inflicted on it by the RAF. The arrogance of it struck a nerve in Calloway. In an instant his experience of war surged through him like a current. He stared at the bombed-out church. Serves you bloody well right, he thought.

The driver turned into Kurfürstendamm, a wide boulevard of shops and cafes that seemed oblivious to the damage that encircled it. Neon advertisements for German radios, American cars and French cosmetics cast a glow as bright as daylight. People promenaded, window shopping, or sat at cafes drinking beer and eating ice cream. Last time Calloway was here it was a dim and decaying strip of half-lit windows, where war-ravaged Berliners pretended life was normal again. What a difference a few years of American occupation makes.

The driver asked for the name of their hotel. He drove another hundred yards and pulled the Volkswagen over. Pat gave him a generous tip. They stood under the faded awning, beneath a sign which said *Hotel Pension Ritz*. The stonework either side of the double doors was peppered with bullet holes from wartime street fighting. Calloway ran his fingers over the damage. It sparked memories of war. Pat peered through the doors into a darkened lobby.

'Not my idea of the Ritz,' she said. 'And they say Germans don't have a sense of humour.'

Calloway carried their bags into the lobby and up a flight of stairs. The reception, such as it was, was on the first floor.

A thin, sad-looking woman, who looked sixty but was probably in her forties, handed them two keys.

'Klaus will show you to your rooms,' she said. She smiled for no longer than was courteous.

Klaus shuffled up to them wheezing. He had one arm. He picked up one of their cases and led them down a dim corridor. Calloway rolled his eyes and picked up the other bags. Pat sniggered. It didn't help his mood.

Klaus showed them to two tall doors that faced each other

across the corridor. Pat tipped him the same as the taxi driver. Her largesse irritated Calloway. She flicked the light switch inside the door and peered in. She wrinkled her nose.

'Smells like someone died in there,' she said.

'Someone probably did,' said Calloway, thinking of the bullet holes around the hotel entrance.

Pat shrugged.

'I'm going to freshen up,' she said. 'I'll meet you downstairs in an hour. You can buy me dinner.'

They ate at Cafe Wien. A passenger on the flight from Frankfurt had recommended it to Pat. It was just warm enough to sit outside.

'I want to watch the world go by,' said Pat. 'That way I don't have to talk to you all night.'

She winked at him. Her tone had softened, at least he thought so. The aggressive coldness of their reunion at the stadium had been replaced by a tolerant courtesy, with the occasional joke at his expense. It might just be enough to get them through this ridiculous escapade.

A chubby waiter with a pencil moustache made a fuss of them as they ordered. At least he made a fuss of Pat. He offered Calloway the wine list. Calloway waved it away.

'Beer for me,' he said.

'And I'll have the strongest thing you've got,' said Pat.

The waiter concealed his surprise with an ingratiating pout.

'That would be *Doppelkorn*,' he said, with a small bow.

'Make it a large one,' said Pat. She looked at Calloway. 'If I'm going to get through the evening looking at your ugly face, I'm going to need Dutch courage.'

'I believe *Doppelkorn* is German courage,' said Calloway.

She looked out across the busy street and sighed.

'I reckon we both need it,' she said. He sensed this wasn't one of her quips. Perhaps the penny was dropping. Two ex-lovers come to a strange city seeking the truth behind the mysterious death of a man they hardly knew, who was at best a chancer and at worst God only knows. This wasn't a holiday by any sane person's measure.

Pat frowned at the menu and asked the waiter for a recommendation. He suggested *Konigsberger Klopse*, a local meatball dish with potato. That would at least soak up the *korn*, thought Calloway. He ordered schnitzel with asparagus for himself. The schnitzel when it came was tasteless and the asparagus was tinned, but he ate it eagerly. He'd not eaten since leaving London.

Pat ordered more liquor and insisted Calloway join her. He didn't refuse.

'Does this relieve the boredom?' he said, waving a hand towards the city life in front of them.

'Ask me tomorrow,' she said. 'When I've tackled the wall.'

They made small talk as they ate and kept it civil. Calloway let the *korn* relax him. He started to feel better, if not something approaching good. Pat excused herself, asking the waiter for directions to the bathroom. Calloway's eyes wandered over to an adjacent table where two women sat drinking and smoking, wearing sunglasses like Hollywood starlets, despite the sun having set more than two hours ago. One was blonde, with shoulder-length hair, plump lips and a rounded face. The other was brunette, her hair falling over her shoulders in waves from beneath a small black felt hat. She wore a belted herringbone trench coat with shoulder pads and elaborate pleating, and a skirt cut short enough to show off the legs she was stretching in Calloway's direction. She drew on a cigarette with red-painted lips and tapped her peep-toe heels in time with an imaginary dance tune. She caught Calloway's eye through her tortoise shell sunglasses and smiled.

Pat returned to her seat.

'Put your eyes back in, Reg, or they'll fall in your schnitzel,' she said.

She gave the woman in the trench coat a predatory smile. The woman took the hint and turned back to make conversation with her friend.

They ordered strudel for dessert and *Underberg* as a digestif, which the waiter took great pride in saying was back in production after its cessation during the war. Pat took a sip of the digestif.

'It's bitter,' she said. She held Calloway's gaze. 'A bit like me, really.'

He'd been waiting for it. The more she'd drunk, the more they'd forced polite conversation, the more he knew it was coming.

'Why did you walk out, Reg?' she said.

He felt a knot in his guts. He took a slug of the bitter liquor.

'I wouldn't have been good for you,' he said.

'Shouldn't I have been the judge of that?'

'By the time you'd realised, it would have been too late. There's a side to me that isn't pretty.'

She laughed, incredulous. 'Who are you, Dr Jekyll?'

There was more than one Calloway, he knew that much. His stoic, dependable facade masked the violence inside him. It had always been there. The war had made it far, far worse.

'I'd settle for Mr Hyde, some days,' he said.

'And what made you think I wouldn't?' she said. She reached over and put her hand on top on his. 'I'm made of sterner stuff than you think, Reg.'

He drew his hand away and lit a cigarette. The brunette in the sunglasses looked over at him and made a sad face.

They walked back to the hotel in silence. Pat unlocked the door to her room and stepped over the threshold. She turned to wish him goodnight. In the half light of the corridor he thought he saw the hint of a smile.

Someone pulled the knot in his guts tighter.

THIRTEEN

The snowdrop at the gates examined their papers. Snowdrop because of his white helmet, British army slang for an American military policeman that Calloway knew well. It wasn't a term of endearment and usually preceded a fight. The snowdrop called them 'sir' and 'ma'am' in that insincere tone every US serviceman seemed to use when dealing with civilians. He asked them to wait while he returned to his sentry box and made a phone call. Satisfied their papers were in order, he waved them through.

It was a typical barracks. A confident, two-storey building which stretched the full length of the parade ground. Imperial German architecture was little different from its Victorian counterparts in Britain. Places like this had been Calloway's world, but perhaps without the level of amenity these Americans seemed to enjoy. Calloway read the signs. Snack bar, club, indoor ranges, gym. Craft shop, library, swimming pool, cinema. This place was better appointed than a holiday camp.

A platoon practiced drill on the parade ground. They drilled well, with precision and flair. They wore peaked caps and white silk scarves tucked into the tunics of their dress uniforms.

'Now there's something you don't see every day,' said Pat, looking at the soldiers.

Calloway had to agree. There were about fifty of them and all of them were black.

The drill lieutenant dismissed his men and walked over to Calloway and Pat.

'Your men are good,' said Calloway. He knew good drill when he saw it. He'd done enough himself.

'We should be,' the lieutenant said. 'It's the only reason we're here.'

'What d'you mean?' said Pat.

The lieutenant smiled. He looked around as if to check whether other soldiers were within earshot.

'The 7800th Infantry Platoon is an honour guard. All we do is greet visiting dignitaries.'

Pat raised a pencilled eyebrow.

'I never knew I was that important.' She nodded at Calloway and laughed. 'And he certainly isn't.'

'Sorry, ma'am,' said the lieutenant. 'We're just here to practice. I'm afraid it's a coincidence you arrived at the same time.'

'I'm only pulling your leg,' said Pat.

'Sometimes I think General Clay is pulling ours,' said the lieutenant, lowering his voice. 'He keeps us here to counter Soviet propaganda about segregation.'

Calloway watched the honour guard leaving the parade ground. Some white soldiers stopped what they were doing and stared at them as they passed. The lieutenant straightened his cap, although it didn't need straightening.

'I came to ask if I could direct you anywhere. You looked pretty lost.'

'We're here with the fairground,' said Pat, holding out her papers.

The lieutenant waved them away. He said, 'The show's out back. On the training field. Are you a performer?'

'Stunt rider,' she said. 'On the wall of death.'

The lieutenant whistled. 'Then you're some brave lady.'

She gave him a wink. 'Come to the show and find out,' she said. 'It's a thrill a minute. You'll have a great time.'

The lieutenant looked apologetic. 'I don't think so, ma'am.'

'Oh well,' she said. 'We've got passes to the NCO's mess. Maybe we can buy you a drink sometime.'

The lieutenant smiled with regret. Calloway guessed what was coming.

'We have our own mess,' he said. He turned and pointed. 'The training field is behind the main building. Turn left at the chapel and walk on past the motor pool. You can't miss it.'

He turned on his heels and followed his men.

The drome was pitched at the centre of a ring of stalls and sideshows. It was identical to Shuman's drome in London. Same lights, same slogans, same gaudy signage, but instead of Cyclone Sid, the main attraction was Hannelore von Hölle.

Calloway laughed. 'Hannelore from hell,' he said. 'There's your double act partner.'

'It got a ring to it,' said Pat. 'Who shall I be?'

Calloway thought. 'Heidi Himmel.'

'*Himmel* means heaven, yes?'

He nodded. She huffed.

'Well, I reckon that's the nearest I'm going to get to a compliment from you.'

A man appeared at the top of the stairs that led into the drome. He was around forty, wearing a voluminous flat cap, a vivid shirt under a sleeveless Fair Isle jumper and high-cut trousers.

'Pattie?' he shouted.

'That's what they call me,' Pat shouted back.

The man slid down the stairway with his hands on the rails and his feet barely touching the treads. He bounded over.

'Pretty Pattie Moxon, Queen of the Dirt Track.' Pat winced. Calloway knew she hated the name. The man held out his hand. 'Milt Harper,' he said. 'I run this show.'

'Call me Pat,' she said. 'And this is my mechanic, Reg.'

Harper looked Calloway up and down. 'You don't look like a grease monkey.'

'I'm still learning,' said Calloway.

'You want to watch this guy,' said Harper, looking at Pat. 'One loose bolt and you could be over the safety line and through the roof of the officers' mess.'

'If they sever a good Manhattan, I shan't complain,' said Pat.

Harper slapped his thigh. 'Atta-girl.'

The sound of engines rumbled out of the drome.

'Hannelore is working out a new trick,' said Harper. 'Backwards, no hands.'

Pat nodded. She looked unimpressed.

'I need to get some wall time in,' she said. 'Can I use the drome for the afternoon?'

He waved a hand towards the sound of the engine. 'Be my guest. You can work with Hannelore. She's got a couple of two-handed routines she wants to try out with you. Tricks she used to do with Stanley, before the sonofabitch did a midnight flit.'

The three of them climbed the wooden stairs, ducked through the doorway of the brightly-coloured tent and stood in the gallery leaning over the safety rail. Hannelore was circling the drome. She stood on the footrests and raised her arms with a flourish, as if to welcome them to her world. Her long red hair flowed behind her. She crouched back down onto the seat of the motorcycle, swivelled until she was facing backwards. Then she threw out her hands again.

Harper clapped his hands. Pat put her fingers between her teeth and whistled. Hannelore gave a small bow. She swivelled forwards and brought the bike down the ramp and onto the ground, before killing the engine and handing the machine to a grease monkey in overalls who stood ready to receive it.

'She's good,' said Calloway.

'Nothing I haven't done before,' said Pat. 'I just need to get my wall head back. It takes a few good rides to get over the dizziness.'

Hannelore joined them in the gallery. She stood next to Pat. She was the same height and build, with the same hard diamond eyes. Only the hair colour was different.

'Look at you two,' said Harper, beaming. 'You're gonna make an A1 double act.'

Hannelore leaned down and took a Zippo lighter that was tucked inside the top of her knee-length lace-up boots. She pulled a pack of Lucky Strikes from the pocket of her jodhpurs and lit up.

'Welcome to the Devil's Drome,' she said. Her German accent had hints of cockney.

Harper made the introductions. The two female riders eyed each other, as if sizing the other up. Pat lit one of her cocktail cigarettes. The four of them exchanged pleasantries until Harper suggested Hannelore show Pat the ropes. He shouted down to the grease monkey to get a second motorcycle ready.

Pat whispered to Calloway, 'They've got their own mechanic. Looks like you're off the hook.'

Calloway was relieved. His knowledge of motor mechanics was rudimentary at best. Hannelore led Pat by the arm to the stairway. Calloway offered Harper a cigarette and lit up for the pair of them. Harper took a good look at Calloway's suit. Hardly Savile Row, but it wasn't a pair of overalls.

'You really her mechanic?' he said.

'More of a chaperone,' said Calloway.

Harper screwed up his face then gave a nod of understanding.

'I getcha,' he said. 'The lady didn't want to travel alone to a strange city. And boy is this a strange city.' He gave Calloway a sly grin. 'Are you and her, you know, are you…?'

Calloway shook his head.

'Just old friends.'

Even that was stretching a point. She may have shown signs of thawing after a skinful of Doppelkorn, but there was still an inch-thick layer of frost between them.

'Did you know Stan Deakin?' said Harper.

'We were on nodding terms.'

'The bastard sure dropped me in it when he left.'

'Did he give any hint he was leaving?'

'None whatsoever,' said Harper. 'We started the tour here in Berlin, at the McNair Barracks in Lichterfelde. Then moved out to Frankfurt, then Heidelberg, then back here. By that time I'd lined up extra dates at the British and French barracks in their sectors. It was gonna be a long tour for good money.'

'Were there any signs something might have been wrong with Stan? Did he seem troubled, or bothered by anything?'

Harper shrugged. 'You know Stan,' he said. 'He's the life and soul. A joker, a charmer, a real showman.'

'How did he get on with the crew?'

'Okay, I guess. He's a likeable guy.'

'No trouble? No fallings out?'

'Not that I know of.'

A motorcycle started up in the drome below them. The

mechanic held the bike for Pat as she mounted it. She'd changed into a check shirt and leathers, with knee-length motorcycle boots. She revved the engine and stated circuiting the circular ramp. When she'd picked up enough speed, she let the bike glide up the wall. She made it look effortless.

'Looks like she's still got it,' said Harper.

Calloway watched her making circuits. She gave him a wink as she passed. She was pleased with herself. He shared her satisfaction. He enjoyed watching her ride. Harper caught the expression on Calloway's face. He grinned again.

'You sure there's nothing between you two?' he said, above the noise of the engine.

'Sure,' said Calloway, hearing the hint of doubt in his voice. He changed the subject.

'Stan was a gambler,' he said. 'Is it possible he got into debt with one of the crew?'

Harper frowned and shook his head. 'I don't allow it. This whole setup works on trust. There's lives at stake. I can't have debts or grudges getting in the way. If Stan had a card school going, I'd have known and I'd have stamped on it.'

Calloway didn't doubt it. Harper was no flake.

'How did Stan get on with Hannelore?' he said, knowing that gambling wasn't the late Stan Deakin's only vice.

'Fine, I guess,' said Harper. 'They were a good double act.'

'And that's all they were?'

Harper looked surprised at the question. Then he smiled, as if realising what Calloway was implying.

'I get you,' he said. 'I kinda made him for a pussy-hound. He'd disappear on his free nights and I could guess where he was heading. But Hannelore? No, nothing doing. I would have known. If anything there was a little tension there. Something I sensed as the tour progressed.'

'I thought you said they got along fine.'

'And they did, for the most part.' He drew on his cigarette and thought. 'There was this one time, though. They had some kind of argument. They were a little cool around each other after that. Nothing terrible, but I noticed it all the same.'

'Do you know what the argument was about?'

'Something stupid. Hannelore got pissed at Stan for taking tools from her toolbox. I put it down to stress.' He gestured towards Pat. She was doing circuits with no hands. 'Riders can get pretty uptight taking these kinds of risks night after night.'

Calloway reached in his pocket and passed Harper the nightclub flyer that Vera had found in the pocket of Stan's best suit.

'Did Stan ever mention this place?' he said.

Harper looked at the flyer and shook his head. 'Looks like a typical Berlin titty bar. Why are you so interested in Stan anyway? Was he a friend of yours?'

Hannelore joined them on the gallery. Calloway pocketed the flyer, ignoring Harper's question. Harper gestured towards Pat. She was sweeping up at full speed, crossing the safety line then plunging down again.

'Fräulein von Hölle, it looks like you've got competition,' he said.

Hannelore gave him a tolerant smile, the kind you give a child that's playing up.

'I got to leave you guys for moment. I need to speak to the entertainments officer over at the mess.'

Harper disappeared through the door in the tent and descended the stairs.

'Let's go down too,' said Hannelore to Calloway. 'I need a break from the noise.' She looked down at Pat. 'She's not so bad,' she said.

Once they were away from the noise, Hannelore said, 'I have coffee in my trailer. Would you like some?'

Her tone was courteous, but there was a coldness behind it. Calloway said yes, he would like coffee. They walked to the rear of the drome. Hannelore's trailer was in fact an old war-surplus radio truck, stripped out, refitted and painted in Shuman & Harper's red and cream fairground livery. The fit-out was modern, with veneered panelling, a small kitchenette and a table between upholstered benches that Calloway assumed converted into a bed. It was neat and tidy inside, with framed photos of

Hannelore in action fixed to the walls. There were also flyers pinned to a small, felt-covered pin board, one for the current tour of the bases, another for a recent tour of eastern England. An illustrator had drawn Hannelore on a motorcycle, exaggerating the size of her thighs and breasts, and picking out her lips in bright red ink. Beneath the illustration were the words *Hannelore von Hölle, the Devil Queen of Danger.* She saw Calloway looking and said, 'They make me look like a hooker.'

'I wonder what they'd make of Pat?' he said.

Hannelore took him literally. 'It is too late to have posters made,' she said, turning to fill a coffee pot and place it on a small gas ring in the kitchenette.

He read the place names on the English fairground tour. Peterborough, Bury St Edmunds, Newmarket, Cromer.

'You certainly get to see the sights,' he said, with a hint of irony she seemed to miss. Perhaps it was lost in translation. He switched to speaking German. 'You live in England now?' he said.

She nodded. 'And you speak German?'

'They taught me in the army.'

'Isn't that unusual?' she said.

'Not if you're in the Intelligence Corps.'

He caught a flicker of something more than causal interest in her face. She busied herself with the coffee.

'Why brings you here to Berlin?' she said.

'I'm keeping Pat company.'

'Milt told me you were a mechanic.'

'I dabble,' he said.

'A wall rider needs more than a dabbler for a mechanic,' she said. 'I would prefer if you didn't touch my motorcycle.'

'I'm happy to oblige,' he said, meaning it. 'How about you? You speak perfect English. What's your story?'

'I live in England now. I came there after the war.'

'After the war?' he said. 'Not an obvious move for a German at that time.' Unless you were built like Trudi Trauber, he thought. 'There was a lot of bad feeling. There still is.'

She shrugged. 'I had bad feelings too. I wanted a new start.'

'It couldn't have been easy getting travel documents.'

She poured the coffee. The aroma filled the trailer. She settled herself in the bench seat opposite him.

'When the British army came to my town in 1945, I worked for them as a translator. My family had been circus people. They travelled and spoke many languages. They taught me English. Because of the work I had done for the army, I was able to get a special permit to move to England. Germany wasn't a place for fairgrounds just then, but I had heard there were dromes up and running again in England. I had saved enough money from the translation work to pay my passage. I travelled to London and met with Alfie Shuman. He gave me a job touring with his second drome.'

Through the open window they could hear the sound of a motorcycle. Pat was riding the wall again.

'So what was Stan like as a wall rider?' said Calloway.

'Stan?' she said and laughed. It was derisive. 'Stan was reckless. An egotist. The show was all about him. But we were a double act and there is no room for ego in a double act. Ego can be a dangerous thing when you're riding a motorcycle ninety degrees from a vertical cylinder at fifty miles an hour.'

'It sounds like you were glad to see the back of him.'

She sipped her coffee without answering.

'Any idea why he left?' said Calloway.

Hannelore shook her head.

'It was a week or so into our second run in Berlin,' she said. 'He just failed to show one afternoon.'

'Was that after you and he had an argument?'

She looked put out by the question. She raised her eyebrows.

'You've learned a lot in a morning,' she said.

'Just something Milt said when we were chatting about Stan.'

She dismissed the subject with a wave of her hand.

'It was nothing,' she said, in a tone which made clear this was the end of the matter. He persisted.

'It must have been something,' he said. 'A man doesn't just walk away from a well-paid job like this for no reason.'

She put her coffee cup down and stared at him. 'Did I say he left after we argued? No. Then why do you think the two things are connected? In fact, why are you asking this at all? Is that why you came here? To find out where your friend Stan went?'

He was playing this badly. Too heavy-handed. She was no pushover and he'd made her suspicious.

'Just making conversation,' he said.

She went to speak, then paused a moment. 'Then make a different conversation.'

He dug deep for some idle chit-chat and she seemed to soften. She reminded him of Pat. The steely eyes, the commanding personality, the handsome face. In fact, only her flame red hair and the absence of jibes at his expense separated them.

'What's it like being back in Germany?' he said.

'Is this Germany?' she said, looking out of the trailer window in the direction of the city beyond the barracks. 'It's the carcass of a city torn to pieces by the occupying armies. They all have their piece of it, with their flags flying and their soldiers patrolling, to remind the Germans of their place.'

'Their place?' he said. 'They're alive and they're no longer at war. All things considered, that's not a bad place.'

'Maybe,' she said. She was quiet for a moment. He caught a faraway look, as if in her mind she was somewhere else. 'Germany will be a better place one day. Perhaps then I will return.'

There was a knock at the trailer door and Pat stuck her head through the doorway. Her hair was tied back and she had a grease smudge on her face. She looked at Hannelore and then at Calloway.

'Well isn't this cosy,' she said.

FOURTEEN

There were two goons minding the door. One was ruddy-faced and rustic-looking. If it weren't for the dinner suit, he could have been a pig farmer. The other just looked like a pig. The piggy one opened the door for Calloway and ushered him in without any hint of welcome. It was dark inside, lit only by candles in wine bottles on the dozen or so tables in front of the stage, where a bored-looking stripper was performing a half-hearted routine under a single spotlight. The audience were mostly men, although some were accompanied by women who looked like they came with the house. A waitress in a cheap, revealing cocktail dress showed him to a table. He declined the house champagne and ordered a beer. The waitress looked disappointed. She asked him if he'd like company, gesturing to two young women seated on stools at the bar. He said no. She said perhaps later then.

He imagined the late Stan Deakin in the place. He'd built a picture of the man in his mind. He would be sitting near the front, talking himself up to a hostess that was sipping watered down *Sekt* from a reused champagne bottle. He might flash the cash, or invite another girl to join them. He would try to impress them with his wall riding stories and they would feign interest and order more of the exorbitant sparkling wine on his tab. He'd ogle the strippers and feel up the hostesses. Stan was the kind of punter they would remember.

Calloway gestured to the women at the bar to join him. They exchanged looks as if agreeing whose turn it was. One of them crossed to floor and sat at his table. She smiled a practiced smiled and said her name was Magda. He offered her a drink and she asked for champagne. He had a pocket full of Webber's money, so he agreed.

My friend recommended this place, he said. He was here a few weeks ago.

That's nice, said Magda, looking slightly surprised that anyone would recommend Club Continentale.

'Name of Stan. He was here with the fair. A motorcycle stunt man.'

'I don't remember,' she said, without thinking first.

He took the photo of Stan from the inside pocket of his jacket and showed her. He saw a head turn from the corner of his eye. The piggy doorman was eyeing him with suspicion.

'I bet you wouldn't forget that face, eh? He's a handsome devil, Stan is.'

She took the photo and looked at it by the light of the candle.

'Maybe,' she said. 'I don't know.'

Calloway saw the doorman speaking to the barman. The two of them were looking at him now. Piggy walked causally past Calloway's table and glanced at the photo. Then he returned to the bar and conferred with the barman. The barman left and disappeared through a door next to the stage.

'Perhaps one of the other girls remembers him,' said Calloway.

'Ask one over, why don't you?' she said, in a tone that dismissed the suggestion. She wasn't sharing her commission on the overpriced *Sekt* with another girl. He took the hint, for now, and put the photo back in his jacket pocket. One of the hostesses drinking at another table rose, taking her punter by the hand. The punter walked with her to a curtained doorway at the back of the house. They disappeared and Calloway heard footsteps on stairs above the piped music. Club Continentale had private rooms, which didn't surprise him.

Piggy the bouncer appeared at Calloway's table.

'The manager invites you to join him for a drink,' he said. He stood over the table waiting, until Calloway accepted. Calloway's hostess looked disappointed. He left the price of the *Sekt* and a generous tip on the table. By the time he stood up, the tip had disappeared and the hostess was on her way back to the bar.

Calloway followed the bouncer through the door by the stage. Behind it was a dim corridor with an anteroom leading off it, where half-naked strippers were changing into their costumes for the next routine. There was another door at the end of the corridor. Piggy knocked and entered.

The room inside oozed cheap opulence. Deep carpet, flock wallpaper, chandelier wall lights and gilt-framed prints of American pinup girls. The air was thick with cigar smoke. There was a large desk by the far wall. From behind it, a man in a dinner suit rose and bowed. He had longish grey hair swept back over his ears and a matching kaiser moustache. His eyes were a steely blue. He fixed Calloway with a calculated smile and beckoned him to sit. Piggy the bouncer stood with his back to the door. Calloway sat and accepted a cigarette from a jewelled box, the kind of tat they sell in Egyptian bazaars. The manager poured two generous measures of whisky from a bottle Calloway recognised. PX whisky, supplied to the US army, and clearly black market. He took a large sip. The whisky was good enough.

The manager sat. He lit a cigarette.

'Thank you for joining me, Mr…?'

'Calloway.'

The manager nodded and repeated Calloway's name, as if trying it out for future use. He swallowed the *w*, rather than pronounce it with a *v* like German stereotypes in films.

'I understand you are asking about a friend of yours. A visitor to the club.'

'Yes. Someone I know in London who recommended this place. I was just making conversation with the young lady.'

The manager put on a look of apology. He flicked ash from his cigarette into a heavy glass ashtray on the desktop.

'I'm afraid that's not the sort of conversation we encourage at Club Continentale. Discretion is very important to us, as I'm sure you will appreciate. Our clientele are discerning gentlemen who come here to enjoy our glamorous stage shows and stimulating company. We respect their privacy.'

The only thing those punters out there could discern would be a blonde from a brunette, thought Calloway. The manager continued. 'You must understand that for us to comment on any gentlemen that might or might not have visited us, would be a gross infringement of the trust they place in us.'

'I'll be straight with you, Mr...'

'Vogel,' said the manager. He gave Calloway an ingratiating smile.

'Mr Vogel, I'm keen to find Stan Deakin. He's gone missing.'

Vogel frowned. 'You sound like a policeman, Mr Calloway. Or perhaps a military official. Are you with one of the occupation armies?'

'I'm with the fairground,' said Calloway.

Vogel looked surprised, then feigned delight. 'Ah,' he said. 'So we are both in the entertainment business.' He dropped the look of delight and frowned again. 'To me, you sound like a policeman.'

Calloway heard piggy behind him grunt.

'You're a shrewd man, Mr Vogel, but I'm not a policeman. I'm with a travelling fairground and so is Stan Deakin. He's a motorcycle stunt rider who rides the wall of death.' He kept it in the present tense. He was keeping Stan's death to himself, at least for now. 'He disappeared from the fair and hasn't been seen since. I'm just asking after him. His family is concerned.'

Vogel gave a knowing nod. 'Men tend not to mention visits here to their families.'

'And I'm sure he didn't. But he told me.'

Vogel appeared to think for a moment. 'The name means nothing, but I understand you have a photograph. May I see it?'

Calloway handed the snap over. Vogel made a show of looking at it. Then he shook his head.

'I'm sorry,' he said. 'I've never seen this man.'

'Perhaps your doorman has,' said Calloway, turning in his chair and holding up the photo for piggy to see. The bouncer looked to his boss for a signal. Vogel gave a small nod. The bouncer glanced at the photo, grunted then shook his head.

'There, you see,' said Vogel. 'I think it very unlikely this man Deakin is one of our clientele.'

Calloway reached in his pocket and pulled out the leaflet Vera had found in Stan's best suit.

'He gave me this,' he said.

Vogel recognised the leaflet and waved his hand dismissively.

'Our leaflets are distributed freely in Berlin. He could have picked one up anywhere.'

Vogel gave the bouncer a look. It was a signal. Calloway heard piggy step towards him. He sensed the big man's presence looming over him. Calloway stood up. The manager spoke. He'd dropped the obsequious tone.

'Berlin is a dangerous town, Mr Calloway. And its entertainment business is not without its, shall we say, criminal elements. I, of course, run a respectable establishment.' He stood and walked around his desk until he was eye to eye with Calloway. 'Not all businesses like mine are as respectable. You should exercise caution before continuing with your enquires. You are not, after all, a policeman.'

'No' said Calloway. 'But I can smell bullshit when I'm served it. You run a cheap strip joint with a knocking shop upstairs. Hardly respectable, by any standards. And if you were telling the truth about Stan never having visited here, you wouldn't be playing the intimidation card right now. You know something, Vogel. You're just keeping it to yourself.'

Calloway pushed past the bouncer and opened the door. He turned back to face the two men.

'And for the avoidance of doubt,' he said, 'I'll ask what the bloody hell I want, to whoever I want, until I get a straight answer.'

He walked back down the corridor. A stripper in a revealing *Brünnhilde* outfit gave him a smile which he didn't return.

The air outside was damp. There was a slight mist through which the dirty neon of Potsdamer Strasse tried its best to glow. Calloway walked towards the U-Bahn station at Kurfürstenstrasse. It was the station on the ticket found in Stan's pocket. The fact cast even more doubt on Vogel's claim not to know anything about Stan. Calloway felt light-headed. The beer, the diluted *Sekt* and the black-market whisky were mixing up a sickly cocktail in his empty stomach. The smell of bratwurst from an *imbiss* kiosk at the corner of the street reminded him he needed to eat. He ordered sausage in a bread roll and stood at the counter smearing on the mustard. He heard footsteps on the cobbles behind him. The sudden look of fear on the *imbiss* vendor's face told him something bad was coming. He felt a hand grab his collar and yank him backwards. The bratwurst hit the cobbles. From the corner of his eye he saw his assailants. Piggy and the farmer were dragging him into a side street. The street was dark and stank of bins. Calloway lashed out but his punches failed to connect. The two bouncers bundled him to the end of the side street and onto a bomb site, well away from the glow of the streetlights. He stumbled over the rubble and lost his footing. He fell face down onto the floor of jagged bricks. They started kicking. He felt their boots in his ribs, guts and kidneys. He grabbed at their legs but the kicks kept coming. He took a kick to the head. Lightning flashed behind his eyes. He felt himself falling. The onset of unconsciousness pulled him down into the rubble.

A shrill whistle pierced his eardrums, then another, then the rumble of boots on cobbles. The kicking stopped. His attackers ran. Someone knelt beside him and put a hand on his shoulder.

'Can you hear me, sir?'

A man's voice, with an American accent.

'Sir, can you hear me?'

Then darkness and silence.

He came to in the rear seat of a jeep. The same voice said, 'Easy, sir. Take it easy, now. We'll get you some help.'

A snowdrop. A US military policeman in a white helmet sat next to him on the rear seat of the patrol jeep. Another MP was at the wheel. Calloway swallowed hard, blinked his eyes and felt his jaw. He felt his ribs and rubbed his back. His head hurt like crazy but he was in one piece.

'I'm fine,' he said. 'Just take me to my hotel.'

'I don't think so,' said the snowdrop, concern in his voice. 'You took quite a beating. You ought to see a doctor.'

'I told you, I'm fine,' Calloway growled. He just wanted to

crawl into bed.

The snowdrop ignored him. 'Do you know the men that attacked you?'

Calloway shook his head. 'I was lost. They followed me. Tried to take my wallet,' he lied. 'I was just unlucky.'

The snowdrop gave a knowing nod. 'It's that kind of neighbourhood,' he said. 'That's why we patrol it. It's the kind of place trouble finds GIs.' He looked at Calloway and smiled. 'And the occasional Englishman.'

The MP at the wheel took a left. Calloway recognised the street.

'This is Kurfürstendamm,' said Calloway. 'My hotel's just there on the left.'

The snowdrop looked doubtful. 'Well, if you're really sure you don't need a doctor, I guess...'

'I'm sure,' said Calloway. He pointed out Hotel Pension Ritz. 'Just drop me there.'

It was late and the hotel doors were locked. One-armed Klaus was on the night shift and let Calloway in. He seemed not to notice his guest's bloodied face. Calloway asked for a bottle of liquor. After some initial reluctance, Klaus agreed to charge a bottle of Bismarck to Calloway's bill.

He locked the door of his room behind him and poured himself a large measure of schnapps in the glass from the wash basin. The liquor burned his throat. It sedated him. He kicked off his scuffed-up shoes and fell onto the bed. His head was fuzzy. He heard the voice of the snowdrop.

'It's the kind of place trouble finds GIs. And the occasional Englishman.'

One thing was clear. It was the kind of place trouble found Stanley Deakin.

FIFTEEN

There was a tap at his door. He lifted his head from the pillow and looked at his watch. His head hurt and he couldn't focus. He lifted himself off the bed. Everything hurt. The tapping persisted.

'Reg, Reggie. Open the bloody door.'

It was Pat. He unlocked the door and flopped back down on the bed. Pat came in the room.

'Christ,' she said. 'What happened to you?'

'Just God's way of telling me girly bars are evil.'

'Looks like he struck you down good and proper,' she said, sitting on the bed beside him and pulling his blood-caked hair off his face.

'He had two gorillas in dinner suits to help him.'

She tutted. 'Where the hell did you get to?'

He'd left Pat and Hannelore in the trailer to discuss their wall routine. He'd killed an afternoon in what was left of the Tiergarten, Berlin's war damaged central park, then found a cafe on Fasanenstrass to kill time, before making his way to Club Continentale.

He passed Pat the nightclub flyer.

'Let's just say Stan's favourite gentleman's establishment didn't welcome me with open arms.'

She looked across the room and through the tall window onto Kurfürstendamm. It was past ten and the street was already buzzing.

'What the hell are we doing here, Reg?' she said.

'Relieving the boredom of your unsatisfied life.'

She looked at him with a half-smile. 'There was a time when

nothing would have given me more pleasure than seeing you beaten to a pulp.'

'I'm glad you've changed your mind.'

'Don't take it for granted,' she said. 'Now get your clothes off. There's a bathroom down the corridor. I'll take your suit to reception and see if they can get it cleaned.'

The soak did him good. He padded back to his room half dry, leaving footprints down the corridor. He dressed in his only other clothes, a sports jacket and trousers, and his remaining clean shirt. It hurt to put the shirt on. He slapped Brylcreem in his hair and combed a parting. He looked at himself in the wardrobe mirror. Despite the pain of the bruising, he could pass for man who hadn't been used as a football by two nightclub goons.

Pat returned with a tray of coffee.

'Don't say I never do anything for you,' she said.

The coffee was good. Better than the ersatz muck he'd had to drink last time he was in Berlin. The strength of it revived him.

'The nightclub manager was hiding something,' said Calloway. 'He claimed never to have seen Stan, but he was lying. He set his two bouncers after me, to give me a good kicking down an alleyway. If it hadn't been for a military police patrol passing, they would probably have finished the job.'

'You think they did the same thing to Stan?'

'Perhaps. The question is why.'

'Did Hannelore have anything to say? Or Harper?'

'Harper knows nothing. That was pretty clear. Hannelore? I'm not sure. Harper mentioned she'd had an argument with Stan not long before he disappeared. He said it was something about taking tools from a toolkit, although I don't buy that. I asked her about it. She shrugged it off, but I got the feeling there was more to it than she was letting on.' He drank more of the coffee. 'How's the routine going?'

'It's the greatest show on earth,' said Pat. 'If you drag your bruised behind up there tonight, you'll see it for yourself.'

'I will,' he said. 'I mean it can't be any more dangerous than Club Continentale.'

She cocked her head. 'Speak for yourself.'

Pat poured more coffee and Calloway gulped it down.

'Do me a favour, will you?' he said.

'Depends what it is.'

'If you get the chance, have a look through Hannelore's toolkit. Just in case there is something in this argument that Harper told me about.'

'What am I looking for?'

'Something other than tools.'

The training field was packed. The autumn sun had set behind the main barracks building and the festoon lights of the fairground cast a vivid glow over the crowd that gathered around the rides and sideshows. The men were American and uniformed, their dates for the night were local women. There were families too, from the married quarters. Well-nourished American kids with freckles and hair shorn short. Dutiful army wives making the most of an evening out. Harper was standing on the small stage at the front of the drome with a bullhorn to his lips. He was giving the crowd the spiel.

'Hannelore von Hölle and Heidi Himmel. The all-girl daredevil double act. There's glamour, there's danger, there's devilish dames on bikes.'

Calloway stood by the side of the stage listening to Harper's pitch. Pat was sitting astride her motorcycle, showing off her no-hands riding as the bike's wheels spun on the rollers, just like he'd seen Cyclone Sid do at the fairground in London. A crowd had gathered in front of the stage. Calloway saw an American officer and two military policemen squeeze their way through the jostling bodies. The officer came up to him.

'Excuse me, sir. Would you be Mr Milton Harper?'

Calloway gestured to the stage. 'The fella with the bullhorn is Harper. He's the boss.'

The officer looked apologetic. 'I don't want to disturb him. Could you maybe pass him a message?'

'Sure.'

'You need to tell your people to stick to the training field while you're here. If you need to leave at any time, just cross the parade ground to the main gate. We've had reports of someone from the fair wandering around the barrack buildings, places that are restricted to US military personnel.'

Calloway nodded. 'I'll tell him,' he said. 'It shouldn't be a problem.'

The officer looked relieved. He didn't strike Calloway as the most robust member of the warrior class. He was puny and pale, with round, gold-rimmed spectacles. He had freckles like the kids from the married quarters. A typical shiny-arse.

'Do you know who it was, this person that was wandering around?'

The officer shook his head. 'The enlisted man that stopped them didn't take their name. It was a woman apparently. A redhead. Quite a looker too, by all accounts.' Calloway caught a slight flush of embarrassment. 'Not that that makes any difference.'

'I'll make sure they get the message,' said Calloway.

The officer nodded.

'We'd be much obliged. While you folks are here we'll put a couple of MPs at the entrance to the field, just to direct people coming and going.' He smiled. 'To keep them on the path of righteousness.'

The American officer saluted by reflex, before realising his mistake. Calloway had been out of the army for five years and he'd only been an officer by grace of a short-lived battlefield commission. But he still had a natural authority. He gave the American a forgiving smile and returned the salute with a wink.

Harper had finished his spiel and was selling tickets hand over fist from the booth. Pat's big night was looking like a sell-out. Calloway felt a pang of vicarious nerves. Then he felt a sharp pain in his ribs, a reminder of the treatment Vogel's boys had dished out the previous night. He wasn't finished with Vogel yet.

He squeezed through the crowd in the arena above the drome. The timbers creaked with their weight. Harper had said with pride that this was an old drome from the nineteen twenties. This didn't sound reassuring. Pat and Hannelore entered through the trapdoor in the base of the wall. They wore matching outfits. Knee-length boots, jodhpurs and tight sweaters. From this distance they looked like the pinup illustration on Hannelore's tour poster. Pat played to the crowd. She blew kisses and wiggled her hips. It drew wolf whistles. She slipped her arm through Hannelore's and the pair of them promenaded around the wall, smiles beaming and eyes twinkling, like two gals looking for a date. GIs hollered. They blew kisses back. The two riders split up and crossed the circular floor to their motorcycles. Pat flung her leg over, wiggled into the seat and kicked the starter. She bent over slowly, as if to make an adjustment to the engine. She looked up at the crowd and winked. The cheers and whistles crescendoed. Harper was in the drome now. He gave dramatic safety warnings to build the sense of danger. The riders kicked into gear and started circling, building up speed, Hannelore ahead of Pat. They needed a good thirty miles an hour to create centrifugal force. By the time they were up, they were doing fifty. They started the tricks. Standing, no hands, side saddle. He had to hand it to Pat. A day's practice and she was on peak form. She matched Hannelore for skill, and beat her on elegance. Calloway felt a tremor of pride, then cursed himself. The pièce de résistance was a no-hands backwards circuit in opposite directions. The crowd went wild. Pat looked ecstatic. If there was ever a cure for boredom, this must surely have been it.

As the riders descended and gave their bows, the crowd threw money into the drome. Yankee dollars fell like autumn leaves in a gale. Harper beamed like the cat that got the cream.

Calloway pushed ahead of the crowd and descended the stairs. Pat was emerging from the drome. She ran to him and flung her arms around his neck. He felt the smack of a kiss on his cheek.

'God, that was incredible,' she said. 'Did you see it? Did you see how good we were?'

She was buzzing with excitement.

'I saw,' he said. He touched his cheek. 'I even got a kiss.'

She let go of him and lit a cigarette. She took a long, deep drag and blew smoke in his direction.

'Adrenalin,' she said. 'That's all. Don't get any ideas.'

She closed her eyes and let the nicotine take effect.

'How long until the next show?' he said.

'An hour.'

'Time for a few adjustments. You'll need to borrow some tools.'

She got his meaning. She nodded towards Hannelore, who was encircled by autograph hunters.

'I'm sure I'll get a chance at some point.'

A cluster of GIs were looking in Pat's direction. All smiles and better teeth than any British soldier Calloway had met.

'Go and talk to your fans,' he said. 'You're a star now.'

She walked towards the soldiers, then turned to blow Calloway a kiss.

'I've always been a star, luvvie,' she said. 'Shame you never realised it.'

SIXTEEN

Calloway stood in the shadows beneath the S-Bahn viaduct and smoked his fifth cigarette. He had a good view of the street. It was late and punters were starting to leave the club. The pig farmer in the dinner suit stood outside the illuminated door nodding a curt good night to everyone that left. He was there to ensure an orderly exit. The last thing a business-like Club Continentale needed was to attract too much attention from the police or a military patrol. Calloway checked his watch by the light of a passing cab, appearing for a moment like a ghost in the headlights. He stepped back behind the big iron pillar of the elevated railway. The darkness swallowed him. He carried on watching as the trains rumbled overhead every few minutes.

He waited another half-hour and smoked another cigarette. His throat felt dirty and his chest tight, but the tobacco kept him alert. Piggy appeared, exchanged words with the farmer and walked away in the opposite direction. A few moments later, the barman and half-a-dozen hostesses left the place for the night. They walked heavy-footed with fatigue after their shift. Then Vogel appeared. He pulled a set of keys from the pocket of his astrakhan coat and locked the door behind him. Calloway peered through the darkness and held his breath. He willed the two men not to leave together. He'd banked on it. Vogel didn't seem the type to treat staff like friends. He was too self-important. Calloway wanted Vogel alone.

Vogel reached in his pocket and drew out a wad of banknotes. He reeled some off and passed them to the farmer. Wages for the night. The farmer gave a surly nod and walked away by himself. Vogel stepped forward to the edge of the pavement and looked up and down the street, searching for a cab, Calloway assumed.

Now was the time. Calloway ran across the street, then edged his way to the entrance of the club, hugging the walls of the neighbouring buildings and treading as lightly as his big frame would allow.

'Herr Vogel,' he said. It startled the club owner, who turned around. Calloway gave him a hard punch to the guts. Vogel doubled over. Calloway grabbed his coat collar and dragged him across the street and into the darkness of the viaduct. He pushed Vogel against one of the big iron pillars. Even in the darkness he could see the fear in Vogel's eyes, the calm assurance of their first meeting absent. Vogel looked around as if hoping that piggy and the farmer might appear.

'Your goons are long gone, Vogel. It's just you and me.'

An S-Bahn train rumbled overhead. Calloway grabbed Vogel's lapels and slammed his head against the iron pillar. The screech and rumble of wheels on rail drowned out Vogel's cry.

Calloway leaned in. 'Hurts, doesn't it?' he said. 'Every time a train passes overhead, I'm going to slam your head into that pillar. If you want me to stop, you'd better give me answers. Straight ones this time.' He lifted Vogel an inch off the ground and leaned into his ear. 'Stan Deakin came to your club. I want to know what happened to him.'

Vogel stammered. 'I don't know this Stan Deakin, I swear.'

'You know him, and you sent your men to give me a good kicking after I'd I asked about him.'

Vogel shook his head. Then his ears pricked up. The next S-Bahn train was approaching. Calloway nodded towards the sound of the train. 'I'd try again, if I were you.'

Vogel's voice went up a tone. 'I know nothing,' he said. 'On my honour, Herr Calloway.'

'Men like you have no honour. Try again.'

The noise of the approaching train grew louder. The train was right above them. Calloway banged Vogel's head against the iron. Vogel winced and started to weep.

'Spit it out, Vogel. I want the whole story, while you've still got a brain that works. If I keep this up, and believe me I will, you'll be a basket case before the night's out.'

He lifted Vogel off the ground again.

'Alright, alright, I will tell you. Just let me have a cigarette.'

Vogel reached in his pocket. Calloway stopped him.

'No you don't,' he said. 'Keep your hands where I can see them.'

Calloway gripped Vogel's lapel with one hand and opened his own cigarette case with the other. He put a cigarette in Vogel's mouth and lit it with his lighter. Vogel drew hard on the tobacco. He exhaled through trembling lips.

'Your friend Stan came to the club,' Vogel said. 'He came several nights running. Stayed a long time. He liked the girls. He went with them, upstairs, you know. Spent a lot of money enjoying himself.'

Vogel stopped. He heard another train approaching.

'I'd carry on if I were you,' said Calloway, cocking his head in the direction of the train noise.

'He was talkative,' said Vogel. 'About why he came to Berlin.'

'He's a wall of death rider with a touring fairground,' said Calloway. 'Tell me something I don't know.' He tightened his grip on Vogel's lapels and lifted him. 'Train's coming.'

Vogel nodded, desperate. He blurted words as the rumble of the train approached.

'I told Baumann,' he said.

'Who's Baumann?' demanded Calloway, although there was something about the name that was familiar.

Vogel looked around him, as if checking they were alone.

'He buys information,' he said. 'Things the girls pick up, you know, from soldiers.'

'This man Baumann pays for intelligence?' said Calloway.

Vogel nodded. 'The men are drunk. They boast to the girls. The girls tell me. I tell Baumann. It's just business.'

The train was overhead. Calloway smacked Vogel against the pillar. Vogel screamed but no one heard.

'What kind of intelligence would Stan Deakin have? He rode a motorcycle with a fairground. What did you sell this Baumann?'

Vogel looked hesitant. Calloway cocked his head as if he could hear a train in the distance.

'It was something he was doing, here in Berlin,' said Vogel. 'Something he'd been asked to do for...'

Vogel hesitated.

'What was he doing? Who for?'

Calloway was shouting now. His words echoed under the viaduct. Something caught Vogel's eye. His head twitched sideways towards the street. Two policemen had stopped and were looking over towards the viaduct.

Vogel shouted. 'Help. Thief.'

The policemen came alert. They looked in the direction of the shouting. They ran towards the viaduct. One was unholstering his pistol.

Calloway let go of Vogel and ran. He ducked between the pillars of the viaduct and stumbled onto a bomb site behind it. It was a cleared site, with an open foreground lit by the half-moon above. Calloway ran towards the line of jagged building facades silhouetted against the sky at the edge of the site. He heard the rumble of boots fifty yards behind him.

One of the policemen shouted, 'Halt.'

Calloway reached the building facade and flattened himself against the walls. He was in deep shadow and he could see the police peering over, looking for him but not seeing him. He edged along until he found a doorway. It led to the remains of a basement. It stank of damp earth and rat piss. He scrambled down inside it. He tried to breath quietly, despite the heaving in his chest. The police were overhead. Their boots clunked over the rough ground above him. They were shouting, telling him to show himself. They found the entrance to the basement and shone their torches in. Light played on the charred walls. The policemen whispered between themselves. He sensed their reluctance to enter the basement, to risk being jumped by a thug with a knife or cosh. They debated whether to continue the search, whether it was worth it for a street thief. It was late after all and they were nearing the end of their shift. They agreed to give up the chase and he heard the sound of their boots retreat in the direction of the viaduct and onto the street behind it.

Calloway let out a big sigh.

'Stanley Deakin,' he said to himself. 'What the hell did you get yourself mixed up in?'

SEVENTEEN

He woke to the sound of knocking on his hotel room door. It was insistent. He climbed out of bed and opened the door. Pat pushed past him and entered the room. She looked him up and down.

'Sleeping in your clothes?' she said.

He looked down at his vest and suit trousers. 'It was a late night.'

He walked to the window and opened the curtains. Kurfürstendamm was bustling. People sat drinking coffee at cafe tables. Others peered keenly into the glass display cases that stood at intervals along the wide pavements, at cosmetics, lingerie or travel posters. Every other car that passed was a shining, egg-shaped Volkswagen. And amid the scene of happy prosperity, reminders of a troubled past. The one-legged street vendor, aged beyond his years, the ravages of war still showing on his face. Old men with hand carts, pulling meagre possessions along the street. The windowless facades of bombed-out buildings, marring the fashionable streetscape with their angry presence.

'Sit down,' she said. 'I've got something to show you.'

He stepped back from the window and sat next to her on the bed. He smelled her perfume. He liked the feeling it gave him.

'I did as you said,' she said. 'I found an excuse to borrow tools from Hannelore's toolkit, when she wasn't around.'

'So you found something?'

She shook her head. 'Nothing you wouldn't expect. But later in the evening I was redoing my make-up before the last show. My lipstick broke as I was applying it. I hadn't got another one with me so I went to Hannelore's trailer. I'd noticed she had a fancy looking make-up box, the proper show business type.' She reached into the pocket of her trousers. 'When I was rooting around inside I found this tucked in one of elasticated lipstick holders.'

It was silver and not much longer than a lipstick, with an aperture along one edge, two circular dials on top, with a small button protruding between them. Calloway took it and examined it. He'd seen something like it before.

'It's a camera,' he said. 'A Minox camera.'

Pat looked doubtful. 'A bit small for a camera.'

'That's the point,' said Calloway. 'Small enough to be concealed. I saw one during the war. We were working alongside the Special Operations Executive, who operated behind enemy lines clandestinely. Their agents were issued with cameras like this, to photograph documents, plans, that sort of thing.'

'Why would Hannelore have one?'

Calloway shook his head. 'I've no idea, but the longer I'm here, the more I'm coming to realise that there was more to Stan Deakin and his associates than motorcycle stunts.' He handed the Minox back to her. 'Do you reckon you could put this back where you found it? I don't want to set hares running.'

'Or stunt riders,' said Pat. She pocketed the camera. 'I'll find a way. I'm on my way up there now. We'll be getting some practice in. I'll put it back when Hannelore's riding the wall.'

They sat in silence for a moment on the unmade bed. He felt slovenly sitting there in his vest and trousers, the smell of the rank, bomb-site basement still on him. She turned and looked him in the eye.

'I hope Bert Webber's paying you enough,' she said.

'It's enough,' he said. 'But I'm not doing this for the money.'

He'd got other plans for that.

'What's your reason then?'

He thought for a moment and shrugged. 'Similar to yours, I suppose. I need the distraction.'

She gave him a sympathetic look. 'Life lacking a bit of sparkle?'

'It's not that,' he said. 'It's just that sometimes my head's not a good place to be. I need to keep busy.'

He'd not spoken like this to anyone about how he felt. The things he'd learned to do, to stop the bad memories filling the chasm in his soul. But he could talk to Pat. He was realising this, the more time he spent with her. A big part of him didn't like it. He shouldn't open up. Not to her, not to anyone. His business was his business, his burden to shoulder. Sharing it wasn't good for anyone.

'You need cheering up. Forget about Stan for the night. Come out with us.'

'Who's us?'

'Me, Milt, Hannelore, and Isaac and some of his men.'

'Isaac?'

'The American lieutenant we met on the parade ground. The one drilling the honour guard. He came to the show after all. He's got some tickets for tonight, to a club he knows.' She had a twinkle in her eye. She seemed excited. 'You'll never guess who's playing.'

When Pat had left, he took a bath and put on fresh clothes. Well, different clothes at least. His Berlin wardrobe was lacking, much like his London wardrobe for that matter. He decided to go for a walk. He needed to clear his head.

As he was leaving the building, the thin, sad-looking manageress stopped him.

'Herr Calloway,' she said. 'A gentleman called and left a message for you.'

She passed him a slip of hotel notepaper. The message was short.

I think we should talk. Meet me tomorrow evening at eight o'clock, Cafe Friedrich, Jägerstrasse, in the Soviet sector.

Franz Baumann

Vogel hadn't wasted time. He'd clearly been rattled enough by Calloway's questions get straight onto his contact who bought information from loose-lipped occupation soldiers.

'Did Herr Baumann call personally?' Calloway asked the manageress.

'Yes, Herr Calloway.'

'Can you describe him?'

Her face suggested she found the question odd. 'He was not a tall man like you, but not short either. He wore a loose overcoat, but I could see he was well-built beneath it. He had thick black eyebrows and a shaved head.'

Calloway pictured the man in his mind. The description had the same ring of familiarity as the name Baumann when he first heard it. But he couldn't place either.

'It was not a kind face.'

She said this as if it were purely a statement of fact, rather than a judgement. It was an odd postscript. Calloway thanked her and left.

He managed to waste the day. He made a trip to the zoo, which he found depressing. Then he killed a couple of hours at a small, newly-completed cinema called the KiKi, where he watched a new release called *Export in Blond*. It was about a young woman trafficked to Rio de Janeiro for auction. He thought it was lousy and couldn't help thinking of the hostesses at Vogel's club. He spent the rest of the afternoon back at Hotel Pension Ritz sleeping off the beers he'd drunk at a dingy bar after the film.

Pat called for him at nine. They took a cab to an address she had been given by the lieutenant called Isaac. When the cab pulled up, Pat said to the driver, 'Are you sure this is it?'

Calloway looked out of the taxi window. They had pulled up beside a cleared bomb site flanked by the remaining walls of the neighbouring buildings. The flank walls bore a familiar patchwork of mismatched wallpapers and paint colours, and the outline of rooms and stairways. They looked like a cross-section diagram that an infant had coloured in with chalks. There was a cleared path across the bomb site lit by festoon lights hanging from a rudimentary pergola which led to a small door in what Calloway assumed was the remainder of the bombed building.

The taxi driver, sensing their doubt, said, 'Yes, yes, this is the place. Most of it is gone, but the show must go on, eh?'

Pat paid him and gave him a handsome tip. She took Calloway's arm and walked with him to the door beyond the lights. They exchanged looks before entering. They were in a quiet part of the city, and this was not a typical entrance to a night spot.

Inside it was a different story. They got a friendly welcome from the doorman. Pat gave their names to a young woman behind the counter. She checked down the list and nodded with a smile. 'Please,' she said. 'Upstairs,' gesturing to the grand-looking staircase that led up towards the rhythmic beat of live music. The stairway was lit with candles, fixed with melted wax to the stone treads, casting a warm glow on the peeling paint work.

'It's a bit of a ruin,' said Pat. 'But the place has got something about it.'

Calloway agreed. In spite of its state of disrepair, the remains of this building were welcoming. They climbed the stairs, following the sound of the music. Pat gave his arm a squeeze.

'You're in for a treat,' she said.

Calloway wasn't convinced. The music emanating from the top of the building was jazz, not the classical music he liked.

A tall, relaxed-looking man in an ill-fitting tuxedo beckoned them towards a set of double doors. Calloway opened the door for Pat, and they both entered. Pat looked around the room with surprise and delight.

'I wasn't expecting this,' she said.

It was a *Spiegelsaal*. A mirrored ballroom with ornate decoration and chandeliers, dimly lit by candles on tables clustered in front of a small stage. Like the stairway that led to it, the grandeur was faded, with peeling paint and flaking plasterwork. But it exuded a warmth which engulfed the pair of them the moment they walked in. There was a band on stage, a small jazz orchestra, and its leader was a face that even Calloway recognised. He turned to Pat.

'Is that…?'

She beamed at him. 'Duke Ellington,' she said. 'It's a secret show, a warmup for his tour of Europe. Isaac has a friend at Radio Free Europe who heard about it on the grapevine.' Calloway looked around the room, through the haze of cigarette smoke. He saw Isaac and a couple of his men at a table with their dates, together with Hannelore and Milt. He and Pat pushed between the tightly-packed tables and joined them.

Isaac and his men stood and offered their seats. One of the men was dispatched to find more chairs. Isaac introduced three young German women, who dressed like the shoppers on Kurfürstendamm. Calloway spoke to them in German. They enthused about Duke Ellington. Pat looked over to the orchestra and turned to Isaac.

'I can't believe this,' she said. 'I can't believe it's really him.'

'What did I tell you?' said Isaac. 'Up close and in the flesh.'

They sat and Isaac poured them cheap German wine from one of the bottles on the table.

'You a jazz fan, Reg?' said Isaac.

'I need to be converted,' said Calloway.

Isaac laughed. 'If this doesn't convert you, nothing will.'

'Reg is a Philistine,' said Pat.

Calloway looked offended. He said, 'I enjoy the romantic composers.'

Isaac gave him an appreciative nod. 'A man of culture and taste,' he said. 'We just need to broaden your horizons a little.'

They watched the band and made idle chatter. The cheap wine relaxed Calloway. And he enjoyed the company of Isaac and his two fellow GIs. They traded the kind of stories that soldiers do. One of the men, a corporal called Joe, had been with an all-black tank battalion in the Ardennes, at the same time as Calloway's unit. Calloway remembered the battalion. It was a rare sight. Meeting Joe in a Berlin *Spiegelsaal* was one of those coincidences that happen with war. You meet a guy for the first time in peacetime and then realise he'd been in the next foxhole along from you, with the same hell raining down upon both of you. Although from the reports Calloway had heard, Joe's battalion rained a whole lot of hell of its own down on the enemy.

But Isaac and his friend had other stories. Stories that were beyond Calloway's experience of military life.

'America's a Jim Crow nation and the army's no different. We're here to promote democracy, but I tell you Reg, the army's as segregated as the Deep South. Forget democracy. We're peddling hypocrisy and the Germans know it.'

'And what do the Germans think?' said Calloway.

Isaac pulled his chair closer and leaned in. 'Here's the thing. Me and my men like it here. We like the people. Sure, there are Nazi die-hards who'll never appreciate us. But for the most part, a German posting is a pretty good thing. You won't catch me getting homesick for the South.'

He looked around the room and smiled. Calloway hadn't noticed the number of black occupation troops in the audience.

'You don't see whites-only signs in Germany,' he said. 'We go where we want, and we drink with who we want. The only people stopping us are our fellow Americans, when they decide we're not welcome some place. That's when the slurs fly and the batons come out.'

'Does that happen?'

Isaac nodded with a hint of solemnity. 'Oh yeah, that happens.'

Calloway felt Pat's hand on his arm. She leaned forward shouted into his ear.

'Go and speak to Hannelore, will you? Milt is boring the pants off her with shop talk.'

They swapped seats and Calloway ordered more wine from a waiter that was weaving his way between the packed tables. Hannelore was more relaxed than the first time they spoke. She was leaning back enjoying the band, one arm slung across the hooped back of her chair and the other raised high, with a cigarette between her fingers. She wore a long-sleeved dress, her vibrant red hair styled in a soft, full pompadour. She reminded him of Greer Garson.

'I like this place,' she said, nodding her head to the music.

'It's a shame Stan's not here,' said Calloway. 'I reckon he'd like this too.'

'Stan likes other kinds of places.'

The wine arrived and Calloway topped up her glass.

'It strikes me that you didn't like Stan.'

'We didn't click,' she said.

'I think there was more to it,' said Calloway. 'I think Stan found something you didn't want him to see. Something from your toolkit, which you then hid in your make-up box alongside your lipsticks.'

She turned her head slowly to face him. 'Aren't you the curious one,' she said, taking a sip of her wine. 'I shall have to start locking my trailer.'

She looked back towards the band, who were finishing a number. The crowd applauded, some whooped. Their leader stepped forward from the piano and announced the next number. He described it as part three of a jazz symphony. This caught Calloway's attention. It was the musical language he understood. A trumpet player stood and played a lazy refrain which built to a taught climax, then the orchestra joined with a relaxed but confident swing. Calloway's ear wasn't attuned to the style but he had to admit you couldn't fault the quality. He'd always dismissed jazz as glib and immature. The music he was hearing had a level of sophistication that challenged his snobbery. He was not quite a convert, but a barrier had fallen. Pat caught his eye. Her expression said, *See? I told you.*

Hannelore brought him back to earth. She said, 'So, I have a camera? What of it? I take photographs for my album.'

'People take photos for their albums with a box brownie, not a miniature camera designed to be concealed. Where did you get a camera like that?'

She took a drag on her cigarette and blew smoke above his head. 'It was a gift, from a British officer I worked with when I was a translator. We dated for a while. I liked him. I liked him a lot. He was a nice man.' She sipped her wine. 'But he was married.'

She turned to face him again. 'Would you like any more episodes from my life story?'

'Perhaps,' he said. 'I'm certainly wondering about you. I worked in intelligence during the war, like I said. I was in field security. One of my jobs was to sort the bad Germans from the good. We compiled lists. Blacklists and whitelists, based on information from our sources. The blacklist was for the Nazis, the SS and the Gestapo. The whitelist was for the ones we trusted, the ones who checked out. You needed to be on it to get a job with the British occupation forces. I'm interested in what qualified you for the whitelist.'

She sighed as if his question was tiresome but she would tolerate it, just this once. She unbuttoned her cuff and pulled her sleeve back.

Calloway turned cold. He recognised the tattoo on the inside of her arm. He'd seen enough of them for one lifetime and very few of them on the living.

'You were in the camps?' he said.

She looked at him as if he was stating the obvious.

'Dachau,' she said. 'Nazi population policy extended to fairground folk which, as a wall rider with a fairground, extended to me.'

Calloway felt uncomfortable. It was hard to find things to say when presented with such a difficult truth.

'I was with an army unit that liberated a camp,' he said. 'I saw it first-hand.'

She stared into his eyes, as if reaching into his soul. 'As a liberator,' she said. 'Not as a prisoner. There is a difference.'

After that, they watched the band in silence. Pat looked over, sensing the tension. She gave Calloway a questioning look. He shrugged it off. Calloway lost himself in the music. He let it speak to him. He needed the distraction. Denton, Hannelore, Vogel and now a man called Baumann. Stan's story was clouded and obscure. He was involved in something bad, Calloway knew that much.

The band finished the number and the audience showed noisy appreciation. Calloway tried to pour more wine but the bottle was empty. He sat up and looked around the room for a waiter but he couldn't see one. What he could see was the woman in the sunglasses and peep-toe heels he'd seen at Cafe Wien. She was seated at a nearby table, her long legs outstretched, and she was looking right at him.

EIGHTEEN

A sign told him he was leaving the British sector. Ahead of him a Soviet flag flew above the Brandenburg gate. It had been there since 1945. A British army scout car was positioned at the border between the two sectors. A military policeman in a red cap peered into the Soviet zone through binoculars.

'What's happening?' said Calloway to the redcap.

The soldier looked down from the small turret of the scout car and gave a weary sigh.

'Not much, pal. Just a bit of tension over there. A strike by some of the workers over conditions. More people's police on the street and Ivans lurking in the shadows.'

'Safe for a visit? A bit of sightseeing?' said Calloway.

The redcap nodded. 'You can walk straight through the gate. Just mind yourself when you're over there. The authorities might be a bit twitchy about foreigners.'

Cars were passing freely through the gate, directed by traffic police on each side, wearing their respective uniforms. Pedestrians walked casually through beside the traffic. Calloway thanked the redcap and walked eastwards across the wide-open stretch of Charlottenburger Chaussee.

Two *Volkspolizei* eyed him as he passed under the gate. They wore murky, field grey uniforms, German in cut but styled with the peasant utility of the Soviet military. Behind them, the expressionless faces of three red army soldiers stared through the windscreen of a Gaz jeep parked at the entrance to Unter den Linden. Calloway saw the machine pistols on their laps as he passed.

He walked along Unter den Linden beside the newly-planted

saplings, there to replace the mature lime trees, from which the boulevard took its name. The old limes had been removed by Hitler to make way for grandiose Nazi parades. The new limes might have symbolised East Germany's rebirth under socialism. To Calloway they just looked sad.

The Soviet sector bore the same scars of allied bombing and Soviet artillery bombardment as the western sectors, but the pace of restoration seemed slower. For every repaired or replaced building there were two that stood derelict amid piles of rubble. Lines of women in pinafores, as if straight from the kitchen, passed buckets of debris hand to hand to others who lined the pavements chipping mortar off the bricks, preparing them for reuse. *Trümmerfrauen*, they called them. Calloway remembered them from his last trip here. In the western sectors this work had passed to commercial contractors. In the east, these 'rubble women' still cleared sites by hand for the equivalent of fourpence ha'penny an hour.

He turned off the main drag onto a side street, following directions the hotel manageress had given him. The manageress knew the restaurant Baumann had suggested. 'It was once good,' she had said with a snort, as if dismissing it as no longer relevant, being inside the Soviet sector and therefore below a standard acceptable in the west.

It was a grand street, or had been, with bold Wilhelmine architecture that echoed the ornate, stone-faced Victorian buildings of London. Every doorway and window was peppered with bullet holes from the furious street fighting of the final days of the war. No attempt had been made to repair or conceal these blemishes. They were worn like duelling scars on aristocratic faces.

Cafe Friedrich was a double-fronted restaurant on the ground floor of one of the buildings. It had an awning and tables outside, in spite of the autumn chill. Diners sat wearing overcoats, none of them smiling. Whether this was due to the cold weather or the restaurant's lack of ambiance, Calloway couldn't say. A stocky man in his thirties with a shaved head sat alone at a table for two. He was toying with a coffee cup and reading *Neues Deutschland*, the Soviet approved newspaper of the east. Stalin's face covered half the front page. Baumann furrowed his thick black eyebrows as he read. He looked up when Calloway approached his table.

'Herr Calloway,' he said. It was a statement, not a question.

Calloway nodded.

'Herr Baumann,' he said.

The man's face was familiar, just as his name had been when Calloway had first heard it from Vogel. He was sure he had never met this man in his life, but he recognised him. There was a connection between them that Calloway couldn't place. It nagged at him.

Baumann gestured to the empty chair.

'I hope you've brought an appetite,' he said, in German. 'The pork knuckle here is very good.'

Calloway glanced over at the other tables, where diners were tucking in to mean portions of insipid-looking food. Baumann pushed a menu towards him.

'Order. Then we can talk.'

Calloway ordered *jägerschnitzel* and a glass of *Radeberger* beer from a waiter, who nodded, just managing a polite smile from his dull, colourless face.

Their food arrived quickly. It was lukewarm. Set dishes plated up until they were ordered. Baumann pushed a serviette into the collar of his shirt and tucked in. He ate noisily. Between mouthfuls he said, 'Why are you in Berlin, Herr Calloway?'

'I'm with the travelling fairground.'

Baumann laughed. 'You don't look the type.'

'What were you expecting?'

'Oh, I don't know. A clown costume at the very least.'

'I'm no clown.'

Baumann thought for a moment. 'No, you're smart and inquisitive, at least from what I've heard. And quite violent.'

'Your friend Vogel's been talking. How is his head by the way?'

'Sore, I imagine. You use the interview techniques of a secret policeman.'

'How would you know? Are you a secret policeman?'

Baumann had the whiff of an official about him. A man enjoying the sanction of his role, his license to probe and pry, perhaps to coerce. He moved his shaved head from side to side as if weighing up the question.

'I'm just a man who is interested in what goes on in this city.'

Baumann's accent was curious, one that Calloway couldn't place. It wasn't a Berlin accent.

'Go and talk to Herr Vogel,' said Calloway. 'He seems like a mine of information. Especially if there's a price on it.'

Baumann smiled.

'Vogel is just a friend. I was concerned to hear that you had caused him some...' He paused as if searching for the word. 'Inconvenience,' he said. 'I'm interested in his wellbeing. You, clearly, are not.'

'Vogel is a grubby parasite that runs a strip club with a brothel above it. I couldn't care less about his wellbeing. What I do care about is how my friend Stan Deakin fits into the picture. Vogel knows more than he told me. I suspect you do too. You buy intelligence. What intelligence did you buy from Vogel? What did Vogel's hostesses tease out Stan that was so interesting to you?'

Baumann gave a theatrical shrug. 'I don't remember. I hear so much tittle tattle.'

'You remember. You're the type that remembers everything.'

Baumann looked up from his plate and gave Calloway a knowing smile. It said he knew but wasn't telling.

Calloway said, 'What's the accent? You don't speak like a Berliner. You don't have any German accent I recognise.'

'You've met a lot of Germans?' said Baumann.

'I was here at the end of the war, with the British army. Yes, I got to talk to a lot of Germans. There's a reason I sound like a secret policeman.'

Baumann smiled. 'Then we are not so dissimilar.'

'So where are you from, Baumann? I'm curious.'

'I've moved around. How's the *jägerschnitzel*?

'Less than satisfying. Like the answers you're giving me.'

'I think it would be best if you stopped asking questions, Herr Calloway. In fact, I think it would be best if you were to leave

Berlin. I'm sure your fairground can survive without you, whatever it is you are supposed to be doing there.'

'That sounds like a threat.'

Baumann scraped the last of the flesh off the pork knuckle with his fork. 'Not so much a threat as a firm suggestion.'

Calloway downed the last of his beer and rose to leave.

'Thanks for the lunch,' he said. 'I'll leave Berlin when I've got some answers. Not before, and certainly not because of any firm suggestion from you.'

Baumann smiled and spoke in English. 'Alright cocker, have it your way,' he said, in a perfect Midlands accent.

NINETEEN

The hotel manageress was anxious to see him. She scuttled over from the reception desk as he appeared at the top of the stairway.

'Telegram, Herr Calloway,' she said holding a folded piece of paper in her hand. She passed it to him and waited while he read it. It was from Bert Webber. It was four words long: *They have taken Vera.*

'They' meaning the man called Denton and his colleague that claimed to be a doctor, Calloway assumed. He tore up the telegram and stuffed the pieces in his pocket. The manageress hovered at his side, expectant for news. He turned his back on her and went to his room.

The *jägerschnitzel* lay heavy on his stomach. He felt queasy and jittery. Baumann had unsettled him. The name, the face and the accent. All familiar to him but a million miles from his grasp right now. And he was no closer to understanding what Stan had been mixed up in. It was something serious, he knew that much. Something Vogel was too scared to spill. Something that got Calloway followed, by Denton in London and by the woman in the sunglasses in Berlin. He was convinced her appearance at the Ellington concert wasn't a coincidence. His radar was good like that. He'd had a career in intelligence based on suspicions. They had proved right more times than not. And now, this character Baumann wanted him out of the way. A man who frequented the Soviet sector, read a Soviet-sponsored newspaper and acted like he owned the city. An Englishman too, or near as dammit, which just added to Calloway's unease.

Then there was Hannelore. A displaced victim of the Nazis who sought refuge in Britain, or a snoop with a spy camera? The jury was still out on Hannelore in the courthouse of his befuddled mind.

He lay on the bed staring at the ceiling, letting the sounds of the Ku'damm wash over him, a soothing soundtrack of near normality in this anything but normal city. He wanted to sleep but he couldn't settle. He crossed to the wash basin and splashed water on his face. The man who stared back at him in the mirror looked tired and drawn. He picked up the half-drunk bottle of Bismarck from the bedside table and poured a big slug in his tooth mug. Medicinal, he told himself.

He flagged a taxi on Ku'damm and told the driver to take him to the barracks. It was mid-afternoon and they'd be getting ready for the early show in the drome. He held out his papers to the snowdrop at the gate and got a business-like nod in return.

'I hope you're feeling better, sir,' the MP said. It was the driver from the patrol that pulled him from the clutches of Vogel's goons.

'Yes, thanks,' said Calloway, ignoring the ache in his ribs and gut. 'I owe you a drink.'

'All part of the service,' the MP said, smiling. 'You take care now.'

Nice guy, he thought. A Southerner by his accent. Then he remembered what Isaac had told him.

'When they decide you're not welcome some place, that's when the slurs fly and the batons come out.'

He crossed the parade ground and walked past the motor pool towards the training field. He heard motorcycle engines as he approached the drome.

Hannelore was working on her bike by the side of the drome. She looked up as Calloway approached.

'Have you come to search my trailer again, Reg?'

'No, but I need some answers. Straight ones. You need to level with me.'

'For someone who claims to be a mechanic, you sound more like a policeman.'

'I'm not a policeman. I'm not an official, or a soldier. I couldn't care less about sectors, or politics, or armies of occupation. I'm just a friend of Stan's family and I want the truth. You're hiding something.'

She threw down the wrench. 'This is ridiculous.'

'It's not ridiculous. It's deadly serious. Stanley Deakin is dead.' This caught her attention but didn't seem to surprise her. 'All the signs point to him being killed in Berlin. I need to know why. For what it's worth, I don't think you killed him. I've met enough killers to know the sort. But you know something you're not telling. And that might just be where the truth lies. I need the truth right now, because there's some people out there making it very clear they don't want me to find it. Don't be one of them. Level with me. You have my word I'll not cause trouble for you.'

She pulled a pack of cigarettes from the pocket of her jodhpurs and took the lighter from inside her boot. She lit up and took a long hard drag.

'You need to leave Berlin,' she said.

'Another threat,' he said. 'That's the second I've had today.'

'Not a threat. Just advice. This isn't the city to go prying. You mean well, Reg, I can see that. But you need to leave things be. It's not safe here.' She glanced behind her towards the sound of the motorcycle. 'Not safe for you or for Pat.'

'Then the sooner I get some answers, the sooner we can go home.'

'Answers about what?' she said.

'About what you're up to. An American officer told me a woman had been poking her nose around the barracks, in restricted areas, claiming she was lost. A woman whose description sounded a lot like you. That in itself wouldn't be remarkable were it not for the fact that you keep a Minox camera in your make-up box.' She fixed him with a look of defiance but beneath it he saw anxiety. He'd struck a nerve. He played a hunch. 'Are you selling information to Franz Baumann? Was Stan Deakin your go-between?'

'Who is Franz Baumann?' she said. The question sounded genuine.

'A man who pays for information. A man who bought information that originated from Stan.'

'I don't know this Baumann and I don't know what you're talking about.'

'Perhaps you don't. But there was more between you and Stan Deakin than you're owing up to.'

She picked up the wrench and returned to working on the bike. 'I don't have time for this.'

He felt a hand on his shoulder. It was Milt Harper.

'Are you distracting my star attraction when she's got work to do?' he said with a smile.

'Just chewing the fat,' said Calloway.

'Go see what the lady Pat is up to. She's working on something good.'

There was no point staying. Hannelore wasn't going to say any more with Milt there. Calloway was half-convinced by her denials. But only half.

He climbed the stairs to the gallery at the top of the drome. Pat was high on the wall, riding backwards with no hands. She gave him a small nod of acknowledgement. She swivelled in the seat and straightened her legs so that she was standing on the footrest, then bent forward, gripped the seat with her hands and flung her legs upwards to perform a head stand. The motorcycle trembled with the movement. Calloway felt a pang of anxiety. Pat adjusted her balance and let the bike circle the wall three times before sitting back into the saddle. She cocked her head and gave him a wink. Calloway clapped his hands and shouted, 'Bravo.' He forgot Baumann, Vogel and Hannelore in that moment. Watching Pat was exhilarating. She gave a small bow as she descended the wall onto the circular ramp below it. Calloway descended the stairs and met her by the exit hatch of the drome. She pulled out her hip flask and took a nip.

'Steadies the nerves,' she said, offering him the flask.

'You're a bloody maniac,' he said, taking a slug of the liquor.

'Living dangerously is not without its thrills,' she said. She was trembling with excitement.

'I wish I could agree. People keep telling me Berlin is a dangerous place, but I'm not getting much of a thrill.'

The light was fading and the festoon bulbs of the fairground sideshows twinkled. They cast a warm glow over the barrack blocks at the perimeter of the training field. Pat took his arm.

'Let's walk,' she said. 'I need to do something to stop my legs shaking.'

'I need to see Vogel again,' he said.

'The clip joint owner?'

He nodded. 'I'm getting nothing out of Hannelore and I've been warned off by a man called Baumann, who Vogel peddles information to.'

'What kind of information?'

'Titbits from loose-lipped soldiers.'

He offered her a cigarette and lit one for both of them. 'Vogel's the weak link,' he said. 'I need to break it.'

A man who goes scuttling off to his paymaster at the first sign of trouble is a weak man. An anxious man. The kind of man that will break if you apply enough pressure. Baumann would never give Calloway the answer. Vogel was his best chance of finding out what Stan had been involved in and how he had died.

Calloway looked at his watch. 'I'm going to miss your big performance.'

She shrugged and smiled. 'You've had a private view.'

He leaned forward and kissed her cheek. 'Break a leg.'

'Try not to do the same. But if you do, make sure it's someone else's.'

He took a taxi to Potsdamer Strasse and a found a bar which served food. He ordered beer with a schnapps chaser, and bratwurst with sauerkraut and *kartofelsalad*. The food was better than the bar's appearance implied. There were British soldiers at the counter, chatting up two young German women, although in this neighbourhood it was probably the other way around and there would be a price involved. He managed to kill an hour and a half. He checked his watch, paid the barman and walked out of the bar. The street was alive with the kind of life you'd expect in a red-light district. Servicemen of three nationalities in various states of inebriation. Maître d's lurking in doorways, luring their prey into overpriced fleshpots. Street walkers on the corners, underdressed for the chill autumn night, hopping from foot to foot to keep warm.

The neon signage of Club Continentale bathed one end of the street in a wash of sleazy red. The pig farmer was minding the door. Calloway turned up the lapels of his trench coat to conceal the lower part of his face. He pulled his hat down low over his eyes.

The pig farmer was looking in the opposite direction. Two randy-looking American soldiers were hovering ten yards up the street, summoning the courage to enter the club. The pig farmer gave his best attempt at a beckoning smile. It fell flat and the soldiers disappeared. He shrugged and lit a cigarette. He hadn't noticed Calloway sidle up to him.

The first blow bent the pig farmer double. The second floored him. He slumped in the doorway. Calloway dragged his unconscious body inside and dumped it in an alcove where punters' coats hung from a wooden pole. Calloway threw one of the coats over the unconscious doorman. He entered the door into the main room of the club. There was no sign of pig face, just a skinny barman and half-a-dozen punters showing more enthusiasm than the act on the stage deserved. Calloway crossed the darkened room as if to take one of the tables, then ducked through the door that led to Vogel's office. Two women eyed him from the open door of the dressing room. One wore a harem veil and translucent pants, the other had just left the stage and was naked, save for her shoes and a feather boa. Calloway said good evening, like he was supposed to be there. He opened the door at the end of the corridor.

Vogel was behind his desk. Pig face sat in the chair opposite, reading the sports pages of a Berlin newspaper. Both men looked up. A look of consternation spread over Vogel's face, then turned to fear. Pig face rose from the chair. Before he'd straightened up, Calloway grabbed the heavy glass ash tray from the desk and smashed it over the doorman's head. Pig face fell back in the chair unconscious.

'Time for another talk, Vogel,' said Calloway. Vogel looked towards the door. 'Your other little friend is taking a nap too, in case you were wondering.'

Vogel pulled one of the desk drawers open. Calloway reached over and grabbed him by the wrist. He slammed Vogel's hand down onto the desk. A small automatic pistol fell onto the desktop. Calloway took it and flipped off the safety catch. He pointed it at Vogel.

'I should sit down if I were you.' He nodded to the bottle of PX whisky on the desk. 'Pour yourself one of those. You're going to need it.'

TWENTY

'Who does Baumann work for?'

Vogel stared at the gun in Calloway's hand. His face was frozen. His last encounter with this big stranger was proof enough of just how ruthless the man could be. He went to speak, then hesitated as if weighing up who he was more afraid of, Calloway or Baumann. He picked up his glass and downed the whisky in one gulp.

Calloway nodded to the bottle. 'Be my guest, if it helps loosen your tongue.'

Vogel picked up the bottle. His hand was shaking. Without his two goons, he was nothing. Pig face lay unconscious in the chair, a trickle of blood running down his fleshy face from the blow of the ashtray.

'Let's try again. Who does Baumann work for?'

Vogel shook his head. 'I don't know. He just buys information.'

'Who's he buy it for? The Americans, the British, the Russians?'

'I don't know, honestly.'

His voice was trembling. He was sweating. He was also lying.

Calloway glanced around the room. There was a small sofa against the wall to the side of Vogel's desk. He crossed the room and picked up one of the cushions. He smothered the pistol with it and fired two rounds into Vogel's desktop. Vogel jumped. He spilled his drink. What remained of the colour drained from his face. Calloway gave him a satisfied look.

'No one will hear,' he said.

Vogel blurted, 'You won't kill me.'

'You're right, I won't. Well at least not to start with. I'll put a bullet through your shoulder first. That will hurt, but not half as much as the one I'll put through your kneecap. You'll wish you were dead after that.'

Calloway waited. He said nothing, just looked Vogel full in the face. Vogel breathed heavily. He reached for the cigarette box on the desk. Calloway shook his head.

'Speak first,' he said.

Vogel took a deep breath. 'Baumann's an ex-Nazi who works for East German security. A branch called the Administration for the Struggle Against Suspicious Persons. He keeps a watch on foreigners from the west.' Vogel took a gulp of the whisky and forced a wry smile. 'He wouldn't be the first Nazi thug to sell out to the Communists.'

A former Nazi thug with a perfect English accent.

The realisation hit Calloway like a truck. He knew Baumann. He knew his story. He'd recognised the name and the face but couldn't place them until now. He reached across the desk and took a slug of whisky from the bottle.

'Why was an East German spy catcher interested in Stan Deakin?' he said.

'Your friend Deakin was shooting his mouth off one night. Trying to impress the girls. He said he was a British agent who was here to crack a spy ring.'

Calloway laughed. 'Deakin was a truck driver who moonlighted for a fairground. The most he could crack was a dirty joke.'

He was speaking of Stan in the past tense. Vogel was either too scared to notice, or it was a fact he already knew.

'All I know is what the girls told me. I sold the information to Baumann.'

'Then what did you do?'

Vogel was wrong-footed by the question. He hesitated. He stared at Calloway as if trying to read him, to understand the motive behind the question.

'What do you mean?' he said.

'Come off it, Vogel. We both know Stan Deakin is dead. Did

you kill him?'

Vogel paused for a moment. He composed himself. 'Why would I kill him?' He took a sip of the whisky. 'I'm not a killer, Herr Calloway.'

Calloway nodded at the bouncer slumped in the chair. 'I bet he is, given half a chance. Him and his pal tried to kick the life out of me.'

'It was only meant as a warning. When dealing with a man like Baumann, it's best to avoid complications. I just wanted you away the club.'

'It didn't feel like a warning,' said Calloway, taking another swig from the bottle. He heard sounds from the corridor outside. Heavy footsteps getting louder.

The door opened behind him. The pig farmer piled into the room. He pulled Calloway out the chair and hit him hard in the face. Calloway recoiled from the blow. The crack of a pistol shot echoed off the walls. The farmer clutched his arm. Calloway smelled the cordite from the gun in his hand. He felt Vogel's arm around his neck. He jabbed his elbow back into the club owner's guts. Vogel groaned and fell back in the chair. The pig farmer took another swing but missed. Calloway struck him with the butt of the pistol. The farmer reeled. His legs buckled. Calloway ran through the door and down the corridor. The women in the dressing room saw the gun in his hand. One grabbed the other and pulled her away. He crossed the main room of the club towards the exit doors. The music was loud. There was a stripper on stage reaching the climax of her routine. Punters wolf whistled. Calloway pushed through the double doors into the lobby, pocketed the gun and stepped out onto the street.

He stood for a moment in the glow of the neon, catching his breath. A car pulled up and two men got out. They were broad-shouldered and ugly, wearing cheap ill-fitting suits.

'Herr Calloway,' one of the men said.

Before Calloway could reply, he felt a sharp blow across his neck. He stumbled on the kerb. Hands grabbed him and bundled him into the back seat of the car. Someone stuck a gun in his ribs.

'I told you to leave Berlin, Mr Calloway, for your own good.'

It was Baumann. His two thugs climbed back in the car. Baumann nodded to the driver through the rear-view mirror. The driver floored the accelerator. The car shot forward, its tyres screeching. Calloway looked out of the window. Heads turned. One of the onlookers caught his eye. She was standing in the shadows at the corner of a side street, a look of shock her face. Calloway recognised her. It was the woman with the sunglasses and the peep-toe heels.

TWENTY-ONE

Calloway sat in silence. He knew better than to ask Baumann where they were going. It wasn't going to be another indigestible meal, he'd figured that much. They drove east, slowing as they crossed into the Soviet sector, getting a nod from the two uniformed *Volkspolizei* at the border. The car was clearly known to the border police. They crossed a bridge over the Spree, with its rusting barges and ink-black water, and sped down a darkened side road. The road narrowed, the carcasses of bombed-out buildings seeming to close in on the car. What little street lighting there was cast more shadow than light and only served to make the surroundings more ominous. The silence in the car was more threatening than any words Baumann might have spoken. Calloway's mind raced. The sour taste of fear filled his mouth. He knew how this story ended. He needed to act. There was a sharp bend ahead. The car would need to slow. He remembered his parachute training, jumping off a moving truck at thirty miles an hour onto hard ground. It was a damn fool idea, but he hadn't the time to think up a better one. He grabbed the door handle and yanked it, throwing the full weight of his big frame against the door.

He hit the road surface side-on and rolled into the gutter. His already bruised ribs erupted into pain. He scrambled to his feet, the leather soles of his shoes struggling to grip on the well-worn cobblestones. The car skidded to a halt and he heard the sound of its doors opening. Baumann was shouting.

Calloway stumbled over brick rubble between the facades of two windowless buildings. The passageway led to a courtyard, surrounded on four sides by what had once been a tall apartment block, four or five stories high. Now they were just shells. He darted into one of the doorways and up a flight of dark, communal stairs. The stairs led to a landing beyond which was a void. The entire rear wall of the block was missing, the jagged edge of the first floor leading to a twenty-foot drop. The remainder of the stairway had been destroyed. He couldn't go higher. There was a door to his left, a high apartment door hanging loosely by a single hinge. He pushed past the door and into the hallway of the apartment. The rooms to his right were missing, their doorways opening onto thin air. He took a door to the left, into a room the size of a generous bedroom. It stank of damp and brick dust. Two tall, glassless windows looked onto the courtyard below. Through the gloom he could see Baumann and his two heavies. They were all holding pistols. Baumann gave instructions. The three men split up, each taking a block to search. Baumann was heading towards the stairway Calloway had just ascended.

The sound of Baumann's feet crunching broken glass echoed around the empty shell of the building. Calloway flattened himself against the wall beside the door of the room. He pulled Vogel's pistol from his pocket. Baumann's goons had been fools not to search him. Calloway heard footsteps entering the apartment. He breathed small, shallow breaths, trying his hardest not to be heard. It was hard. His chest was heaving, his heart pounding. He could hear Baumann checking the adjacent room, then re-enter the hallway. He braced himself. The nose of Baumann's pistol appeared in the doorway, then his forearm. Calloway grabbed his arm and yanked it. He struck Baumann's wrist with the edge of his hand. The pistol fell to the floor. Calloway kicked it away. He slammed Baumann's head against the wall. Baumann lost his footing. Calloway shoved him to the far end of the room and levelled the pistol at him.

'Don't make a sound,' he said. From across the courtyard he could hear the goons searching the other blocks floor by floor.

Baumann spoke in German. 'You fire that pistol, my men will be here in seconds. You won't know what's hit you.'

'I've been hit enough lately not to care.'

'Then shoot me now and get it done with,' said Bauman. He looked at Calloway and grinned. 'Or don't you have the guts?'

Calloway levelled the pistol at Baumann's chest. 'You're going to talk to me first,' he said. 'After that, I might just let you go.'

Baumann scoffed. 'Why should I talk to you?'

'Because I know your story, Baumann. I know who you are.'

Baumann sneered. 'You know nothing about me.'

'Oh, believe me I do. You see I had the misfortune to meet a friend of yours a year or so back. He was a speedway rider who went by the name of Ray Simpkins.'

Baumann was suddenly alert. 'Yes, I thought that might get your attention,' said Calloway. 'I was head of security at the speedway stadium where Simpkins raced. He was being blackmailed. I was asked to look into it. Another rider had photographs you see. Photographs from an old wartime album. You were in those photos. You, Simpkins and a third man called Wood. You were soldiers. Soldiers with skulls on your caps.'

Baumann looked towards the window. 'You'd better finish your story, Herr Calloway. My men will come looking for me soon.'

'You can quit with the German. You're as German as I am. You're British and your real name's Belper. You, Simpkins and Wood were members of the Britische Freikorps, a volunteer unit recruited into the Waffen SS. You were a fascist and a traitor. Your name rang a bell when you left the note at my hotel. When I met you I recognised your face. It took me a while to figure out where from. I've seen the photographs of your exploits during the war. They were in the album being used to blackmail Simpkins. They weren't pretty, believe me.'

Baumann seemed to relax now the truth was out. 'War isn't pretty.'

'No, but your war was uglier than it's possible to be. You're a sick bastard, Baumann. You're lucky you didn't face a war crimes trial. You were lucky you were picked up by our intelligence services.'

Baumann raised an eyebrow.

'Yes,' said Calloway, 'I know about that too. I know the story.

They let you settle in the East as a German called Baumann, let you embed yourself in a nice cushy job within East German state security. You've been their man on the inside ever since.'

Baumann looked incredulous. 'How can you possibly know that?'

'Ray Simpkins wasn't our only mutual friend. I know Sammy Mackay too.'

This startled Baumann. 'Sammy was my old commanding officer,' said Calloway. 'He's now a spook. You're one of his assets.'

Baumann gave Calloway a look of grudging respect. 'It seems you are a step ahead of me.'

'I can blow your cover, Baumann. Just one phone call to a Stasi informant line and you'll be digging salt in Siberia for the rest of your life.'

Baumann was silent. He was thinking.

'So what do you want?' he said.

'I want to know how Stan Deakin died.'

Baumann gave a dismissive wave of his hand. 'Deakin was a fool. He was shooting his mouth off. He was causing trouble for everyone. Vogel's men killed him.'

'Why Vogel's men?'

'Because I told them to. It was tidier that way. In my position the last thing you need is a loudmouth that knows a little too much.'

Baumann looked towards the window again. The sound of the two other men searching the blocks was closer now.

'There's still a few more floors to go,' said Calloway. Now that he had Baumann, he should have asked more questions about Stan's death. What Baumann had told him was half an explanation. But Calloway was remembering the worst of the photographs. He couldn't shake the image from his head. It was taken in a forest somewhere in Central Europe. Simpkins, Wood and Baumann stood in a line, their pistols pointing at the heads of three kneeling figures. Two men and a young boy.

'Tell me,' said Calloway, 'what's it like to kill a child?'

Baumann seemed emboldened by the question. He appeared

to almost welcome the opportunity to give an answer. He gave Calloway a satisfied smile and composed himself.

'You make them kneel, facing away from you,' he said. 'It's how you dominate. They must recognise your superiority. You don't want to see the fear on their faces or hear their prayers. That would be...' he grappled for a word. 'Inelegant,' he said. 'It would detract from the ceremony of the act.' He looked down at his palm. 'The pistol feels good in your hand. As you squeeze the trigger the full force of your power is concentrated in your fist. You squeeze hard. You feel it. A tingle of excitement spreading through your fingers, your arms, down through your heart, your belly. It's almost sexual. In that moment your superiority is proven.'

Baumann took a long, slow breath, then continued.

'It's good to see them dead, face down and lifeless. All your bad, painful, awkward childhood memories dying with them in that moment.'

Baumann gazed into space, as if transported back to the times he was describing. Calloway could barely believe what he was hearing. The man was deranged.

'I don't like children,' Baumann said. 'Their milky smell, their soft cheeks, their careless, unkempt hair. Vulnerable, powerless and dumb.' He paused as if something had just occurred to him. 'Some survive the first shot. They lie there twitching on the ground.' He made a pistol with his thumb and forefinger and levelled it at a spot on the floor. 'You deliver the coup de grace in a single elegant move. Like a noble duellist, in your fine uniform. You light a cigarette and inhale with satisfaction. Your brothers offer congratulations and you share their sick jokes as they point at the bodies. One will have a camera, capturing the kill as a trophy. Then,' he said, 'you turn and leave. There are lesser men to drag away the corpses and sweat to dig their graves.'

Calloway pointed the pistol at Baumann's head and fired two bullets into his brain.

TWENTY-TWO

Baumann's heavies burst into the room. They grabbed Calloway by the arms and wrenched the pistol from his hand. Only then did they notice the body on the floor. Blood trickled from two clean holes in Baumann's forehead.

There was no fight left in Calloway. The heavies dragged him down the stairway, across the courtyard and out into the street towards the car. They bundled him into the back seat. One of them took handcuffs from his pocket and chained Calloway's wrists. He pushed the barrel of his pistol into Calloway's ribs. Calloway barely felt it. He was numb.

They drove for fifteen minutes, heading further east. The heavy behind the wheel pulled the car up outside the pockmarked facade of an old office building. The new East German flag hung limply from a pole above the doorway. They dragged Calloway up the steps and through the double doors. It was bright inside. The brightness of officialdom, like a police station. A uniformed officer nodded at the heavies from behind a tall reception desk, as if the appearance of a bloodied man in handcuffs was not unusual in this place. The heavies pushed Calloway through another set of doors and dragged him down a corridor. The overhead lights flickered. There were stairs at the end, leading downwards to a basement. Calloway stumbled on the steps as they descended. His legs were weak and he felt lightheaded. There was an iron gate at the bottom with a uniformed guard outside it. The guard acknowledged the heavies and unlocked the door with a key from a big ring on his belt. The clank of the key in the lock echoed off the painted brick walls. The heavies led Calloway through the gate and the uniformed guard locked it behind them. They pushed Calloway into a darkened cell and slammed the door.

The cell stank of stale sweat and urine. The smell of fear. Calloway groped in the darkness and found a hard wood bench along one wall. He lay on it, shivering.

He slept fitfully for perhaps an hour. The cell was cold. He pulled his jacket tighter around him. His eyes adjusted to the darkness. He made out a slash of dim light from under the door. There were voices in the corridor outside, then the flick of a switch. A bulkhead light filled the cell with a dazzling glare. Calloway squinted. The light hurt his eyes. He heard the slide of bolts. The door opened. Two men stepped in, one uniformed, a holstered pistol on his belt, and the other in a civilian suit. The suited man was burly, with close-shorn hair and a thick neck. He smelled of a cheap cologne with a chemical tang. He stood over Calloway and told him to sit up. The uniformed guard stood with his legs apart, one hand on the pistol holster. The man in the suit asked Calloway his name and nationality. Calloway answered truthfully. No point doing otherwise. He saw no way out. He'd killed Baumann. In Calloway's mind Baumann had deserved it. He was a sadistic thug and a traitor who'd escaped justice. But the East Germans knew nothing of this. As far as they were concerned Calloway was a foreigner and a murderer. There was only one way this was going to end.

The two men left the cell. The light went out. Calloway lay back on the hard wooden bench and closed his eyes. He thought of Bert Webber and his sister-in-law Vera, who would never know the truth, not even the fragments of truth Calloway had uncovered. He thought of Pat, throwing her arms around him, exhilarated from riding the wall. He thought of the tenderness she had shown after his bruising from Vogel's goons. He heard her voice saying, *'Why did you walk out, Reg?'* He wondered why himself. What had he feared? Why couldn't he allow himself some happiness? These were pointless questions. He knew why, deep down. He'd never let go of Miriam, the love he'd lost, the woman he'd met in the camp who had reached into his soul like no one before or since. He mourned her and he carried the constant guilt that he had survived when she had died. The guilt pained him, the anger that it spawned terrified him. That anger was the reason he was here, alone in the dark cell. When he'd killed Baumann he was taking his revenge on all the other Baumanns that had caused Miriam's suffering. The persecution, the imprisonment, the violation. The fate he now faced was a small price to pay for vengeance. The thought calmed him. He fell into a deep, dreamless sleep.

The bolts slid back and the light came on. The glare roused him. He'd been out cold for hours. It might have been the morning. He couldn't tell. The same two men stepped into the cell. The uniformed man told him to stand. Calloway complied. The man in the suit held a sheet of headed paper. He read out a series of charges, some criminal, some political. He asked Calloway if he understood. Calloway nodded. The two men left the cell, slid the bolts and switched out the light.

An hour later footsteps sounded in the corridor outside. Voices conferred. They reached agreement. A small hatch in the bottom of the cell door opened, casting a long rectangular light across the concrete floor. Calloway heard the scraping of metal. Someone on the other side of the door pushed a tray into the cell and closed the hatch. The light came on. On the tray was a bowl of weak stew, a chunk of bread and a plastic beaker full of water. Calloway ate. It was no worse than army food.

The same routine continued for several days. He tried to count them but failed. Five, perhaps six. He couldn't be sure. The lights would come on, the men would enter, they would ask questions, he would give non-committal answers. No coercion, no brutality, just procedure. Food came twice a day. The dishes varied up to a point. All of them could be eaten with a spoon.

After what could have been a week, a third man came to see him. He came twice a day. He was better dressed, self-assured, with an air of superiority. The other two men deferred to him. He spoke English to Calloway, with a strong Russian accent. He asked interrogator's questions. Calloway knew the game. He played along, feeding small amounts of information to keep the interviews civil. The questions implied Calloway was acting for a foreign power. An agent or freelancer. Calloway revealed nothing to support this assertion. He gave the Russian nothing more than the impression he was a hot-headed thug who'd messed with the wrong people. If he was to be hung, he'd be hung as a murderer, not a spy. The Russian kept his temper. His demeanour was, at worst, one of frustration and irritation. Calloway worked hard to keep it that way.

The Russian didn't come again. Calloway was left alone in his cell. He gave up any attempt to count the days. Then one day, as he slept, he was woken by the sound of the bolts sliding back once again. He peered through the doorway into the dimly-lit corridor. There were three men. Two uniformed guards with machine pistols in their hands, and the East German in the suit, with the close-shorn hair, who smelled of cheap cologne.

'Come with us, please,' he said.

It was night outside. They were in a small parking lot at the rear of the building. One of the guards ushered Calloway into the back of an unmarked van, then got in behind him. The second guard slammed the doors and locked them from the outside. Through a small portal window between the cab and the back of the van, Calloway saw the East German in the suit climb into the passenger seat. The second guard sat in the driver's seat. The engine started.

'I don't suppose you're going to tell me where I'm going,' Calloway said in German. The guard opposite said nothing. His hand tightened on the grip of the machine pistol.

They drove for twenty or thirty minutes. Calloway could make out the headlamps of oncoming traffic through the portal window. There wasn't much traffic to start with. There was virtually none as they neared their destination. Calloway felt the truck's wheels mount the kerb and bump over rubble. The driver changed down and revved. They were heading up an incline. The van seemed to bump over a threshold and level off. They drove at no more than a few miles per hour then stopped. Calloway heard the rasp of the handbrake. The two cab doors clunked open. The sound of footsteps approached the back of the van, then the sound of the rear doors being unlocked. The doors opened. The guard opposite gestured with his machine pistol for Calloway to dismount. Calloway climbed down onto the rubble floor. He let his eyes adjust to the darkness.

They were in the ruined shell of a massive oval building. Its outer walls had survived but its roof was gone. Above them a charcoal sky offered little light. Calloway looked around. The building had been some sort of arena. A *Sportpalast.* Now it was open to the elements, the smell of damp weeds and mould circulating within its walls. The van's headlamps cast two harsh, conjoined circles of light on the wall in front of them.

'Stand over there,' the man in the suit said, pointing towards the illuminated wall.

Calloway hesitated. 'Do you have a cigarette?'

The man nodded. He pulled a pack of Juwels from his jacket pocket, passed one to Calloway and lit it with a match.

'Now go,' he said, nodding towards the circles of light.

Calloway walked to the wall and turned to face the men. He squinted through the light. The two guards had stepped forward a few paces. They were training their machine pistols on him. The man in the suit lit a cigarette for himself and drew on it hard. The man checked his watch.

Calloway savoured the cheap East German tobacco. He closed his eyes and waited. This was it, he thought. No people's court. No show trial. No diplomatic complications. He would just become one of the missing. He took a last drag on the cigarette, flicked it into the darkness and watched the orange glow of the burning tip fade to nothing.

TWENTY-THREE

The sound of an engine neared. A car drove slowly over the threshold of the building and into the oval centre ground. Its tyres rumbled over the rubble, its headlamps sweeping the inner walls as it turned. The car parked. It kept its engine running. Calloway peered through the glare of the headlamps and saw three people climb out of the car. A man and two women. The light was too bright for Calloway to get a proper look at their faces. The man walked over to the East German in the suit and exchanged words. The East German nodded. The man then gestured to one of the women, who took the other woman by the arm and walked her towards Calloway. He recognised them as they approached. The woman being led was Hannelore. The one holding her arm was the woman that had seemed to be following him around Berlin, only this time she'd ditched the movie star glasses and heels. She wore trousers and boots, with a heavy reefer jacket. She had a pistol in her hand. Hannelore looked at Calloway, tired and expressionless. She stood next to him and faced the beam of the headlamps. The East German in the suit looked at her for a moment and beckoned her over.

'Goodbye, Reg,' she said. 'I hope you found what you were looking for.'

She walked over the rubble and climbed into the back of the van. One of the armed guards climbed in after her. The van revved hard and bumped over the rubble floor and out through the *Sportpalast* entrance.

No longer dazzled by the light, Calloway could make out the face of the man who'd arrived in the car. It was Sammy Mackay.

'You know, Cab,' he said, 'I had a feeling our paths might

cross. Now get in the car, will you.'

Calloway climbed into the back seat. Mackay took the passenger seat. The woman drove.

'This is Carmichael, by the way. One of my people here.' The woman acknowledged the introduction with a cock of her head as she drove. 'She's been keeping an eye on you since you arrived at Templehof. We see all the passenger manifests for the incoming flights. Your name rather jumped out. You have a habit of turning up, don't you. Like an oversized bad penny. Or perhaps that should be bad *pfennig*.'

Sammy was SIS, otherwise known as MI6, the part of the intelligence community that didn't exist officially. He'd been Calloway's CO during the war. They'd done their best not to keep in touch, but it hadn't always worked out that way.

'You really have fucked things up good and proper this time, old man,' said Mackay.

'Where are we going?' said Calloway.

'We need to debrief you. But first, I expect you'd like a drink.'

They drove west into the British sector, through the Tiergarten towards Charlottenburg. Carmichael pulled the car up outside what had once been a grand town house. Now its upper windows were boarded and its crumbling stucco bore the scars of shrapnel.

'It's not much, but it's home, as they say,' said Mackay. His conviviality would be hiding a seething resentment at the trouble Calloway had caused. Calloway knew his old CO well enough to know the signs. The three of them walked up the steps of the house and through the heavy front door. A man sat behind a desk in the high-ceilinged hallway. He was military in all but uniform.

Sammy said, 'Sign us in, will you, Geoffrey. One visitor, name of Calloway.'

The man behind the desk nodded.

'Anyone in the mess?' said Mackay.

'It's all yours, sir.'

They crossed the hallway towards a door at the far end. Sammy stopped halfway.

'You and Carmichael go ahead. I just need to get something from the ops room,' he said. He opened a door onto a busy room, where more young men with a military demeanour fussed around wirelesses and teleprinters, which crackled and clacked above the hum of voices. There were maps on the walls, divided into the sectors of the occupying forces, with coloured pins and scrawlings in chinagraph pencil. Carmichael led Calloway away, towards the room Sammy had called the mess. It was a long, narrow drawing room that looked onto what was left of the garden, now a jumble of building debris, broken crates and jerry cans from the war.

'Nice view,' said Calloway.

'The budget won't stretch to a gardener,' said Mackay, closing the door behind him and crossing the room to the window. He drew together a pair of dusty velvet curtains.

The room was furnished with a collection of salvaged armchairs and sofas, with cheerless prints on the walls. Standard lamps with frayed shades shed sepia light. It resembled what Calloway imagined a common room at some minor public school might look like. A dark and ornate sideboard served as a bar, with a row of spirits and a dozen bottled beers. Sammy poured three large scotches and set them down on a low table between two threadbare sofas. He brought the bottle with him.

'Sit down, Cab,' he said.

Calloway sat and sank into the deep horsehair upholstery. It was the most comfort he'd experienced for a fortnight. Every muscle ached, every tendon groaned with dull pain. He downed the whisky in thirsty gulps. Sammy poured him another.

'You've certainly made your presence known here, Cab,' he said. 'Berlin hasn't buzzed so much since Grigori Tokaty defected.'

Calloway had heard the name, a Soviet rocket scientist who'd walked into West Berlin with his family and applied to the British for asylum.

'I like to make an impression,' he said.

Sammy's expression changed. Here it comes, thought Calloway.

'You've done more than that,' said Mackay. 'You've made a bloody mess and I've had to clear it up.' He slammed his glass on the tabletop. 'For Christ's sake, man, you nearly started a war.'

'I just asked some questions.'

Sammy slopped more whisky into his own glass. He gulped it down in one.

'Questions that left a member of the East German security services dead in an abandoned building in the Soviet sector. They found him with two bullets through his head.'

'That must be an occupational hazard in his line of work,' said Calloway.

'Quit the bloody jokes. Do you realise where you are? Peace in our time hangs by a thread in this city. A thread that can snap with a single wrong move. You've made several, from what I've heard.' Sammy looked at Carmichael, who gave a faint nod of agreement. 'You're a bloody nuisance and I was the one that had to bail you out. It's my balls on the line if this doesn't blow over.'

Calloway thought of the exchange at the *Sportpalast*, the image of Hannelore climbing into the unmarked van.

'You made your swap,' he said. 'The slate's clean now.'

Sammy scoffed. 'The slate's never clean. You're not so long out of this business not to realise that. Forget the swap, that's just a short-term fix. As far as the Russians are concerned, we've killed one of theirs. That means one of ours in return. That's how it works here. Tit for bloody tat. You've put lives at risk.'

He knew Sammy was right, but old habits die hard and he took the dressing down from his old CO with a stone face and a hint of defiance.

'And to boot,' said Mackay, 'you've dispatched an asset we've been embedding in East German security for the last five years.' Mackay put his head in both hands. 'What the hell were you thinking, man?' he said.

The last thing Calloway remembers thinking was that Baumann's death was a small but necessary vengeance on him and his kind. He kept these thoughts to himself.

Mackay composed himself. He took a sip of the whisky. 'You recognised Baumann from that other business?'

He meant the blackmail case at the speedway stadium. That was the first time Mackay's and Calloway's paths had crossed since the war. That's when Calloway heard about the deal that Baumann, real name Frank Belper, the psychotic traitor in the blackmail photos with his Britische Freikorps comrades, had struck with the British intelligence services.

Calloway nodded. 'I remembered him from the photographs,' he said.

Mackay sighed and shook his head. 'Sod's law he'd be the one East German you ran into on this wild goose chase of yours. What the hell's it all about, Cab? What's Stanley Deakin to you?'

'A friend of a friend,' he said.

'And you came here looking for who killed him?'

'I came here to find out how he died. It wasn't in a road accident in England, like his wife has been told. Why don't you tell me what it's all about, Sammy.'

Mackay refilled their glasses. He turned to Carmichael. 'Tell him what we know. I've had enough.' He lay back into the sofas and rubbed the muscles in his neck, wincing.

'It's not an SIS matter,' said Carmichael. It was the first time Calloway had head her speak. She was well-spoken but with a cavalier air, like a bad girl from Rodean. The type Sammy would like, Calloway thought. 'This is strictly Curzon Street territory.'

'MI5?' said Calloway. 'What are they doing stomping around Berlin?'

Mackay looked up. 'Same as you probably,' he said. 'Sticking their nose where it doesn't belong.'

'We only found out about it when Deakin was killed,' said Carmichael. 'Curzon Street had to own up to Berlin Station that they had a live operation gone sour in our bailiwick. They needed our help to clean up the mess.'

'How does Deakin connect to MI5?' said Calloway. 'The man was a truck driver. A pretty unreliable one, from what I've heard.'

Carmichael exchanged looks with Mackay. Mackay nodded. She handed Calloway a file with a few flimsy sheets, copies of a file on Stanley Deakin. Calloway read in silence.

Deakin was arrested by the military police in Alexandria,

Egypt in 1940 for selling army radio valves to local civilians on the black market. This much Calloway knew, from what Webber had told him. Deakin was sentenced to six months in a military prison somewhere in the desert with an Arabic name Calloway didn't recognise. It was a hard regime. Endless PT, drill and beastings from the redcap guards. After three months he was visited by a major in the Queen's Own Hussars. He offered Stan a way to cut short his sentence. The major was recruiting for a new unit, a highly irregular one. A deep reconnaissance unit that would disappear into the remotest parts of Egypt and Libya for weeks on end to observe enemy activity. It was called the *Long-Range Desert Group* and, the major said, they were short of skilled radio operators. Despite his petty criminality, Stan was one of the best wireless men in Egypt. He agreed to join the new unit and was released from prison the same day, leaving in the major's jeep to the chagrin of the redcaps, with whom he'd developed a less than respectful relationship. There was some training to follow, on the minutiae of desert warfare, the use of weapons like the Lewis gun and the Boys anti-tank rifle, and the best ways to dig trucks out of deep sand. He also had to get to know the stripped-down Canadian Chevrolet trucks that would be their home, their fortress and their camel train for weeks at a time. He was encouraged to grow his hair and beard and was issued Arab garments to wear over his battledress, should they need to pass themselves off as Bedouin when encountering an enemy patrol. Stan adjusted well to irregular warfare. He liked its informality, the comparative equality between officers and men, and the maverick bloody-mindedness the group were allowed to exhibit in their dealings with more regular units. He was placed under the command of the major that had recruited him and the two men struck up a good working relationship with moments of friendship, in spite of the difference in their rank and social class. Stan spent the best part three years with the LRDG, before returning to the signals corps for the remainder of the war.

He received an honourable discharge in late 1945 and resumed his civilian life. He had no contact with his former comrades in the years following his demobilisation. Then, in 1948, he was again contacted by the major. They arranged to meet and Stan was offered a proposition. The major was now an operational officer with MI5 and as such he needed reliable freelances to take on arm's-length assignments suited to their experience, capabilities and type. Stan qualified on all three counts for some very deniable work and, thanks in part to the decent sums of money involved, agreed to the major's proposition. He had been used three times since then, although details of these operations were not included in the file. The report was dated and signed by the major himself. His name was Patrick Denton.

Calloway passed the file back to Carmichael. 'Do you know this man Denton?'

'Never set eyes on him,' said Mackay. 'Our dealings on this mess have been higher up the chain of command. Issues like this tend to get kicked upstairs.'

'Denton's been following me around, in London.'

'I'm sure he has,' said Mackay. 'I can imagine you've been as much of a pain in his arse as mine.'

'What was Stan doing for Denton? What was he working on when he died?'

Carmichael lit a cigarette and offered one to Calloway. 'Denton had assigned him to keep close to Hannelore Schneider, that's her real name. MI5 has been watching her for some time. A former member of KPD before the war who joined the Communist Party of Great Britain soon after settling in England. A staunch anti-fascist, not surprisingly given her experience, who saw communism as the antidote. She quit the party after a couple of years and steered clear of politics, at least as far as appearances are concerned. She was recruited by the Russians sometime around 1947 we think. Her role is believed to be gathering intelligence on the deployment of British and US air forces in the UK. Touring with a fairground takes her around the country to places within an easy motorcycle ride to our air bases. The fairground is a perfect cover.'

Calloway remembered the place names on the tour poster in Hannelore's trailer. Peterborough, Bury St Edmunds, Newmarket, Cromer. All within easy reach of bases in the east of England, places Calloway had heard of, like Alconbury, Lakenheath and Mildenhall.

'MI5 weren't interested in Schneider *per se*. She was a small fish who they could have lifted at any time. They wanted her network. It was Deakin's job to get close to her, with a view to turning her. His name showed up on MI5's radar when he applied for papers to travel to Berlin with the fairground. That's when Denton saw his chance. He hired Deakin to shadow Schneider on the German tour and thereafter on the English dates.'

And all the while, thought Calloway, Vera believed her husband was driving a truck in Stratton-Fenwick, sending the postcards that were no doubt pre-written.

'The plan was to expose her, so that Denton and his people could work on her to turn double,' said Carmichael.

'It should have been plain sailing,' said Mackay, 'as far as these things ever are. But your friend Stan's fondness for cheap champagne and the local *fräuleins* threw a spanner right in the works.'

'He blabbed, in other words,' said Carmichael. 'He tried to impress the girls with his Dick Barton story, which in this case happened to be true. He told them enough for the club owner Vogel to see the value. That's when Baumann got involved.'

'Baumann said he had Stan killed.'

'He did.'

'Baumann was your asset, Stan was working for MI5, couldn't you have stopped him?'

'Oh yes, Cab, it's that bloody easy,' said Mackay. 'We didn't even know of Deakin's existence. Curzon Street were flying solo, operating on our turf without our knowledge. Baumann saw Deakin as a complication that might compromise his position. His solution was to remove the complication. Frankly I can't say I blame him.'

'I'll tell Deakin's wife that. I'm sure it will be a great comfort to her.'

Mackay shook his head. 'Reg Calloway,' he said. 'The thug with a heart of gold. That was always your problem, Cab. You cared too much and it clouded your judgement. You let your anger get the better of you.'

'Next to your friend Baumann, I'm a fucking angel. Don't talk to me about judgement, Sammy.'

Calloway took a long drag on the cigarette. 'Was it your idea to trade Hannelore for me?'

'There's no need to thank me, if you were considering it.' Calloway wasn't. 'I did it to avoid an almighty diplomatic stink, not to save your neck. Believe me, that's of little value to me.'

'What did MI5 think?'

'They weren't happy, as you might imagine. But frankly, she was as good as blown the minute Vogel tipped Baumann off that Deakin was onto her. He might have been our man, but there are some things he couldn't have sat on. It was a fair assumption he'd have told the Russians.'

Sammy lit a cigarette and sat back in the sofa.

'MI5 can fuck themselves. They shouldn't have been operating on our patch without telling us.'

Calloway had smoked Carmichael's cigarette down to the butt. He nodded at the pack on the table. Sammy passed him one and lit it.

'So what happens next?' said Calloway.

Carmichael spoke. 'You disappear as soon as possible. We'll get you on a plane from Templehof and send you back to London.'

'And Pat Moxon, the woman I came here with?'

'She's no concern of ours.'

'I need to speak to her.'

Carmichael shook her head. 'You'll stay here until it's time to leave.'

He needed to see Pat. He couldn't walk out on her again.

'What about Denton?' he said.

Mackay shrugged and looked irritated. 'How the bloody hell should I know? He's MI5, I'm MI6. There's not a lot of love lost between us at the best of times.'

'He's taken Deakin's wife off to some kind of clinic.'

'Not my worry, old boy,' said Mackay.

Calloway downed the last of the scotch. 'I need to sleep.'

‘There’s a room upstairs with a camp bed for the duty officers on the night shift,’ said Mackay. ‘You can have that. The duty officer can sleep in here if he needs to.’

Carmichael showed Calloway to the room. It faced onto the rear garden, although its blown-in window was boarded up. There was a fresh pillow and two blankets on the rickety canvas bed.

‘Try to stay out of trouble,’ said Carmichael, closing the door as she left.

TWENTY-FOUR

Wind whistled between the cracks in the boards on the window. Calloway tested the bottom plank, which gave a little, its nails sitting loosely in the damp window frame. It came away easily as he pulled on it. He worked on the other boards until there was a big enough opening to for him to fit through. He climbed out backwards, finding a small parapet with his feet. It was just big enough to stand on. He flattened himself against the outer wall and eased himself over to a small balcony beneath an adjacent window which was also boarded. He judged that if he hung off the balcony with his hands, the drop to the garden below would be manageable. He slung one leg over the parapet, then the other, then took a deep breath and let himself drop. He fell to the uneven ground below, snagging his ankle on a broken brick. He cursed. He tested his foot on the ground. Sore but not broken. There were voices coming from the mess. Its curtains were still drawn closed. There was no sign that the garden was overlooked by any other windows.

The weak glow of the moon behind the clouds was enough to see by. He watched his footing as he negotiated the piled debris in the garden and made it to the far wall. It was six foot high. He dragged a crate over and up-ended it. It gave him the leg-up he needed. He heaved himself up with his arms and rolled over the top of the wall.

He had no money and no papers. He didn't know what time it was, other than that it was late. He navigated the dark streets by instinct, ducking into doorways or cutting across bomb sites to avoid the headlamps of the few cars and taxis that passed. It took him an hour to reach Hotel Pension Ritz. He did his best to smarten himself up. He had a fortnight's growth of beard but there was nothing he could do about that. Old Klaus was asleep behind the reception desk. Calloway reached behind him and took his room key from the rows of hooks. Klaus stirred, smacked his chops noisily, then settled. Calloway stepped lightly on the hard parquet floor down the hallway towards his room. There was light shining under Pat's door. He tapped softly. He heard stirring inside. The door opened a crack.

'Jesus Christ, Reg, look at the state of you,' she said.

She held the door open and ushered him in. He flopped on the bed, and she sat beside him.

'What the hell happened to you?'

'Been worried about me?'

'I wouldn't go that far,' she said. There was a half-bottle of whisky open on the bedside table. She poured him a glass.

'Thanks,' he said. He took a sip. 'The less you know the better.'

She looked him up and down. His suit was stained, his shoes scuffed. His shirt was grimy at the collar. His hard face was pallid beneath the growth of beard.

'You're probably right. I don't want to go the same way as Hannelore. The military police came for her.'

'I know,' he said. 'They swapped her for me. That's why I'm here and not on trial in the east.'

She paused for a moment, taking this in, then nodded. 'The less I know the better. Now go and get yourself cleaned up.'

Her room had a bathroom. He ran a bath to the rim and let the hot water soothe him. He lay there for an age, slipping in an out of a bleary half-sleep. Then he dried himself and wrapped the bath towel around his waist.

Pat had undressed. Her clothes lay on the floor. She was in bed. The cover was turned down on one side like an invitation. Her eyes beckoned him over. He sat on the bed beside her and she took his hand in hers. She pulled him towards her.

'Don't think I'm not still angry with you,' she said.

He slept through the night, the first decent sleep he'd had in days. Pat nudged him awake. She had ordered coffee. He sat up and lit a cigarette. The gravity of his situation came back to him.

'What's happened since I've been away?' he said.

'You've had callers. Two men looking for you. They've been here most days.'

'They speak to you?'

'The receptionist told them we were travelling together. She called me down to see them.'

'What did you tell them?

'That I knew nothing.'

'Did they accept that?'

'No, they looked like they were going to turn nasty. But I guess they didn't want to do anything in front of a witness. I'm just glad I wasn't on my own. I can handle myself, as you well know, Reg, but these two were bruisers.'

'Describe them.'

'Big, ugly, German.'

'Does one look like a pig?'

She laughed and nodded. 'More than I thought possible.'

'They're trouble,' he said. 'They killed Stan.'

Pat didn't often look shocked. She was made of sterner stuff. But the colour had drained from her face.

'Did they say they'd be back?'

She nodded. 'Today.'

'We need to leave. Pack some essentials.'

He climbed out of bed, wrapped a towel around his waist and crossed the room to the door.

'Listen, Reg...' she said.

He cut her off. 'We'll talk later. Right now we need to move.'

He went to his room and put on a change of clothes, all he had left. He would leave the soiled suit behind. There was a mouthful left in the Bismarck bottle. He swilled it down. He reached under the mattress and took the last of the cash Webber had given him for the trip. Then he fumbled in the drawer of the bedside table and pulled out the signet ring on the chain that Trudi had given him. He put the chain around his neck and fastened the clasp.

When he returned to Pat's room she was still in bed.

'I'm staying here,' she said. 'I'll change hotels to be on the safe side, but I'm not leaving Berlin. I'm going to finish the tour.'

'You're mad,' he said. 'These men are killers. They killed Stan and tried to kill me. They're coming back to finish the job.'

'Then perhaps it's best I keep away from you.'

There was no arguing with the look she was giving him. Pat had determination in spades.

'If I go, Milt doesn't have an act,' she said.

He looked incredulous. 'So what?' he said. 'It's a sideshow. This is life and death.'

'It's my life, Reg. It's not yours to own.'

She climbed out of bed and walked over to him. She took his head in her hands and kissed him hard.

'Now it's my turn to walk out on you,' she said. 'We're even.'

TWENTY-FIVE

The address Trudi had given him was on a street in Kreuzburg. In reality it was half a street, the other half no more than piles of rubble a good storey high. Laundry hung on makeshift lines on half-remaining first-floor rooms, which jutted out like jagged balconies from the flanks of high buildings. Children played on the rubble piles like kings of the castle. Old women in black coats huddled on street corners to gossip. Tired-looking men in the worn and dirty clothes of labourers strode purposefully to work. Mothers pushed rusting prams, toddlers played in sandpits made from the destroyed footings of buildings. The contrast with the bright shop-window hubbub of Ku'damm was striking. This was slum living, or little better.

Calloway knocked on a heavy wooden door within a tall, Wilhelmine-era apartment building. If it had been grand once, its grandeur was long gone. Its curtains were filthy and torn, half its window broken or boarded. There was no reply. Calloway knocked harder. He heard footsteps and scuffling from behind the door. A bolt slid back and the face of a man appeared in the crack of the half-open door. He had fat lips, jug ears and a toothbrush moustache. His skin was like leather, tanned to a potato-peel brown with deep lines chiselled into it. A hand-rolled cigarette dangled from his lip. He squinted into the light from beneath a Neanderthal brow.

'What do you want?' he grunted, eyeing Calloway up and down.

'I was told you could help me.'

The man frowned. 'Why should I help you?'

Calloway reached inside his shirt collar and pulled out the ring on the chain.

The man in the doorway looked at the ring and back at Calloway. He looked suspicious.

'Who sent you?' he said.

'I'm a friend of Trudi Trauber.'

The man frowned some more. Then his expression softened. He held open the door.

'Come in,' he said.

He bolted the door behind them and led Calloway up the darkened stairway to the first-floor landing. The man ushered him into a shabby apartment which looked onto the street through dirty windows.

'Sit,' he said, gesturing to a small table on which a coffee pot stood. He took a chipped mug from the shelf and poured Calloway coffee.

'Here,' he said, passing Calloway the mug. 'I am Otto.'

'Reg,' said Calloway, holding out his hand. Otto hesitated. He leaned forward and examined the ring around Calloway's neck. He glanced down at his own hand. He wore the same ring. He clapped Calloway on the shoulder and sat down opposite him.

'How do you know Trudi?' he said.

'I work at a wrestling arena in London. She's our star wrestler.'

Otto slurped at the coffee. He wiped the dribbles off his chin with his shirt sleeve.

'Trudi is the best,' he said. 'She give you that ring?'

Calloway nodded. 'For luck.'

'She must like you,' said Otto. 'That ring is important. It means a lot to us.'

'Who is *us*?'

Otto lowered his voice.

'The Kreuzburg *Ringverein*,' he said.

Calloway translated in his head.

'Ring club,' he said. 'What's a ring club?'

'They were started last century,' said Otto. 'Official clubs to help ex-convicts back into decent society. Started by some philanthropic fool who thought it was a good idea to create networks of criminals across the city.' He laughed to himself.

'What this fool created was organised crime in Berlin. Our very own mafia families.'

'And Trudi was a member of the Kreuzburg *Ringverein*?'

Otto smiled. 'Oh yes. A valued member. Loyal and strong.'

'Had Trudi been to jail?'

'Two years in Hohenheck women's prison for assault.'

Calloway was taken aback. Trudi was a devil in the ring, but outside it, she was a gentle giant.

'I expect he deserved it,' he said.

Otto was quiet for a moment. He looked solemn. 'He deserved it.'

The men drank their coffee in silence for a moment. Upstairs a couple argued while a baby cried.

'What kind of trouble are you in, Reg?' said Otto.

'A man called Vogel wants me dead.'

'Vogel the club owner?'

'You know him?'

'He was a member of *Ringverein Immertreu*, until they kicked him out. The man is a snake.'

'He set his two dogs on me.'

'Max and Günter?'

'We weren't on first name terms,' said Calloway. 'I got away from them. Now they want to finish the job. I need to get out of Berlin.'

Otto waved a hand in the direction of the door.

'So leave,' he said. 'Catch a plane from Templehof. I have money if you need it.'

'That's generous,' said Calloway. 'It's not that simple. I have no passport. I also have a friend who is staying behind in Berlin. I believe she's in danger too.'

Otto weighed this up. 'So you want that danger removed.'

'If it can be arranged. I'll also need a passport.'

'Vogel is nothing without his hired muscle. A weak and frightened man. We can deal with Max and Günter. A passport is more difficult. There are still a few good forgers in Berlin but they are busy. People want to leave the east. The wait would be too long. But,' he said, 'I can get you out of West Berlin and across to Hamburg without papers. From there you can take a boat and take your chances. We know people. People who will help us.'

It sounded risky but Calloway had little choice than to trust the criminal Otto. It wasn't just the lack of a passport. He wanted to get back to London without Denton knowing. This seemed like the only way.

'Thank you,' said Calloway. 'I know it's going to cost you. I can send money when I get home.'

Otto waved the offer away. 'Trudi has saved my skin on more than one occasion. I owe her this much. Tell her Otto says hello.'

He laid low in the Kreuzburg apartment until nightfall. Otto was gone for several hours making arrangements. At just after nine o'clock a truck pulled up outside the building. Otto introduced Calloway to the driver.

'This is Lothar. He is making a run to Hamburg to collect goods from the docks. Legitimate freight. You can ride in the cab for most of the journey, but you must hide while Lothar drives through East Germany between the two checkpoints. There's a false floor in the back of the truck, for smuggling contraband. It's just big enough for a man your size.'

'If you breathe in,' said Lothar with a grin.

'You'll be leaving West Berlin via Checkpoint Bravo in the woods at Dreilinden. Then you'll take the autobahn to Checkpoint Alpha at Helmstedt-Marienborn on the border with West Germany. It's the shortest route between east and west.'

Lothar looked at his watch. 'We must get moving.'

Calloway thanked Otto and climbed into to the cab.

Lothar offered him a slug of American PX whisky from a bottle in the glove compartment.

'For the road,' he said.

Calloway declined. He wanted a clear head. This wasn't a pleasure trip.

Lothar was talkative. Calloway could have done without company, but he was grateful to the driver for sticking his neck out to help. He wondered what Lothar's deal with Otto was. Was he *Ringverein* too, or just a hired hand? Either way, Calloway wasn't going to ask. Instead he listened to Lothar talk about football, which Calloway didn't follow, politics, about which Calloway didn't care, and family, none of whom Calloway knew. It was an ordeal of forced platitudes on Calloway's part. He was already exhausted when the truck approached the forest. Lothar pulled over.

'We must stop here,' he said. 'Go and take a piss. A good long one. It will be your last for about three hours.'

Calloway did as instructed. Lothar led Calloway to the rear of the truck and dropped the tailgate. The two men climbed in. Lothar lifted a section of planking on the wood floor. Beneath it was a sunken recess, measuring about five foot by two foot six. It was lined with an oil-stained blanket.

'Are you serious?' said Calloway.

'It's either that or you walk, my friend,' said Lothar, without his usual joviality.

Calloway lowered himself into the small space. He curled up like a foetus. Lothar lowered the planking. Calloway heard the clinking of metal then a loud banging. Lothar was nailing the planks down. Calloway shouted through the boards.

'Jesus Christ, man, what the hell are you doing?'

'If it's loose, they will discover you in an instant,' Lothar shouted back. 'This is the safest way.'

Nothing about being nailed into an undersized box felt safe to Calloway. Trusting a criminal gang was starting to seem like a dumb idea. He heard Lothar place his head against the boards and whisper.

'You must be quiet now. Not a sound.'

He heard the tailgate close and the engine restart. The truck pulled back onto the road.

It was cold in the box and the smell of diesel fumes was overpowering. He wasn't sure he'd survive three hours in Lothar's nailed-down coffin.

He felt the truck slow until it came to a halt. He heard American voices, sounding official. They'd reached Checkpoint Bravo. Calloway could just make out the conversation. The American MPs were telling Lothar the procedures to expect on the East German side of the border at Drewitz.

The procedures on the American side of the border took no more than a few minutes. The truck rolled forward at a few miles an hour then stopped again. German voices this time. More urgent, more authoritative. The wait this side seemed interminable to Calloway, crammed into the small space. He strained to hear the exchanges between Lothar and the East German *Grenzpolizei*. They sounded tense. The Grepos were questioning the validity of Lothar's travel papers. Calloway heard Lothar climb down from the cab and the sound of heavy boots walking to the rear of the truck. The slam of the tailgate dropping shook the truck. Two sets of boots climbed into the back and stomped around. The Grepos tapped and tested. Calloway's mouth went dry. His heart pounded in his chest. If he was caught here, there would be no prisoner swap this time. He'd burned his bridges with Sammy and Carmichael when he'd climbed out of the window in Charlottenburg. The Grepos were on top of him now, tapping the planks with their knuckles and comparing the sound to other parts of the floor. Calloway heard fingernails scrape over the heads of the nails in the planks. The guards' voices got louder. They seemed to be arguing with each other now, one suggesting they should get tools and lift the planks, the other complaining of the cold and saying it was late and they should get back to the warmth of their hut. Lothar was silent throughout the search. He clearly knew better than to remonstrate with the East German border police. A third voice spoke, with the tone of a superior officer. He ordered the two Grepos off the truck. Boots jumped down onto the ground. Lothar exchanged words with the officer who wished him a safe trip and walked away. Calloway heard Lothar grunt as he climbed into the back of the truck. He put his head against the planks and whispered.

'Their officer likes PX whisky.'

Calloway heard the tailgate close. Lothar climbed back into the cab and drove on.

Calloway managed some sleep. It passed the time. He woke with cramp, a searing pain through his calf muscle and no way of stretching it out. He pressed his foot hard against the edge of the box, which brought some small relief, but he had to suffer the pain for a good half-hour before it subsided.

Crossing at Helmstedt-Marienborn was more straightforward. It was late and there was no queueing. The truck rumbled over the border and was waved on by a soldier with an English accent. Lothar drove for a further half-hour and pulled over. He jemmied up the planks and helped Calloway out of the hole. Calloway stretched his limbs. His joints ground like they were rusted.

'Welcome to West Germany,' Lothar said. He shook Calloway's hand. 'Come on, you can ride in the cab now. I have some bread and sausage.'

Calloway scoffed the food. He was starving. He'd not eaten all day.

'We should reach Hamburg in about three hours,' said Lothar. 'You should get some sleep.'

Calloway complied. He fell asleep to the rumble of the engine and the sound of Lothar humming an off-key tune.

TWENTY-SIX

Calloway awoke to the sound of seagulls. It was just before dawn and the light was turning from stifling black to a hopeful blue-grey.

'Hamburg docks,' said Otto, passing Calloway a flask. 'Here, coffee.'

Calloway poured a cup. It was weak but welcome. He looked out of the truck window across the vast swathes of cold black water, criss-crossed with girder bridges and lined with cranes. A timid sun peeked from behind the funnels and masts of some of the biggest cargo ships Calloway had ever seen. The docks were busy, despite the early hour. Merchant seamen bustled around in gangs, uniformly dressed in pea coats and black caps, with shapeless kit bags slung across their backs. They smoked pipes and exchanged words through missing teeth. Otto drove the truck along the dockside road at a crawl, avoiding the cat's cradle of ropes as thick as a man's arm that held the vast freight ships in their berths. Beyond them, tugs belched smoke to a dawn chorus of steam whistles and ship's horns.

Otto gestured to one of the ships. '*The Kurtz*,' he said pointing at the name on the rust-streaked stern. 'Two thousand tons. She leaves in an hour for London.'

'Who's the captain?' said Calloway.

'A man called Steiner. A friend.'

Lothar parked the truck. The two men dismounted and wove their way across the busy quayside and up the gangplank to the ship's deck. *The Kurtz* had seen better days, its steelwork battered and rusting. Lothar exchanged words with a pint-sized deck hand who pointed up to the bridge of the ship. Lothar and Calloway climbed the stairway and ducked through the low door.

Captain Steiner was alone on the bridge. He slouched in a high chair, watching the activity on deck with a bored expression. He was perhaps fifty, with a ruddy face and a paunch beneath the straining brass buttons of his bridge coat. A mop of greasy grey hair stuck out from beneath his braided cap. He stood and looked Calloway up and down.

'Is this our cargo?' he said to Lothar.

Lothar nodded. Calloway held out his hand. Steiner shook his head.

'Best we don't do introductions. As far as I'm concerned, you don't exist.' He turned to Lothar. 'You have the money?'

Lothar reached inside the pocket of his pea coat and pulled out a grubby envelope. Steiner took it, counted the money and pushed it into his own pocket. He leaned out of the door and hollered down to one of the hands, who scrambled up the stairway two treads at a time.

'Take our guest to the fore hold,' said Steiner. The hand gave a curt, *'Jawohl, Herr Kapitan,'* then gestured for Calloway to follow him below. Calloway shook Lothar's hand and thanked him for the ride. Lothar wished him luck. Without thinking Calloway reached inside his shirt and fondled the ring on the chain. Then he clanked down the stairway after the hand.

The fore hold was damp and stinking. It didn't hold cargo so much as all the oily odds and ends that didn't have a place elsewhere on the vessel. A space had been cleared for a camp bed, over which hung a battery lamp that would be the only source of light. There was a thin blanket folded on the bed. The hand passed Calloway a small canvas bag containing a sandwich wrapped in paper and a bottle of water.

'There's a bucket in the corner,' the hand said.

Calloway could smell it.

'You stay here,' said the hand. 'We will come and get you when it's time to disembark.'

Calloway acknowledged the instructions with a nod and settled himself on the camp bed. The hand slammed the hatch shut. Calloway fumbled for the battery lamp and switched it on.

It cast a weak glow outwards for no more than a couple of feet. Shut in a box again, thought Calloway. But at least there's room to stretch. He lay flat on the bed and stared into the half-darkness. The muffled blare of the horn announced their departure from the docks. The anchor chain clanked and water slapped against the hull. The ship's huge engines sent shudders along the lower deck, vibrating the bed beneath him. He didn't relish spending the best part of twenty-four hours under these conditions. He peered through the gloom at the hatch. There were no handles on the inside. He unwrapped the sandwich and ate, then settled himself back on the bed, pulling the blanket around him against the cold and damp.

He slept a fitful sleep, incoherent dreams colliding as he tossed and turned under the meagre blanket. The wall of death spun around him, dragging him down into a vortex of screaming faces – Vera, Hannelore and Pat – all calling his name, desperate and accusing. Then pain, the fierce, intolerable pain of fists and boots pummelling into him, Max and Günter drooling from the mouths of their pigs' heads, squealing with delight.

He was woken by the slow metallic creak of the hatch opening, and the silhouette of a man ducking into the hold.

'Time to go,' said Captain Steiner.

Calloway threw the blanket off. His shirt clung to his back, soaked in a cold sweat. He peered at the face of his watch but couldn't make it out in the darkness.

'What time is it?' he said.

'An hour before dawn,' said Steiner. 'Quickly now.'

It was cold on deck. Steiner led Calloway to the starboard side of the boat. They stood looking over the side under the green glow of the navigation light.

Calloway could just make out a small vessel, a motorboat, perhaps a fishing boat, with a wheelhouse not much bigger than a call box. On the deck of *The Kurtz*, hands were stuffing boxes into a cargo net that hung from the jib of a crane. There must have been three dozen boxes, each a foot and a half square. Whatever they contained, it was something the customs men would never get to see.

Steiner saw Calloway looking towards the net.

'I hope you have a strong grip,' he said. 'That's how you're leaving the ship.'

One of the hands sniggered. Calloway didn't find it funny. He peered down into the black waters between *The Kurtz* and the fishing boat. They looked cold and rough, perhaps not rough by Captain Steiner's standards, but there was enough swell to put the fear of God into any land lubber.

'Put your feet through the squares in the net and hold onto the rope with both hands. You'll be fine if you don't let go,' said the captain with a smirk.

Calloway hesitated. The fishing boat was still far back from the ship.

'Can't they get any closer?' he said.

Steiner shook his head. 'Any closer and they risk slamming into the hull.'

Calloway did as instructed. He slipped the soles of his shoes through the net until the heels caught. He pushed his feet down to test their grip. He caught the rope from the jib with both hands and straightened up.

Steiner read the look on Calloway's face. 'If you know a better way to get to London without a passport, I suggest you do it, my friend.'

'If I did, do you think I'd be clinging onto this bloody rope,' said Calloway.

Steiner clapped him on the back. 'You'll be fine,' he said, signalling to the jib operator.

Calloway felt the rope tauten beneath his hands and the cargo beneath him rise from the deck. The filled net started to sway. The jib swivelled on the mast and swung the cargo out over the water, its momentum rocking Calloway back and forth with more violence than he'd expected. He squeezed the rope tighter. The fishing boat skipper shouted instructions to the crane operator. Wind whipped around Calloway ankles. It was a cold damp wind. It bit at his fingers as they clutched the rope. The wind sent the cargo swaying out even further. The jib operator was struggling to align the load with the meagre deck of the fishing boat. The boat's skipper was swearing, tugging at the wheel, trying to steady the tiny vessel, while at the same time shouting instructions into the darkness. Calloway felt a sudden, violent lunge, which all but wrenched his arms from their sockets. A tall wave threw *The Kurtz* upwards. The jib of the crane snapped backwards towards the ship, the cargo net following. Calloway clung on. The net hit the hull with a jolt. Calloway felt his ankle slam against the steel. He screamed in pain and lost his footing. His legs dangled above the waves, his hands clinging to the cold wet rope. The rope slipped through his grasp. His legs flailed as he tried to find a footing on the net. The jib swung again, this time out over the sea. The inertia flung Calloway horizontal. He felt the sting of rope burns across his palms. He heard shouting all around him. His body slapped back against the cargo and one of his feet snagged in the net. He pushed down hard and found a footing. He heard the high-pitched squeal of the pulley above him and looked down to see the sea rising up to meet him. Then the fishing boat lunged backwards on the waves so that its deck was directly below. The skipper gave a signal and reached up with a boat hook. He snagged the net. The pulley squealed again and the cargo landed on the deck with a mighty thud. Calloway lost his grip on the rope and fell backwards, the boxes in the loosened net tumbling over him. They were light. Lighter than he'd expected. Light enough to spare him the two broken legs a heavier cargo would have dealt him.

'You alright, chief?' the skipper said.

Calloway's subconscious audited the damage. It was a habit from the war and was seldom wrong.

'A few bruises and rope burns,' he said.

'You can help me get these below then,' said the skipper. 'Quickly now.'

The two men tossed the boxes through a small hatch beneath the open wheelhouse. Clearly, they weren't fragile. When they were done, the skipper signalled to *The Kurtz*, which picked up speed, leaving the fishing boat bumping in its wake.

The skipper wrestled with the wheel and, satisfied all was well, reached into his coat and passed a hip flask to Calloway.

'You'll need a nip of that I expect,' he said.

TWENTY-SEVEN

'What are we carrying?' said Calloway.

The boxes were too light for liquor, probably too light for drugs.

'Nylons,' said the skipper.

'Stockings?'

The skipper nodded. 'It's bloody ridiculous, if you ask me,' he said. 'Britain manufactures loads of them but exports them to Europe. The racketeers buy them in Europe and smuggle them back to Britain to sell on the black market.'

'Who's picking them up?'

'Bloke called Freddie. He'll have a van waiting by a jetty near Maldon.'

'Essex?'

The skipper gave an affirmative grunt. 'The Blackwater,' he said. He cackled to himself. 'Takes someone as old as me to navigate the Blackwater by night. I've been navigating these waters since I was a boy.'

Calloway felt reassured, at least by the skipper's confidence in getting him back on dry land. He kept an open mind about Freddie.

Dawn was breaking behind them, but the dull grey light didn't make the Blackwater any less black. It remained dark and threatening. Calloway wasn't a natural sea goer. He could jump out of an aircraft with a parachute on his back or plummet to the earth in a glider, but he'd happily leave the sea to the mackerel and the matelots, especially after his ride on Steiner's cargo net. He was relieved when the skipper gestured to a jagged black line against the low horizon.

'The jetty,' he said.

Calloway could see the van beside it and a man standing. The red glow of a burning cigarette beamed like a lighthouse. The skipper pulled alongside the jetty. Calloway picked up the ropes and jumped out of the boat. He tied up fore and aft. Freddie approached the jetty and gave Calloway a cautious nod.

'You the stowaway?' he said, drawing on the butt of the cigarette and flicking it into the water. He was about five foot eight with slits for eyes and a gap in his teeth. He wore a broad-shouldered coat that covered his knees. The coat was made of a tweed that was too loud for this early in the morning. Its lapels were wide enough to touch his arms. He wore his stingy-brimmed trilby at an angle. If the intention was to advertise that he dealt in black market nylons, he was succeeding. He looked incongruous amid the sodden marshland.

'I'm here,' said Calloway. 'Let's just leave it at that.'

'Freddie will take you to London,' said the skipper.

'I could do without company, if I'm honest,' the spiv said, looking at Calloway.

'A deal's a deal, Fred,' said the skipper, with an air of authority he'd not shown before.

Freddie shrugged. 'S'pose so,' he said, like he supposed quite the opposite. He looked at Calloway and cocked his head in the direction of the van. 'You can help me load up,' he said. 'Earn your passage.'

They transferred the boxes from the fishing boat to the vehicle. Freddie reeled off a wad of banknotes and handed them to the skipper. The look on his face said it pained him to do so. The skipper shook Calloway's hand and bade him farewell. Freddie started the van and Calloway climbed in beside him.

'What's your story then?' Freddie said, tugging at the wheel as the van bumped over the uneven ground towards the road.

'Just a man who needed to get home,' said Calloway.

'Sounds like I could get in some bother if I got found with you in my van.'

'So keep driving and don't get found.'

The van bumped onto the hard surface of the road. The boxes

thudded around behind them. Freddie took his hands off the wheel and lit a cigarette.

'Cocky sod aren't you?' he said.

Calloway ignored him. They drove in silence for close to an hour. They were on country roads. Freddie looked in his rear-view mirror and said, 'We'll stop here. Stretch our legs.' He turned off into a narrow track. He pulled the van up on the verge, in a small patch of woodland that shielded them from the main road.

'We've only been going an hour,' said Calloway. 'Hardly worth stopping.'

'I need a piss,' said Freddie. He climbed out of the van and relieved himself against a tree. Calloway got out and lit a cigarette. Freddie buttoned his fly and wiped his hands on the back of his coat. He walked back to where Calloway stood.

'Got money on you?' he said.

'That's my business,' said Calloway.

'Course you've got money. I'm going to need a fee.'

'That wasn't part of the agreement.'

Freddie scoffed. 'With the krauts? Don't make me laugh. They don't count for nothing here.'

It wasn't worth the argument, thought Calloway.

'How much do you need?' he said.

'All of it.'

'Don't be stupid, son.'

Freddie reached in the pocket of his overcoat and pulled out a pistol. A Luger. He pointed it at Calloway's belly.

'You're the one being stupid,' he said. 'Hand it over.'

He cocked the pistol.

Calloway reached into his jacket pocket for the last of Webber's cash. There was plenty left and he had plans for it. But he wasn't inclined to argue. He'd seen a single round from a Luger rip a grown man's skull in two and spatter his brains like sauerkraut. He tossed the small bundle on the ground. Freddie bent to pick it up then hesitated.

'Don't you fucking move,' he said.

Calloway looked at the gun.

'I wasn't planning to,' he said. 'I've seen the holes those things make.'

Freddie grinned. He reached down towards the money.

Calloway seized the moment. He took a step forward and kicked the spiv in the head. It was a good hard kick. The spiv reeled then fell flat on the ground. Calloway kicked the Luger out of his hand and picked it up. He tucked it into his waistband, retrieved his cash, then riffled through Freddie's pockets for the keys to the van. He found the keys and a wad of five-pound notes. He left the money. No point starting a feud with a gang of black marketeers. Calloway prodded the prostrate spiv with the toe of his shoe. The spiv was out cold. He opened the rear doors of the van and chucked out the boxes of nylons. If stopped, he could say the van was borrowed. He couldn't explain twenty-four boxes of contraband stockings. Or the Luger. He stuffed the pistol down the back of the passenger seat.

The drive to London took more than two hours. The van was a pig to drive. He had to wrestle it into top gear through a series of grinding gear changes. But it was better than hitch hiking with empty pockets.

He hit central London in the morning rush hour. The clock that told Guinness Time at Piccadilly Circus said a quarter to eight. Freddie would be conscious by now. Calloway hoped his head hurt. He parked the van in a side street in Victoria. He pulled the Luger from the back of the seat and tucked it in his waistband. He then left the van and took the tube to Kensington High Street. From there it was a short walk through busy streets to the hotel.

There was no crowd outside, nor any police. Since he'd left for Berlin, the squatters must have won a stay of execution. He went to his room, splashed water on his face and changed into his one remaining set of clothes. His guts felt queasy with hunger. He left the building, found a cafe and ordered breakfast. Then he called Webber from a phone box. Elsie answered.

'It's Calloway. I'm back in London.'

She sounded relieved to hear from him.

'Did you get Bert's telegram?' she said.

'I did. Have you heard anything from Vera?'

'Not a peep. We're so worried, Mr Calloway. Her neighbours said those men came and took her away.'

'The man called Denton and the doctor?'

'Sounded like them. The local kiddies recognised the car. They don't miss a trick.'

'And you've no idea where Denton and the doctor have taken her?'

'One of Vera's neighbours asked, because Vera seemed distressed when they were leading her to the car. The doctor told the neighbour they were taking Vera to a clinic for some rest. That's all we know.' There was silence on the line. Then Elsie spoke quietly. 'Can you help us, Mr Calloway?'

His answer might have been no, under any other circumstances. The favour he'd agreed to do Bert when the little rider had first shown up at the arena had long since been used up. But something compelled him to help. It might have been friendship, but if he was honest, he'd long since forgotten what that really felt like. It might have been the death of Stan, a pointless casualty in a new kind of war that seemed more like a game to Calloway. Or it could have been the hatred he felt for Vogel, Baumann and Freddie the spiv. Jumped-up little caesars with guns instead of guts. They reminded him of Jimmy Jenks. Whatever the reason, he wanted resolution. He wanted to draw a line under the whole sordid business.

'Tell Bert to meet me at this address,' he said.

He gave Elsie the location of the squat and put the phone down. He made another call, dialling the number on the calling card Denton had given Vera. He knew he wouldn't make it past the switchboard, but he wanted Denton to know he was in London. Then he called the arena and asked for Trudi Trauber. When she came to the phone, he made her a proposition.

He went back to the squat and slept. He woke at dusk, the streetlamps casting a comforting glow through the widow. For a moment or two, in the mist of half-sleep, he thought Pat was beside him. He reached across the bed, finding no one. He felt a sudden, overwhelming loneliness. There was noise from the corridor. The Poles had their door open and were playing music on their gramophone. Calloway recognised Chopin. The piano music was soothing. He went to his bathroom and ran a bath. It was a luxury he seldom enjoyed. He scrubbed the oily stink of *The Kurtz* off his skin and lay there soaking. Two nights ago he had bathed in Pat's hotel room, while she undressed and turned down the bedsheets for him. He hoped that Otto had been true to his word, that Max and Günter were out of the picture and that Pat was safe. As safe as a wall of death rider could be.

He went out and bought a bottle of scotch from a wine merchant and borrowed three glasses from the Poles when he returned. He poured himself a slug and waited. Webber arrived at just after seven.

'A Kensington hotel?' he said, looking around the room. 'You going up in the world, Reg?'

'It's a squat,' said Calloway.

'A squat with hot water and a tub,' said Webber, poking his nose around the bathroom door.

'I struck lucky,' said Calloway.

'Noisy neighbours, mind.'

A crying baby was competing with Chopin in the corridor outside.

'I like it,' said Calloway.

He poured Webber a drink. Webber raised his glass.

'Welcome home,' he said. They drank in silence for a moment, listening to the muffled sounds of piano music, then Webber said, 'You going to tell me all about it?'

'You're better off not knowing,' said Calloway.

'But you went there to find out. To put Vera's mind at rest.'

'I'm not sure the truth will do that, Bert.'

Webber reached into his pocket. 'If it's more money you want...'

'Don't be stupid,' said Calloway. 'Put your money away. I'll tell you the story, but it's not pretty. I'll leave it up to you what you tell your sister-in-law.'

He told Webber everything, from Stan's debt to Spanner, to his death at Baumann's behest. The small rider listened to it all, his usually expressive face completely blank. When Calloway had finished, Webber shook his head.

'I know he's family and I know I shouldn't speak ill of the dead.' He took a large gulp of the scotch. 'But what a silly cunt.'

It took a man like Bert Webber to see the world like that. Calloway admired him.

'In truth, there's nothing silly about it, Bert. Stan had a whole other life you didn't know about. A secret life, full of deception and lies. A dangerous one too. A very deniable life, where nothing's what it seems. It's all smoke and mirrors in that world, Bert. Don't try to understand it. Stan's gone and we need to find Vera. I'm going need your help. It won't be without its risks.'

Webber looked down at the glass in his hand. He swilled the last of the whisky around then drank it.

'Well,' he said. 'It's not as if I have much to do, now the season's over.'

Calloway smiled and poured them both another slug.

'You expecting someone else?' said Webber, nodding at the third glass.

There was a knock at the door. Calloway opened it. Trudi filled the door frame. He beckoned her, introduced her to Bert and poured her a drink.

'Otto says hello,' said Calloway. Trudi smiled. He unfastened the chain with the ring and handed it to her. 'Thank you,' he said. 'It brought me luck.'

In truth, he didn't feel too lucky right now, but at least he was home. And alive. Trudi laughed and clapped him on the back.

'You are now a member of the Kreuzberg *Ringverein*,' she said, raising her glass in toast. '*Prost!*'

Calloway clinked her glass. He sensed Webber's discomfort at Trudi's presence. Whether it was because she was German or that she was a woman twice Webber's size, Calloway didn't know. He got to the point.

'Trudi's a friend, Bert,' he said. 'We can trust her. And what we've got to do is going to take more than the two of us. Trudi's agreed to help and I've persuaded her to accept a fee. I know you're good for it. What we need to do carries a level of risk that's unreasonable to expect as a favour.'

Webber looked a little confused but nodded his agreement. Trudi thanked him.

'You don't need to pay me any more,' said Calloway.

He charged their glasses and told them his plan. He adopted an air of outward confidence. It hid the grave unease he felt about what he was proposing.

TWENTY-SEVEN

For three days Calloway waited. He watched the street below from the window of his room. He eyed faces in the crowd as he moved about the city. He cast sideways glances into parked cars everywhere he went.

Then Denton appeared. He sat in a Ford Prefect parked in a side street opposite the arena, its bonnet poking out from behind a corner giving him a clear view of the arena entrance. Calloway watched him from a small window on the third floor of the building. Denton was alone. It was time.

Trudi and Calloway had prepared for this. They had agreed on a plan beforehand. Calloway collected her from the dressing room and walked with her to the foyer. They stood in the shadows of the unlit entrance and looked towards Denton's car.

'You see him?' said Calloway.

'Ripe for the plucking,' said Trudi with a grin.

'Off you go. I'll be right behind you.'

Trudi walked out into the street towards Denton's car. Calloway watched Denton pick up a newspaper and pretend to read. Did they really teach them this Boys' Own nonsense at MI5, he thought. Trudi crossed the road until she was a yard or two from the car. She glanced back in Calloway's direction. He gave her the nod. She wrenched open the car door, grabbed Denton by the arm and yanked him onto the pavement. She got him in a body lock, which probably had a name in wrestling circles although Calloway didn't know it. Calloway ran over to them. Together they frogmarched Denton into the arena. They led him through the foyer into the auditorium. It was dark inside, save for a shaft of light which struck the canvas of the ring from a skylight high in the roof. They ignored Denton's protestations. He shammed innocence and indignation. Calloway parted the ropes and Trudi tipped Denton into the ring then jumped up behind him.

'Seconds out, round one, Mr Denton,' said Calloway.

Trudi swung Denton by the arm onto the ropes. The force catapulted him back onto the canvas. Trudi fell on him, pinning him to the ground. Denton looked up at the six-foot female wrestler with a combination of fear and astonishment. Calloway leaned down and spoke into Denton's ear.

'Our friend Bert Webber wants his sister-in-law back. Where have you taken her?'

Denton gasped for breath under Trudi's weight. 'I don't know any Bert Webber.'

Calloway nodded at Trudi. She gripped Denton by the shoulders and slammed him down hard on the canvas.

'You know Webber and you know his sister-in-law, Vera. You and your doctor friend led her to a car and took her to a clinic. We want to know where.'

'I tell you, man, I don't know what you're talking about.'

'Think again, Denton. I'll give you some names to jog your memory. Stanley Deakin and Hannelore Schneider.'

The names got Denton's attention but he feigned ignorance. 'This is all some kind of mistake. You need to let me go.'

Calloway smiled. 'We've only just started,' he said, signalling to Trudi. She picked Denton up off the floor, flipped him around and slammed him back down again. The impact sucked the air out of Denton's lungs. He gasped like a beached fish.

'Where is Vera Deakin?' said Calloway. 'You took her away. Her family wants her back.'

Deakin spat.

'Fuck her family. And fuck you.'

Trudi didn't need a signal. She dragged Denton off the floor and flung him onto the ropes. He rebounded into her clenched arm, spasmed and dropped onto the canvas. Calloway bent down.

'There's no wrestling matches tonight. It's just the three of us here. We can go on like this for hours.'

Denton was dazed. He pushed himself onto his hands and knees and swayed like he was going to collapse again. Trudi flipped him over and dropped down onto him, pinioning him to the ground with her knees.

'Where is she Denton?' said Calloway. 'Where's Vera Deakin? Where's this clinic you took her to?'

Denton summoned strength and shouted, 'Get this fucking Amazon off me.'

Trudi laughed. Calloway gestured to her to move over.

'That was just a bit of sport,' he said. 'Now it's serious.'

He hit Denton hard in the face.

'Every bullshit answer you give me, you'll get another one like it,' he said.

Denton shouted through bloodied lips. 'Go to hell.'

Calloway hit him again.

'Seems like you need softening up a bit,' he said. He nodded to Trudi. Again she grabbed Denton's arm, dragged him to his feet and flung him into the ropes. She tripped him on the rebound so he fell face down on the deck. Calloway grabbed Denton's hair and slammed his face onto the hard canvas. Denton gave a muffled yelp. He went limp. He was breaking. Calloway knew the signs. A sharp blow to the kidneys bought his compliance.

'She's at the fort,' Denton mumbled. 'The clinic at the fort.'

'What fort?'

Denton mumbled words Calloway couldn't make out.

'Speak up, man,' he said. 'We're all ears.'

He cuffed Denton around the head.

'Grain Tower Battery. At the mouth of the River Medway,' said Denton.

Then he passed out.

'Take him to the dressing room and lock him in. Can you keep him here for a few hours?'

Trudi nodded. She hoisted the unconscious body over her shoulder as if he weighed no more than a child and climbed down from the ring.

Calloway went to his office. He made two phone calls. The first was to Bert Webber. Calloway told him to be ready at the prefab in an hour. The second was to Johnny Suskind, his old paratrooper comrade from the boxing booth. He made Johnny a proposition, like the one he'd made Trudi. It meant asking Webber for more money, but the stakes were high and he needed Johnny's kind of muscle on the job. He banked on Webber understanding.

Calloway took Denton's car. He met Johnny at the entrance to the fairground. There was no fair today. The rides were shrouded in faded canvas and the sideshows were shuttered. Johnny wore his old paratroopers Denison smock. He clearly meant business.

'I owe you for this, Johnny,' said Calloway.

'Forget it, mate. Sounds like a laugh, this caper.'

'I can't promise any laughs. But you'll be helping some good people out of a bad situation.'

'It'll stop me getting bored.'

Johnny was another one. Couldn't settle back into civilian life. The war had shaped him so that he no longer fitted. He wasn't a nine-to-fiver. He was neither factory fodder nor a shiny-arse. He'd lived on instinct, wits and adrenalin for nigh on six years. That kind of living doesn't leave you in a hurry. The boxing helped, Calloway imagined. It channelled Johnny's aggression. The same applied to their scrapes with the fascists in the East End. And now this mad fool plan. Any normal man would have run a mile, but Johnny didn't need persuading. A good word from Calloway and the promise of a few extra quid was enough.

They picked Webber up outside his prefab.

'Elsie's down the shops. I've left her a note.'

Johnny laughed. 'It's not like you're leaving home,' he said. 'Unless you plan to run off with her sister.'

Webber looked embarrassed, then gave an impish grin. 'Might have crossed my mind a couple of times.'

He laughed for a moment, before the seriousness of the situation struck him.

'Do you reckon she's alright, Reg?' he said. He tapped his

temple. 'You know, up here I mean.'

It was a rhetorical question, an excuse to fish for a reassuring word.

'Grief's a poison, Bert. It can turn your head inside out.' Calloway knew grief. He'd never been right since his own loss. But what he'd seen of Vera's condition troubled him more than he was letting on. He'd seen many kinds of madness. It was as much a product of war as death and maiming. Hysteria, melancholia, rage, even blindness. Vera was in a different state, like nothing he'd seen before. It was way more than grief, if he was any judge.

They drove for almost an hour, leaving the Dover Road before Rochester and heading northeast along a scrubby minor road. They pulled over in a village that was little more than a cluster of sad, isolated cottages and asked directions. They were on the right road. The three men were tense now. Conversation had long since run out. They smoked one cigarette after another looking intently through the windscreen. Heavy grey clouds hung over the flat and marshy peninsula. They could see the estuary ahead of them, a cold and murky expanse that stretched to the featureless coastline beyond it.

'There's the fort,' said Johnny, pointing across Calloway as he drove.

It wasn't so much a building as a mutation of concrete, brick and stone. From what Calloway could see, it had started life as a Martello tower, on whose round stone base newer defensive structures had been added during successive conflicts. On one side a brick-built barracks block floated on stilts, beyond that a concrete tower rose up four or five stories with open stairs up to an observation post.

Webber, who was sitting in the back seat, poked his head between the two men and peered through the windscreen.

'Fuck me,' he said. 'It's got to be a mile out to sea.'

He was right. It was something they hadn't banked on. Calloway had assumed the battery was on dry land, facing out to sea from the coast. This was a sea fort.

'I hope you can swim, Bert,' said Johnny.

'It's not funny, mate,' said Webber. 'How the hell are we going to get over to that?'

'Maybe it's walkable at low tide,' said Johnny.

'Low tide could be hours away,' said Calloway.

He'd been a fool. He'd not planned properly in his haste. He was strung out since his experience in Berlin and his judgement was way off. Bert and Johnny had trusted him. But he was leading them on a wild goose chase.

Webber drew breath, as a thought occurred to him. 'We could get a boat,' he said. 'You know, nick one.'

Calloway didn't like the idea. His experience on *The Kurtz* didn't endear him to another jaunt on the water.

The wind whistled around the car and the sea ahead of them was rough. Even at this distance he could see the white peaks of waves lapping against the base of the fort.

'We're all ex-army, Bert,' he said. 'We're not exactly seafaring types. I don't fancy our chances out there, looking at that swell.'

Bert grinned. He bristled faintly with pride. 'Speak for yourself,' he said. 'When I was in the service corps I did a stint with *No.2 Motorboat Company* over at Mersea Island.' He pointed to the other side of the estuary. 'Somewhere over there, I reckon.'

'The service corps has boats?' said Johnny, looking quizzically at Webber.

'The army's little navy,' said Webber.

'So you reckon you could handle one?' said Calloway.

Webber nodded. 'And hot-wire one too,' he said. 'I know me way around engines thanks to the Corps.'

A mad fool idea. Another one. But they were committed now. Each knew they wouldn't forgive themselves if they'd not given their best shot to bringing Vera home, whatever the consequences.

'The light's going,' said Johnny. 'If we're doing this, we'd better get moving.'

They drove in silence down to the outskirts of a small town, which stretched along the western bank of the River Medway. It was a ramshackle place, with half-a-dozen jetties with small boats moored to them.

'We'll pull up here,' said Calloway. He checked his watch. 'Half an hour till it's dark, I reckon. Then we'll see what we can find.'

They chain smoked while they waited. They had parked alongside an old marine workshop, in amongst the rusting and rotting hulls of broken-down craft which sat haphazardly on the quayside. The workshop was shuttered and dark. The boats moored along the adjacent jetties bobbed up and down on the swell, straining at their ropes.

'It looks quiet enough,' said Johnny.

Webber opened the car door. 'Come on,' he said. 'Let's do a recce.'

The three men climbed out and walked along the quayside. The air was damp and smelled of diesel fuel. The wind was up and the boats clanked together as they were jostled by the swell. Johnny stopped as they approached the first jetty.

'You go ahead,' he said. 'I'll keep an eye out.'

Webber surveyed each boat like he was hunting for bargains at a street market. He shook his head and tutted.

'Flotsam and bleedin' jetsam,' he said. 'A load of floating junk.'

They tried another jetty. This one was longer and the vessels were larger. One caught Webber's attention.

'That's more like it,' he said.

He was looking at a fishing boat, newer than the rest, about thirty or forty feet long, with a small round-fronted wheelhouse and a cabin in the bow. A tarnished name plate on the transom said *Strood Lights.*

'You keep watch,' he said. 'I'm going aboard to check her over.'

Webber hopped over the rail onto the deck and tried the wheelhouse door. It was open. He gave the thumbs up to Calloway and ducked inside.

Calloway stood waiting. Bert was taking his time. It made Calloway uneasy. He lit a cigarette and held it between his thumb and forefinger, concealing the glowing tip in the palm of his hand. His suit flapped in the wind like a sail. It was cold. He pulled his jacket tight around him.

Johnny gave a low whistle. Calloway peered into the darkness towards the sound. Two figures were walking over to the jetty. They were maritime types, with woollen caps and heavy, loose-fitting jumpers. One was sucking on a pipe, the other smoked a roll-up that dangled from his lip. Johnny said hello and gave them some chat about looking for a good pub for the evening. They bought the line. One of the men mentioned a place called the Five Bells. The other laughed and made a disparaging comment. Johnny kept them talking. Calloway heard Webber clunking around inside the fishing boat. He had no way of telling him to keep quiet. Then the boat's engine started up. It was as noisy as hell. Webber stuck his head out of the wheelhouse. He'd not noticed they had company.

'Untie the ropes and jump aboard,' he shouted above the noise of the engine.

One of the men looked over.

'Who the hell's that on the *Strood Lights*? That's not old Billy.'

The other man, the bigger of the two, grabbed Johnny by the arm.

'What the fuck's going on pal?' he said.

Johnny shook free. He jabbed the big man in the guts, doubling him over. He kicked the other man's legs from under him, sending him face down onto the boards of the jetty.

'Sorry gents, needs must,' he said, running towards the fishing boat.

Calloway was untying the ropes.

'Did you hurt them?' he said. He knew what Johnny was capable of.

'Only their pride.'

'Jump aboard and help me push us off.'

They pushed against the slippery timbers of the jetty and felt the boat move out a foot or two. The bigger of the two men was running towards them.

'Shit, here he comes,' said Johnny.

There was a boat hook pole on the deck. Calloway grabbed it. The big man was level with the boat. He made to board it. Calloway jabbed him in the chest with the pole. The man lost his footing. He slipped and plunged into the water. Calloway and Johnny watched him splashing around, looking for a hand hold.

'Christ, I hope he doesn't drown,' said Johnny. He sounded genuinely concerned.

Calloway looked around. There was a lifebuoy hanging by the wheelhouse door. He pulled it off and flung it towards the man in the water. The man grabbed it. His mate was there now, reaching down to offer a hand.

'He'll live,' said Calloway. 'Mind you, I wouldn't want to be in their shoes when they tell whoever old Billy is that they let three strangers steal his boat.'

Three strangers driving a car stolen from an MI5 operative, thought Calloway. Damn fool plan.

TWENTY-EIGHT

'She's got a tank full of diesel,' said Webber, tapping the fuel gauge.

The three men stood in the wheelhouse peering through the rain-spattered glass into the darkness. The boat lunged back and forth with every roll of the waves.

'You ever navigated these waters, Bert?' said Johnny. There was a hint of unease in fearless Johnny Suskind's voice.

Webber shook his head. 'We'll stay in the middle and hope for the best,' he said. 'That usually works.'

Suskind exchanged glances with Calloway. Best give him something to do, Calloway thought.

'Search the boat, Johnny. See if you can find anything useful.'

The big boxer said 'aye-aye' and squeezed himself through the hatch, down into the cabin below. Calloway stared through the arc of half-clear glass with every sweep of the fishing boat's inadequate wiper.

'You reckon we'll make the fort in this light?' he said.

'Keep looking left,' said Webber. 'She's bound to pop up.'

Calloway knew Webber's jocularity was a sham. Pure bravado. It hid the gut-wrenching nerves they were all feeling. Johnny appeared in the hatch.

'A torch, a wrench, some rope...'

'If all else fails, we can play Cluedo,' said Webber.

'Oh,' said Johnny, 'and some Dutch courage, courtesy of old Billy.'

He waved a half-drunk bottle of navy rum at them.

'Pass it round, mate. My mouth tastes like a zookeeper's boot,' said Webber.

Johnny passed him the bottle. The little man uncorked it with his teeth, spat the cork out and gulped down a good measure. He passed the bottle to Calloway.

Johnny laid his finds on the ledge in front of the wheel. Calloway pulled out Freddie's Luger.

'Just for show,' he said. 'We're not leaving any bodies behind.'

Calloway thought of Baumann, dead on the floor of the bombed-out apartment. He wasn't sure he trusted himself.

'You take it, Johnny,' he said.

Suskind was the level-headed one.

'Look,' said Webber.

They could now see the fort a few hundred yards ahead of them. Calloway felt his stomach churn. An assault on a fixed position took a certain sort of courage. Assaulting a sea fort took two dozen commandos.

Johnny coiled the rope across his chest like a mountaineer. He slipped the Luger into the pocket of his camouflage smock. Calloway put the wrench in his trouser pocket.

'There's a landing stage between the stilts,' said Webber, pointing to a concrete platform lined with old tyres as fenders, under a three-storey, brick-built block. 'I'm going to drop you two off and then circle the fort. I'm not mooring up. We can't risk them getting hold of the boat.'

Calloway agreed. He left the wheelhouse with Johnny and the two men crouched on the deck. Webber grappled with the wheel, bringing them alongside the landing stage. The choppy waters buffeted the small boat against the fenders. Calloway gave Johnny the signal. They jumped over the rail and onto the wet concrete base. There was an open staircase leading to the first floor of the block above. Johnny led the way. They climbed the stairs. There was a rusting steel door. It was locked. Johnny pulled out the Luger. Calloway banged on the door with the wrench. The sound echoed around them. They heard the bolts sliding on the other side. The door opened a chink. A face appeared. Johnny stuck his boot in the gap. Calloway put his full weight against the door. The two men barged through, Johnny first, the Luger in his hand.

'What the hell...' said a voice.

Johnny silenced him with his left fist. A second blow knocked him down.

'How many in the fort?' said Calloway, leaning over the man on the ground.

'Who are you?' said the man, his voice faltering, his eyes fixed on the pistol in Johnny's hand. He wore a white side-fastening tunic, like a doctor in an American movie.

'How many manning the fort?' said Calloway again. Johnny cocked the pistol.

'Four,' the man on the ground blurted out.

'You and three others?'

The man nodded.

'Armed?' said Calloway.

'What?' the man looked confused. 'No. Lovell, perhaps. I don't know.'

'Who's Lovell?'

'Security.'

'The rest?'

'Two orderlies and a doctor. I'm one of the orderlies.'

'Where are they now?'

'On the ward, or in the office. On the floor above.' He looked at the pistol nervously. 'I don't know for sure. We heard the boat, then the banging. They sent me down to see what the noise was.'

'How many patients?'

The orderly hesitated. He looked from one man to the other. Johnny pushed the barrel of the pistol against his temple.

'One,' said the orderly.

'Vera Deakin?'

The orderly nodded.

'On your feet,' said Calloway.

Johnny grabbed the back of the orderly's tunic and shoved him along the corridor. Their footsteps echoed off the dirt-streaked wall tiles. For a clinic the place had the feel of a public lavatory. There were stairs at the end of the corridor and the sound of voices above.

'Up you go,' said Johnny. He jabbed the barrel of the Luger

into the orderly's back. 'Quietly does it.'

There was a door at the top of the stairs. Johnny gestured to the orderly to open it. The orderly hesitated. Another jab with the barrel of the gun convinced him to comply. As the door latch clicked, Johnny shoved the orderly into the room and he and Calloway piled in behind him. Two shocked faces turned towards them. Johnny raised the gun so they could both see it. Calloway took in the scene. A large open space like a small ward in a convalescent hospital. Three empty beds along one wall, some medical cabinets and a desk. The windows were barred. One man wore an orderly's tunic, the other wore a suit.

'Face down on the ground please, gentlemen,' said Johnny, pushing the first orderly towards the other two men and gesturing with the Luger. The two orderlies complied; the man in the suit hesitated. Calloway saw him slide his hand inside his jacket.

'Johnny,' Calloway shouted. 'The suit's armed.'

Johnny slammed the butt of the Luger across the side of the suited man's head. The man's knees buckled. Johnny grabbed him and pulled a small automatic pistol from inside his suit jacket. He tossed it to Calloway, who turned off the safety catch and cocked it.

'I don't need to tell you what will happen if anyone moves,' said Calloway.

There was a door at the end of the room, half glazed with a frosted panel. Calloway walked towards it. He could make out figures behind the glass. He reached for the door handle and threw the door open.

It was a small office, like a doctor's consulting room. Vera Deakin sat in an armchair, her knees raised to her chin. She was barefoot and wearing a loose hospital gown. She looked up at Calloway, trembling. A grey-haired man of about fifty wearing a white coat sat opposite her. He had a stethoscope around his neck and a notebook on his lap. He started to stand. Calloway gestured with the pistol. The doctor sat back down. Vera stared at Calloway's face, moving her head slowly from side to side as if examining him from many angles. A weak smile spread across her face.

'It's Bertie's friend,' she said and sang, 'Burlington Bertie, I rise at ten thirty...'

'We've come to take you home, Vera.'

The doctor protested. 'She's in no fit state to...'

Calloway cut him off. 'Exactly what state is she in, doctor?'

'Who are you?'

'A family friend who doesn't think much of this clinic of yours. What the hell is this place?'

'That's none of your business.'

'I'm the one with gun, pal. I'd say everything's my business.'

The doctor peered through the open door into the ward. 'Where's Lovell?'

'Face down on the ground, wishing he was better at security.'

Vera sang, '...but my people are well off, you know.'

'What's the matter with her?'

'She's in an altered state.'

Vera was staring at the backs of her hands, reading the veins for some hidden meaning.

'I can see that,' said Calloway. 'Is she mad?'

'A kind of madness, yes. But it's temporary. Chemically induced.'

'Something in those pills you gave her? I assume it was you visiting her with Denton.'

The doctor nodded. 'A small dose, yes.'

'What for? What was wrong with her, apart from the natural grief of losing her husband?'

'I can't tell you that. I'm not permitted.'

Calloway gestured to the pistol in his hand. 'Oh, I think you are. Unless you want to see what *my* temporary madness looks like.'

Vera was staring at the gun now. It seemed to fascinate her.

'You look just like Alan Ladd with that,' she said. 'Are we at the pictures?'

She started to laugh. The doctor looked at the gun. His bravura ebbed away. He hesitated, then spoke.

'She knew too much. She was threatening to go to the press.'

'About her husband Stan being killed in Berlin, chasing Soviet agents for your friend Denton. Yes, I know. What kind of pills do you prescribe for that?'

The doctor shook his head. 'It's all classified.'

Calloway stepped forward and cuffed him around the head, good and hard.

'Classify that,' he said.

Vera giggled. 'You *are* Alan Ladd. I knew it,' she said.

The doctor rubbed the side of his face.

'Let's start again,' said Calloway. 'What have you pumped her full of, and what's it do?'

The doctor swallowed hard. 'Lysergic acid diethylamide.'

'What the hell is that?'

'A hallucinogenic drug.'

'Hallucinations?' Calloway knew of delirious soldiers seeing things. 'Why are you giving her hallucinations?'

'Used in combination with hypnosis, we can create memory loss.'

'Are you serious? Sounds more like something from a cheap B picture.'

'A picture with Alan Ladd,' said Vera, giggling and wiggling her toes.

'The work is experimental. But the Americans have been achieving good results by all accounts. They have an extensive research programme. It builds on work the Germans were doing during the war using mescaline.'

Calloway could imagine who the subjects were. He felt his blood rise. The veins pounded at his temples.

'So you're using this woman as a lab rat?'

The doctor looked offended. 'We work under strict clinical conditions.'

'In a draughty sea fort, cut off from the outside world, with an armed guard.'

'Our work is top secret.'

Calloway scoffed. 'Not anymore, blabber mouth. Those pills were supposed to suppress her memory?'

'We tried small doses at first, hoping that the behaviour

change they induced might discredit any allegations she was making about her husband's death. But she's strong. We couldn't be sure the smaller dose would have the intended effect, especially without concurrent hypnosis.'

'So you abducted her and brought her here for the full à la carte.'

'For longer-term treatment, yes.'

Vera rose from the armchair. She walked up to Calloway and put her arms around him. She nuzzled into him.

'I've always liked Alan Ladd,' she said.

'Get yourself dressed, Vera love,' Calloway said. 'We're going home.'

She smiled then walked through the door onto the ward, opening one of the bedside lockers and removing a pile of clothing. She continued humming the tune, seeming not to notice Johnny with the gun in his hand and the three men lying on the floor.

'Will this wear off?' said Calloway.

'It should do. In several hours.'

He didn't relish getting Vera onto the boat in her present state.

'Can't you give her something?'

The doctor shook his head. 'You'll just have to wait.'

'What are the aftereffects?'

'It's hard to say. We're in the early stages of the programme. It's possible there won't be any permanent change to her mental state.'

Calloway's switch flicked. He hit the doctor hard in the face. Blood spattered onto his white coat.

'Get in there and get down on the floor with the others.'

He grabbed the doctor's collar, dragged him through the doorway and pushed him to the ground. Johnny tied the four men together using the rope he'd taken from the boat. Calloway looked at the door to the stairs. It had a lock. He nudged the first orderly with his foot.

'Where are the keys?'

The orderly stuttered the words. 'The desk, top drawer.'

Calloway opened the drawer and took the keys. There was a

radio telephone on the desk, military issue. Calloway picked it up and smashed it onto the hard floor. He heard the valves shatter.

Vera was in some semblance of dress now. She wouldn't pass muster in the street, but it was better than the hospital gown. Calloway helped her into her coat.

'This is Johnny,' he said, nodding to Suskind, 'and I'm Reg, remember? You stick with us. We'll have you home soon.'

Vera held Calloway's arm, like they were heading out for a walk along the prom. Calloway tossed Johnny the keys. Johnny locked up.

They signalled to Webber from the landing stage. The swell was still high and Calloway sensed Bert was struggling to control the boat. Vera shivered in the cold of the night. Calloway put an arm around her and held her close.

Webber pulled the boat alongside. The swell bumped it back and forth against the fenders.

'She'll never make the jump, Reg,' shouted Johnny, looking at Vera. 'We're going to have to tie up for a mo'.'

Calloway signalled to Webber to tie up. Webber looked anxious. He brought the boat in as close as he could and ducked out of the wheelhouse, grabbing a rope and throwing it. Johnny leaned forward to grab it, but he was short. The rope fell into the water. Webber cursed. He pulled the rope in and tried again.

'Hook a duck,' said Vera. 'Blue picks a prize.'

She laughed above the sound of the engine. The boat strayed out, a good five yards from the landing stage. Webber ran back into the wheelhouse and wrestled with the wheel. He brought the boat in close again and threw the rope once more. Johnny grabbed it.

'Howzat,' he shouted.

Calloway grinned, relieved. Johnny pulled the boat onto the fenders and looped the rope around one of the concrete stilts. Calloway helped Vera onto the prow. He heard a shout behind him. It was Johnny. Calloway turned and saw him grappling with Lovell, the security man. Damn my haste, thought Calloway. There must have been another exit.

'Bert,' he shouted. 'Put Vera in the wheelhouse, then hold the boat steady.'

Bert looked gravely towards Johnny. Lovell was trying to wrest the Luger out of the big boxer's fist. Calloway felt for the automatic in his waistband. It was gone. In the bloody sea when he jumped onto the prow.

'Here,' shouted Webber. He threw Calloway the boat hook pole. Calloway caught it. He held it like a pike and jabbed at Lovell, snagging his jacket on the hook. He yanked the pole towards him, pulling Lovell to the edge of the landing stage. Johnny seized his moment. He gave Lovell a shove. They heard him scream as he plunged feet first into the swell. Johnny released the rope and jumped aboard. Calloway gave Webber the thumbs up. The diesel engine revved hard, exhaust billowing from the pipe above the wheelhouse.

'Take her below,' said Calloway, gesturing towards Vera.

Johnny took her by the hand and led her down the steps into the small cabin.

'How is she?' said Webber.

'Mad as a box of frogs,' said Calloway, 'but that quack doctor said it will pass.'

'What a bloody place, eh? Like being locked up in the tower.'

Calloway looked down into the cabin below. Johnny had his arm around Vera, who was leaning into him, muttering to herself. The whimsy was gone. She seemed distressed now. Johnny was talking her down with calm words. Calloway had never seen that side of the big ex-paratrooper.

'Good job there was a handsome prince to rescue her,' he said, nodding towards the pair below.

'He seems like a good sort, your mate,' said Webber.

'I reckon he is.'

It was pitch dark now, but Webber seemed calm at the wheel.

'It's all coming back to me now,' he said. 'You know, motorboats and that.'

'Can you get us to London?'

Webber shrugged. 'I'll give it a go. What's the worst that could happen?'

Calloway could think of a few things, but he didn't voice them.

All he could do was place his trust in Webber. Of the three of them, he was the only one who knew anything about boats.

'Here, have a nip of this,' Calloway said, passing Webber the bottle they had found.

It was cold in the boat. Calloway pulled his jacket tightly around him. The night was fully dark now and only clusters of lights from the estuary towns gave them any clue as to where they were. They were navigating by instinct, Webber doing his best to control the boat as it lurched through the water, buffeted by the swell.

In time, the clusters of lights merged into two long strips of illumination either side of them.

'We're getting close to London now,' said Webber. 'I reckon that's Tilbury.' He pointed towards the lights on their right. 'Where are we heading for, Reg?'

'We're taking Vera home. She needs to be in her own surroundings. Somewhere she feels safe.'

'What if they're waiting for us?'

'We'll have to take that chance. I smashed the radio at the fort so with any luck they will be cut off for hours yet. And I made sure Denton was out of action before I left London.'

He tried not to think how Trudi, the German gangster turned wrestler, might be restraining their guest back at the arena.

'Can you get us to Deptford?'

Webber nodded. 'But I reckon we should cover our tracks,' he said. 'I'll get us to the Isle of Dogs and tie up there. We can cross the river through the foot tunnel. It's only a short walk from there to Vera's house. If they're looking for the boat at least they'll find it on the other side of the river. It might buy us a bit of time.'

'Worth a go,' said Calloway.

He looked down through the hatch into the cabin. Vera lay on the bench, her head in Johnny's lap. Johnny stroked her hair like a mother lulling a child to sleep. Vera's distress seemed to have passed. Above the sound of the engine, Calloway could hear the faint sound of Johnny humming a lullaby.

TWENTY-NINE

Denton sat on a bench in the female wrestlers' changing room, his head down, his hands in his lap. He looked up when Calloway entered the room. He had a black eye and dark bruises on his forehead. His split lips were crusty with congealed blood.

'You are in so much fucking trouble,' he said.

Calloway lit two Navy Cut and passed one to Denton.

'I could say the same to you.'

Denton winced as he dragged on the cigarette. 'Don't you know who you're dealing with, man?'

'Yes, I do. The scum that inhabit the rotten end of the intelligence world. The grubby little men with dirty raincoats and blood on their hands.'

'Don't sound so pious. We know your record. You're no choirboy yourself.'

'Perhaps not. But I sing a different tune. And boy, have I got a song to sing, should the need arise.'

'That sounds like a threat.'

'Oh, it very much is.' Calloway pulled up a chair and sat facing Denton. 'I've been to your fort. I've seen what goes on there. Sick experiments. Treating human beings like lab rats. Sending them mad with chemicals.'

'The rules have changed, Calloway. We're fighting a different war.'

'Fuck off, Denton. You took a man's wife. His widow. An ordinary woman, grieving for her husband. You abducted her and locked her up. Why? Just because she wanted the truth? Doesn't she deserve that? Does the balance of power between east and west depend on whether Vera Deakin, a truck driver's widow from Deptford, knows her husband died on government service? Did it ever occur to you that you might be able to trust her?' Calloway shook his head. 'You underestimate people, Denton.'

'Don't be naive. She threatened to take the story to the press.'

'You could have slapped a D-Notice on it.'

'It would be no guarantee.'

'So you tried brainwashing her instead. That's what you lot call it, isn't it?' Calloway had read the term in a lurid news report from the war in Korea, claiming US prisoners were cooperating with their Chinese captors though some kind of mind control. 'I bet your doctor mate was rubbing his hands. A human subject. Widowed, working class, no old school tie, no influential friends. The sort that don't count. In other words, expendable.'

Denton sighed. He looked resigned.

'So what do you plan to do?' he said.

'Nothing, if you leave Vera Deakin alone. Same goes for the others.'

'What others?'

'Oh, there's a few of us. We can keep our mouths shut. But if you try anything, you're going to need something stronger than your doctor's happy pills to keep us quiet.'

He watched Denton weighing up the threat. There was a knock at the door and Trudi walked in. Denton flinched.

'Get him cleaned up,' said Calloway. 'We've reached an agreement. Mr Denton can go home.'

Trudi pulled a sponge from a bucket in the corner and turned on the showers.

'Wait a minute,' said Denton. 'We don't have an agreement. We have nothing of the sort. Your threats are meaningless. Who the hell would believe someone like you?'

Calloway sat back in the chair. He took a long drag on his cigarette.

'Perhaps you're right,' he said. 'Perhaps I'm just like Vera Deakin. One of those people that don't count. But you count, don't you, Denton? You count a lot. Major Denton, a hero of the desert war, a chest full of medals and an old school tie. What club do you belong to? Bucks? The Naval and Military? Or the Special Forces Club? You're one of those people with a reputation that counts. So what about your little indiscretion in the ring? I mean, you didn't put up much resistance, did you? You broke good and early. Sang like a subaltern at his passing out party. Not qualities conducive to good intelligence practice. Letting the side down good and proper, I'd say. "Lacks moral fibre". You wouldn't want that in your report, would you? So let's keep all that between you, me and my big lady wrestler friend, eh?'

Denton looked at Trudi. She waved the bucket and sponge at him. Calloway rose to leave.

'I think we have an agreement now,' he said. He pulled a ten-bob note from his wallet. 'You'll be needing a cab. Your car's down by the river a mile outside Rochester. Just watch yourself when you collect it. There's an old sea dog called Billy who might want a word about his missing boat.'

When Denton had left, Calloway went to his office and slept. He curled up on a floor mat in in the corner of the room and slept in the clothes he was wearing.

He woke around eight and treated himself to breakfast at a cafe. He couldn't remember the last time he'd eaten. He went to a barber's shop and paid for a shave, enjoying the smell of the lotion and the warmth of the towel on his face. He tipped the barber well. He had a lot of money in his pocket. Webber had insisted he take it. He couldn't fault the small rider's generosity. He took a trolleybus east and stepped off at the corner of Doreen's street.

She answered the door in her dressing gown. She had bruises on her face.

'What happened?' he said.

'Jimmy brought a friend.'

She let him in and put the kettle on. 'Why did you do it, Reg? Why did you have to hurt him again?'

'So he'd leave you alone.'

'Well that worked, didn't it?' she said, touching the bruised skin with her fingertips.

'I never thought...'

'No, Reg, you didn't think.'

She poured the tea and handed him a cup. He hadn't the stomach to drink it.

'You don't know Jimmy like I do.'

'I know he's scum.'

'You won't change him.'

'But things need to change. For you and little Maggie.'

She rolled her eyes. 'You don't say.'

He took the wad of notes Webber had given him from his pocket and laid it on the table in front of her.

'This is a start,' he said.

She looked at the big white notes, expressionless. 'Keep your money,' she said. 'You can't fix things.'

'I want to help.'

She pointed to her face. 'Look what your help did.'

'It was a mistake. A big mistake. I see it now.'

'Everyone can see it now.'

She turned her face away from him.

'Take the money. It might not fix things, but it won't go amiss, eh?'

She looked at him. He caught the faintest hint of a smile. She picked up the bank notes and put them in the pocket of her dressing gown.

'What do you want from me?' she said.

'Nothing. Just to know that you're safe.'

She laughed. 'Who d'you think you are, the patron saint of lost causes?'

'I lost someone once. Someone who'd been hurt. I wanted to make things right for her, to make up for what had happened to her.' He shook his head. 'But I couldn't. She's gone and that's that. I tried to make things good for her and I guess there's a part of me that just keeps on trying.'

She put her hand on his. 'You're a good man, Reg,' she said. 'You can stop trying.'

He took a sip of the tea. He looked around the room. It was filthy and damp, in spite of Doreen's efforts to make it a home.

'Let me do one more thing,' he said.

THIRTY

Finnegan wasn't best pleased by Calloway's extended absence. But the arena boss agreed to give him his job back. Calloway suspected Trudi had had a word. She was the star attraction and she had influence. He wondered whether Finnegan knew about her criminal past. Probably not, because if he did, she would be known as Jailbird Judi, the Gangland Gorgon, or some such legend.

It had been three weeks since Webber, Johnny and Calloway had snatched Vera from the fort. There had been no word from Denton, no more figures in the shadows, no police at the door. The agreement seemed to be holding.

It was Sunday and Calloway sat in the passenger seat of Webber's Buick with little Maggie on his lap. Doreen was squeezed into the back seat along with boxes and bags filled with the contents of her rented room. She'd given notice to the landlady and handed back the keys. Maggie was thrilled to be riding in the car, staring awestruck from the window as they passed over Tower Bridge heading south. Webber was giving her a running commentary. He seemed to be enjoying himself.

'It took eight years to build, that bridge did, and takes five minutes to raise so the boats can get under. That's clever, innit?' Little Maggie nodded. 'And that street down there,' Webber's voice went up a tone with excitement, 'that's Webber Street. Same name as me, eh?'

They drove for another twenty minutes, Webber pointing out landmarks to Maggie and telling anecdotes. As they turned the corner into the narrow street of dockers cottages, they saw Vera standing on her doorstep. She was dressed in her Sunday best and her hair was newly set. She looked a different woman to the addled figure in the hospital gown they'd found at the fort.

'There's aunt Vera,' said Webber, pointing through the windscreen at his sister-in-law.

'She looks nice, doesn't she, Maggie?' said Doreen.

Calloway could hear the nervousness in her voice. He reached back and took her hand.

'It's going to be fine,' he said.

Vera had set the table for tea. A fruitcake took centre stage. Maggie stared at it with hungry eyes.

'Leave your things in the car for now,' said Vera to Doreen. 'Bert and Reg can bring them in later.'

Webber looked out of the window towards the bomb site on the opposite side of the street. The grubby kids with the fox terrier were staring at the Buick.

'I'll just nip back and lock the car doors,' he said.

The adults sat at the small table making conversation, while Maggie nibbled at the large slice of cake Vera had cut for her. The conversation was stilted, but well-meant, and by the second cup of tea the four of them were starting to relax. Calloway caught Doreen's eye. She smiled at him, looking more at ease than she had been in Webber's car.

'It's going to be nice having guests,' said Vera, taking Doreen's hand. 'It will bring a bit of life to the place.'

'It's very kind of you, Mrs Deakin,' said Doreen.

'Call me Vera, love.'

There was a knock at the door, loud and heavy. A man's knock. It startled Vera. Webber turned to Calloway, with a look of concern.

'I'll get it,' said Calloway.

Vera tensed. Webber put his hand on her shoulder.

Calloway rose from the table, stepped into the small, dark hallway and opened the door.

'Reg?'

A surprised Johnny Suskind stood on the doorstep in his best suit, holding a bunch of chrysanthemums. Calloway gave him a sly grin.

'I'm guessing those aren't for me,' he said, nodding to the flowers.

Johnny's face reddened. 'I thought I'd drop in on Vera. You know, just to see how she's getting on.'

'It's a bit of a houseful, Johnny, but come on in,' said Calloway. 'I'm sure she'll be glad to see you.'

After moving Doreen's possessions into Vera's spare room, Webber drove Calloway back to the squat. Calloway was happy to make his own way back but Webber had insisted.

'It'll be good for her, having people around,' he said. 'That Doreen seems a decent girl.'

There was a hint of uncertainty in Webber's voice.

'She needs another chance,' said Calloway.

Webber nodded in agreement. The answer seemed to satisfy him. Neither man mentioned Johnny's surprise appearance. That was Vera and Johnny's business.

'One for the road, Bert?' said Calloway, when they pulled up outside the old hotel building.

'I'll pass if you don't mind,' said Webber, yawning. 'I reckon the past few weeks is catching up with me.'

Calloway was relieved. He knew how Bert felt. He wanted more than anything to sleep a long, dreamless sleep. The two men said goodbye. Calloway climbed the steps to the hotel portico, pushed the heavy panelled door open and stepped into the hallway. The place was run down but retained a sense of grandeur, with its columns, chandeliers and wide marble staircase. There were worse places to call home and worse people to call neighbours. There was a sense of community forged by common experience. Scarred by war, spurned by peace, homeless, stateless or just unable cope in the world they'd fought to save. He was going to fit right in here.

He turned to climb the stairs when a voice called to him.

'Are you Calloway?'

It was the old boy that manned the reception desk, one of the Vigilantes. He stood in front of Calloway with his arm outstretched.

'You've got a postcard,' he said.

Calloway climbed the stairs to his floor and opened the door to his room. The Poles were playing their music. The sound of Chopin drifted down the corridor. He left the door open so he could hear it better. The bed was unmade but enticing nonetheless. He kicked off his shoes and lay down, holding the postcard to the beam of streetlight shining in through the tall window. The postcard said *Greetings from Berlin*, with a view down Kurfürstendamm towards the Kaiser Wilhelm church, in vivid, unreal colour. On the back, three words.

Miss me? Pat, xxx

THE END

About the author

DDC Morgan lives in South East London. He has written professionally as a journalist and consultant for more than thirty years. Crime writing fills the rock'n'roll-shaped hole in his life left by no longer playing in bands.

You can follow him on Twitter @DDCMorgan

More great books from Fahrenheit Press…

Blood & Cinders by DDC Morgan

London 1949. Speedway fever runs high.

Its stars are the working class heroes of a Blitz-torn city emerging from the ravages of war. With cash in their wallets and hoards of adoring fans, these dirt-track chancers enjoy a life of speed, celebrity and sex.

But as Bermondsey Bullets defend their league title, they are rocked by the death of star rider Des Fenton in a mid-race smash.

It's the start of a new and dangerous chapter for stadium security boss Reg Calloway, as he's dragged into the dark side of life at the track, with echoes of his own troubled wartime past.

Rope & Canvas by DDC Morgan

Six months after his adventure in *Blood & Cinders*, Reg Calloway finds himself working as head of security for a London film studio turning out low-budget Brit flicks.

When the studio boss's car is blown up, Special Branch suspects Irish terrorists are responsible but Calloway doesn't buy it. He saw a woman fleeing the scene. Finding the woman and uncovering her connection to the case becomes his obsession.

Calloway's under pressure from all sides - Special Branch and his studio bosses are convinced that the IRA are behind the bomb but when the terrorists give Calloway an ultimatum to find the real bomber or else, he knows for sure that the mysterious woman who fled the scene is the real key to everything.

His investigation takes him into the dark side of the London film business - its exploitation of starlets, its underworld connections and its Faustian star makers who trade young souls for broken dreams.

As Calloway delves into some of the seediest recesses of 1950s London he risks everything in an attempt to find the truth and see that justice, in some form, is served.

Abide With Me by Ian Ayris

Abide with me is the story of two boys forced to walk blind into the darkness of their shattered lives and their struggle to emerge as men. It's also a story of loyalty, of community, and of powerful friendships shaped by adversity and celebrated on the football terraces of England.

With power, sensitivity and wit, Ian Ayris has crafted one of the most authentic snapshots of working class life you will ever read.

"Ayris brings a depth and level of emotion to his writing that most authors strive their entire career to achieve, and which many never do."

Know Me From Smoke by Matt Phillips

When Stella and Royal meet one night, they're drawn to each other. But Royal has a secret. How long before Stella discovers that the man she's falling for isn't who he seems?

A noir of gripping suspense and violence, Know Me From Smoke is a journey into the shadowy terrain of murder, lost love, and the heart's lust for vengeance.

"Two great characters here in Stella and Royal. Couple that with a psychotic villain and a grudge-bearing cop, and you're gonna be hooked til the end. Happy endings? Well, maybe..." - Paul Heatley,

Slow Bear by Anthony Neil Smith

In the oil fields of North Dakota, times were good during the boom. Some people got rich: Santana the Exile certainly did. A lot of other people got jobs. A lot of bars and strip joints got busy. Then the boom times ended and everything slowly crumbled back to the red dust from which it was built.

This is noir at its deepest, at its most savage, at its most vital, from an acknowledged modern master of the genre.

"More happens in the first two chapters of Slow Bear than in some literary novelist's entire output. Thrills, spills. Twists, turns. Heart, soul. As good as it gets." - Mark Ramsden

Black Moss by David Nolan

In April 1990, as rioters took over Strangeways prison in Manchester, someone killed a little boy at Black Moss.

And no one cared.

No one except Danny Johnston, an inexperienced radio reporter trying to make a name for himself.

More than a quarter of a century later, Danny returns to his home city to revisit the murder that's always haunted him.

If Danny can find out what really happened to the boy, maybe he can cure the emptiness he's felt inside since he too was a child.

But finding out the truth might just be the worst idea Danny Johnston has ever had.

Find out more at **www.Fahrenheit-Press.com**

www.ingramcontent.com/pod-product-compliance
Lightning Source LLC
Chambersburg PA
CBHW020333310726
48979CB00015B/2352/J

* 9 7 8 1 9 1 4 4 7 5 5 3 5 *